What White Boyz Ride

Natalie Dunbar
Karen White Owens
Seressia Glass
Kelly Nyrae
Simone Harlow

Noire Entice is an imprint of Parker Publishing LLC.

Copyright © 2008 by
Natalie Dunbar
Karen White Ownes
Seressia Glass
Kelly Nyrae
Simone Harlow

Published by Parker Publishing LLC
12523 Limonite Avenue, Suite #440-438
Mira Loma, California 91752
www.parker-publishing.com

ISBN: 978-1-60043-055-8
First Edition

Manufactured in the United States of America
Printed by Bang Printing, Brainard MN
Distributed by BookMasters, Inc. 1-800-537-6727

Cover Design by Jaxadora Designs
        jaxadora.com
Type Layout by Candy Vinyl Design
        www.candyvinyl.com

Parker Publishing, llc
www.Parker-Publishing.com

Knight on A Jet Ski

By
Natalie Dunbar

Chapter One

"Gillien's Island is down there, just to your right. It's sort of shaped like a 'D'," the pilot shouted above the half buzz, half whine, and too loud sound of the plane's engines.

Arms folded across her travel sensitive stomach, Alexis Calhoun bent over sideways to peer down at the tiny patch of green mostly surrounded by the beautiful blue-green waters of the Atlantic Ocean and Gulf of Mexico. There were other small irregular patches of green dotting the water like periods, broad dashes, and variations of circles.

With her gaze still glued to the island, she pushed back into the seat. Alexis hated heights and hated riding in this puddle jumper of an airplane, but it had been necessary. Her latest book was due to the editor in two months and barely half of it was done. Five books in the last four and a half years and the last three had hit the New York Times Bestseller list, resulting in breathtaking advances and even higher expectations from her publisher, Pennington Press. She should have been thrilled. She was thrilled, but she was also going crazy. There was little time to spend with her boyfriend, all she could think about was the damned book, and her well of inspiration had run dry.

Closing her eyes, Alexis concentrated on keeping her stomach calm and corralling her scattered thoughts. She was a mess. *Maybe I should be sitting in a shrink's office instead of marooning myself on some damned island.*

The bottom fell out of Alexis' stomach as the plane zeroed in on the tiny patch of green and came down. Her feet pressed hard into the bulkhead in front of her feet, helping him brake on the tiny runway. She sighed gratefully as the plane finally coasted to a stop and the engine noise finally ceased.

Her door opened and the pilot helped her climb out. Glad to be on solid ground once more, she examined her surroundings. The air was steamy. They were in a grass covered clearing. Tall, graceful palm trees surrounded it, waving gently in the breeze. Coconuts littered the ground beneath some of them. Near one of the palm trees a small path winded into an area thick with exotic plants and flowers. The place looked like something out of the television show Fantasy Island.

The pilot lifted her two large cases from the cargo area and placed them on the ground. Handing Alexis her small carry-on luggage, he pulled the handles on her cases and tilted them. "This way, Miss."

No transportation for them or the bags? This is roughing it! Rolling her carryon bag, Alexis followed. When fellow author Miranda Gillien, her new best friend, had described her island, she'd used words like lush, remote, and solitary, and an ideal place to write uninterrupted. Hard up for inspiration and impressed with the very productive and successful La Miranda, as most people were, Alexis had happily snapped up the opportunity to finish her book at the place where Miranda completed many of her bestselling novels.

The path through the mini-rain forest was surprisingly smooth and teaming with wildlife. They went around a bend and came face to face with a gray, contemporary styled cottage surrounded by a covered lanai. Rolling waves gently slapped the sandy beach in front of it.

"Wow!" Alexis stopped to stare. The place was gorgeous.

The pilot kept going. Alexis tore her gaze away from the sun sparkling ocean to see that he'd mounted the steps, opened the door, and was rolling her bags inside. She hurried to catch up.

"The refrigerator and cabinets have been stocked per the list you provided, Ms. Calhoun," the pilot explained as he led her to the modern kitchen that looked like a downsized version of Emeril Lagasse's. "Email the grocery and supply list to the same address and we'll send new supplies on Saturday mornings. Per your request, there will be no boat available and no phone, but I understand that you have a cell phone. We have a generator for electricity here, so charging it should be no problem. If there is an emergency, we have a radio you can use to contact the coast guard." He showed Alexis the radio and went over the instructions. "Any questions?"

Alexis shook her head and thanked him. Her brain wasn't working too well right now. She knew that she should have questions. They'd probably descend as soon as the man left.

With a nod and a grin the pilot turned and headed for the door. "See you in two months."

Two months. Alexis followed the path, arguing with herself. This place was beautiful, but was she really going to be okay all alone for two months? You don't have a choice. You're not giving back that advance.

Swallowing hard, Alexis watched the tiny plane take off. Then she walked back to the cottage with the whispering sound of the ocean filling her ears. "Write, write, write, Alexis," she chanted under her breath. Then she caught herself. There was no one around to hear. Then she threw back her head and screamed, just for the hell of it.

The sound filled the air, shocking her. The scream strained and cracked with self directed anger and frustration. Then it disappeared into the perfect landscape as if it had never existed. Alexis stomped into the cottage, grinding her teeth. She was going to make this work.

In the roomy bedroom with the large, pillow covered bed, she took in the picturesque beach from the large windows as she opened her largest suitcase and searched till she found her new bathing suits. She hadn't been swimming in years for a variety of reasons. Long ago, she'd been an accomplished swimmer, competing at college. Now all she did was write, worry about writing, and scout around for high concept ideas to use for her books.

I need to relax. I won't be able to write until I do. Resolutely, she selected the baby blue bikini with the ruched bottom and the beaded strap top. Stripping quickly, she donned the suit along with her favorite beach sandals, a hat, towel, and a little sunscreen. Then she took the steps and headed for the private beach.

Lying on the beach with the morning sun warming her skin felt good. Alexis lounged for a good hour. Then, unable to help herself, she walked along the beach, digging her toes in the sand and splashing in the water. Not far away she saw a tiny strip of verdant green. That had to be Sailor's Island, the place Miranda said the locals sometimes used for picnics.

Alexis eyed it curiously. Except for size and structures, it looked a lot like the island she was staying on. With her eyes, she judged the distance. She could swim there easily. Adding a swim to Sailor's Island to her list of things to do when she just had to get off the island, Alexis dipped deeper into the water. For a while she swam short distances out and then back to the shore. Then, longing for more of a challenge, she headed for Sailor's Island with the thought that she would turn back at the first hint of fatigue.

Three-quarters of the way, Alexis felt the first signs of fatigue. Her arms were tiring. She eyed the landmass up ahead. She could make it, but she would need to rest. Mentally, she berated herself for wasting time and energy swimming in circles before swimming out to the island. Gathering her strength, she focused her energy, pushing harder with her legs and switching to a different stroke.

Gasping, muscles bunching, and her legs shaking, Alexis made it to Sailor's Island. Despite her exhaustion, she was tentative as she stepped up the sandy beach incline. Warm water sloshed her legs, urging her forward and drawing her back with the action of the waves.

A border of rocks ringed the top of the incline. She stepped over it, her legs threatening to quit. Shifting her weight, she slipped. Her ankle wobbled right, left, and back again. With a painful shriek, Alexis went down.

Sharp pain brought tears to her eyes. Checking the ankle she saw that it was already swelling. Now how was she going to swim back to Gillien's? "Damn, damn, damn, damn!" she cursed between sobs. Then she had a pity party and outright bawled.

The day wore on with no sign of anyone. Alexis crawled to the base of a palm and sat. Along with the pain her head swam with negative thoughts and possibilities. How long would it be before someone came by? Would she be awake and conscious enough to call for help? What if she was stranded her for the rest of the week?

In the moist, oven-like heat she lost track of time. For small periods of time she dozed fitfully, awakened by the throbbing pain or pesky flies and mosquitoes.

The loud lawnmower-like sound of a jet ski penetrated the air. Alexis licked dry, cracked lips and forced a swallow. This might be her only chance. She stood, yelping in pain when her weight momentarily rested her weight on the swollen ankle.

Hobbling to a better vantage point she saw a deeply tanned hunk of a blond man with dark glasses on a Jet Ski. Water arced into the air behind him and the water vehicle like a clear, crystalline tail. He only wore a pair of swim trunks. Unwillingly, her eyes focused on his naked chest, broad shoulders, trim waist, and strong thighs. The man was fine, fine, fine. Eye candy of the highest caliber. "Help!" she screamed, wishing she'd remembered to bring her emergency whistle.

The man lifted his head from the view of the sparkling blue green water, searching the area. As soon as he spotted Alexis he pulled into a rocky area at the bottom of the incline. Their gazes locked and she felt the earth shift.

"You all right up there?" he called.

"No!" she yelled back.

"What's the problem?"

"I hurt my ankle."

He got off the water vehicle and took the sandy incline easily. Alexis felt the masculine gaze behind the sunglasses cover her tear-streaked face, her new bikini and the rich brown skin it left exposed. Then it dropped to her swollen ankle. It was three times its normal size.

"Sit down," he ordered as soon as he reached her. With an arm around her shoulders he helped her to the ground. Then he examined her ankle with gentle expertise. "I used to be a physician's assistant," he explained, "and based on that experience I'd say that it's just a minor fracture or a sprain. If you want to see a doctor I could take you over on the Jet Ski or go back for the boat."

The last thing she needed was a doctor visit complete with mind dulling drugs. Alexis found her voice. "Thanks. I'll take your word for it, but shouldn't it be wrapped or something?"

"Actually you need a cast or a splint and yes, and I can do that. Are you here on vacation?"

"Actually, I'm here working," she admitted. "I'm a writer."

"I didn't see a boat out there," he said looking around. "How did you get here?"

"I swam."

"The closest island is Gillien's and that's at least a mile. You're a good swimmer."

"Not good enough." Alexis glanced at her ankle. "I'm out of shape. I was so exhausted that I slipped, coming up from the beach."

He grinned. "That could happen to anyone. By the way, I'm David."

Pain and all, Alexis found herself returning the infectious smile. "Glad to meet you. I'm Alexis."

"Alexis, where are you staying?"

"Gillien's. Miranda thought it would help me get my book finished."

Considering that for a moment, he shrugged. "No one will bother you. That's for sure. But it's a bit isolated for someone in your condition. You should probably spend the night at my house."

"You don't know me," Alexis said, stating the obvious. She didn't know him either, but for some crazy reason she wasn't afraid of him.

He lifted the dark shades to reveal familiar emerald green eyes that saw clear through to her very heart. Those eyes, that hair. She did know who he was. Alexis realized that she was looking at David Anthony, the actor and he looked better in person than he ever did on the screen.

As he let the shades fall back into place she realized that thousands of women would kill to get in her shoes.

"Any friend of Miranda's is a friend of mine. Besides, what could someone do in your condition?" He stood. "And if you're worried about me, I'm just being a Good Samaritan. I have a live in housekeeper. My girlfriend was visiting, but had to hit back to L.A. for a shoot. She will be back in a couple of days. Okay?"

"Okay."

"Then I'm going to lift you and carry you to the Jet Ski."

Alexis nodded. She wasn't a heavyweight, but no guy had ever risked his back to carry her down an incline, especially a movie star like David Anthony.

Chuckling at her expression, he put an arm under her bent knees and the other around her waist. Scooping her up, he strode across the sand and down the incline.

Alexis found her cheek resting against his naked chest and suppressed a sensual shiver. She could smell the light, oriental scent he used. Silky blond hair that they obviously removed for the picture screen sprinkled the sculpted planes. She wondered that he was obviously such a nice guy. The gossip magazines were full of stories about temperamental actors and their off screen exploits. She'd never heard a bad thing about David Anthony.

He gently set her down on the back of the vehicle and climbed on the front. Taking her hands and placing them on his waist, he started the engine. "Hold tight!" he cautioned as they took off in a rush of water.

It felt very intimate. If not for the painful throbbing in her ankle, Alexis would have enjoyed the ride and her being close to him. David was a natural athlete, swerving and curving the Jet Ski through the water and making sure she didn't get shaken too badly or hit by tree branches.

Alexis watched until Gillien's island was out of sight. This was some adventure for woman who was supposed to be in the cottage writing away. Instinctively, she trusted David, but if she were writing this, where would the heroine end up? What would be waiting when she arrived on his island?

Chapter Two

It took fifteen minutes to get to his island. The house was a lot bigger than Miranda's cottage and painted white. The landscaping along the beach and a canopy structure was made it more unique. Two beefy, sharp-eyed men in camouflage clothing approached from opposite sides of them.

"Don't be alarmed, it's just my security crew," David explained. "It guarantees me some privacy and keeps crazy fans at a distance." Gesturing to the men, he declined help and sent them back to whatever they'd been doing.

"What's the name of your island?" she asked as he got off and tied down the Jet Ski.

"Pepper Island. It's a long story." He carefully lifted her and strode towards the house.

"I'm not even going to ask." Alexis said airily. The view from his arms was wonderful. The house was filled with natural colors and comfortable island style furnishing. They even passed an aroma filled kitchen where a woman was preparing a meal. Alexis' stomach rumbled, reminding her that she hadn't eaten.

"Loni, meet our neighbor, Alexis. She's an author staying at Miranda's until she finishes her book. Alexis, Loni, housekeeper and cook extraordinaire."

Both women nodded, smiled, and spoke. Alexis felt a little bare in her bikini, with David's warm hand around her shoulders and the other beneath her legs, but what the hell? David wore only a pair of swim trunks.

David didn't stop until he had installed Alexis in a chair out by the swimming pool with the offending ankle propped up. "You're invited to our late lunch, of course," he said as he bustled off to get his first aid supplies.

"And I joyfully accept. I'm starving."

"It's almost done." The screen door slammed shut. "Feel free to use the phone," he called out.

Alexis spied the white portable phone on the floor by her chair. Retrieving it, she decided not to call her parents and cause them needless worry. She called her agent. All solicitous concern, he offered to come and get her, or make arrangements to end her setup on the island. Alexis declined. She momentarily considered his offer to provide someone to care for her on the island, but she didn't need the distraction. "I'll be all right," she told him. He made her promise to call him before she left David's island.

Michael, her boyfriend, was already distraught when they talked. A power play was going on at his company and one of Michael's rivals was trying to maneuver him out of a job. Alexis listened while he stressed on for several minutes. "Are you going to be all right by yourself on that island with your ankle sprained?" he asked finally.

"Sure. David's going to put a splint on it and give me something for the pain, and the house on the island has been stocked with everything I need," she explained.

"Good." Michael all but cut her off. "I've got to get ready for a meeting. Call or email me tomorrow and let me know how you doing."

The dial tone sounded in Alexis ear. She stared at it for a moment then switched it off. That was fast. No real worry or concern that she'd been injured and then rescued by one of the sexiest actors on the silver screen? And what happened to I love you, I miss you baby?

The screen door opened and David reappeared with a big first aid case and a swimsuit cover up. "You can put this on," he said, giving her the garment. "It was in a stack of stuff I bought for my girlfriend, Rena, but it's never been worn. She wouldn't mind your wearing it."

Alexis gratefully accepted the black and white designer garment and slipped it on while David set up his supplies.

"I haven't used this stuff in years, but the dates are still good, and the supplies for the cast are fresh since Loni's friend broke his leg a while back," he mused, as he handed her two ibuprofens and a glass of water. Then he opened the case and began getting everything ready.

The man is a saint, Alexis thought, as he cleaned her foot and applied a soothing topical anesthetic. How many women got their injuries tended to by an A list movie star? She swallowed the pills with a couple of sips water, and gratefully drank the rest. "I want you to know how much I appreciate your rescuing me and helping me."

Emerald green eyes captured hers as he glanced up from applying the cast. "It's nothing. I should be thanking you. Sometimes the life I have now makes me feel all but useless. I get a kick out of helping others. That's why I was a PA."

Alexis thought of her own life. She wasn't satisfied with much in it. As she became more successful, her boyfriend grew more distant.

Several of her friends seemed to be suffering the same issue. Her mother was supportive, but occupied with the new man in her life. Her father was busy with his new wife and baby. Then there was the very big issue of the book. She had outlines for all her scenes, character sketches, a detailed synopsis, and even a book of character pictures, but her writing when she managed to write, was dry, dull, and boring. If it didn't interest or excite her, how could she expect to do the same for anyone else?

The screen door opened and Loni came out with a large wheeled tray. "Here's lunch. I have shrimp salad on pita, French onion soup, iced tea, and ambrosia. There's more in the kitchen if you want."

Alexis' stomach rumbled painfully. "It smells wonderful," she said, hoping no one had noticed.

With the cast finished and an ice pack resting on it, David stood. "Thanks, Loni. You can put the table by Alexis."

He drew up a chair as and tossed Alexis a packaged hand wipe as Loni disappeared into the house. "So how long were you stranded on that island?"

In the act of cleaning her hands, Alexis paused. "I got in at about eight this morning and lounged around on the beach for about an hour. Then I swam for at least another twenty minutes before I headed for that island. What time is it?"

He checked his watch. "Two o-clock."

Alexis shivered. She felt the threat of tears. "Three or four hours. It seemed like it was a lot longer. I was afraid that I would be there all week."

David's eyes gleamed with understanding. "You're safe now. Everything okay except for the ankle?"

"Yes." She finished cleaning her hands and lifted the pita sandwich from the plate. "I owe you."

"No, you don't. Anyone would have helped you."

"Maybe, but you did, and I'm not going to forget that. I'll find a way to pay you back."

Alexis ate her lunch with gusto. It was only as she finished that she noticed David watching her with amusement. "You find me amusing?" she asked finally.

He shrugged. "That's not the issue. I just like watching you eat. My girlfriend is always on a diet, so most of the time I eat while she picks at her rabbit food."

Alexis remembered those days. She'd been like that before the first book hit the New York Times bestsellers list. Now she could eat what she liked because nerves and her active schedule kept her from accumulating pounds. "What are you working on?" she asked, changing the subject. "Can you talk about it?"

He set down his glass. "So you know who I am?"

Alexis raised her brows. "How could I not? You're David Anthony and had you were nominated for an Academy Award for your last movie. I knew that I recognized you from somewhere, but it was all over when you took off the sunglasses."

David shifted in his deck chair. "That's why I like to come here. It's away from the paparazzi and fans. Here, I'm just David and people like me for who I am. I can relax."

That was what she wanted to do, relax. Relax enough to finish the book. Alexis put down her fork. "Right now, you're my hero and it has nothing to do with you being an actor. So you don't want to talk about your work?"

David's head tilted in amusement. "Not going to let me get away with that, huh?"

Alexis met his gaze. "No."

"This isn't for public consumption…" he began.

"This conversation is just between us," Alexis replied in agreement.

He curled his fingers around the armrests. "I'm reading scripts, but nothing seems that good. Not getting that award made me focus on my career and the roles I've played. I've had fun and I've made a lot of money. It's time to get serious. Would you agree with that assessment, looking in from the outside?"

Alexis' breath came out in a huff. "I thought you should have won that award."

He smiled in appreciation, those green eyes just sparkling.

"But since you didn't," she continued, "You probably should go for better roles."

"So what are you writing Ms. Calhoun?" he asked.

"Call me Alexis." She said, reminding him that they were on a first name basis while she hid her surprise that he'd recognized her too. Alexis swallowed, the catchy phrase she'd given her agent springing to mind. "Black hero and white partner discover that not only are they related, but so are bunch of people from their past, who are turning up dead. They must discover who's doing it and why before someone kills them too."

"Hmmm. It sounds intriguing, kind of like my kind of story. What's the white partner look like?"

Alexis couldn't hide her smile. "Blond hair, green eyes, sort of like a young Brad Pitt."

'Or David Anthony," he interjected with a laugh.

"I've been using Brad's picture when I write," she assured him with a teasing lilt to her voice.

"Then I'll have to give you one of mine," he countered. He pushed the tray table to the side. "You're going to have to let me read your book."

Alexis laughed. "Okay, but I'll have to finish it first. Remember, that's why I'm here."

"How long do you have to finish the book?"

"Two months."

"Well I'm looking forward to reading it."

Thanking him, Alexis smiled and stifled a yawn.

Watching her reflexively, David stood. "You're tired. Let me show you to one of the guest rooms."

"You could take me back to Gillian's," she reminded him.

His gaze dropped to her ankle. "I have crutches I could loan you, but you really should be somewhere around other people until you can move around better. If you had another accident, there'd be no one to help you."

She ran a hand over her face. She didn't want to intrude on his privacy, but David was right. This was not a time to be alone. Studying his face, she only saw sincerity. "I don't want to be an inconvenience."

He waved a hand. "Don't worry about it. I feel like I know you already and I appreciate the company."

The amazing thing was that she felt the same way. She liked David Anthony in person more than she'd ever liked him as an actor. Then there was the side benefit of being able to enjoy his physical perfection. She nodded. "I appreciate the offer and everything you've done."

David dashed off to find the crutches. When he came back, he showed her how to use them. Then he led her to a guest room and disappeared. Drawing back the silk coverlet, she stretched out on the cool cotton sheets and fell asleep.

Chapter Three

Alexis awakened in an unfamiliar, air-conditioned room. Her ankle throbbed, but it wasn't really painful till she put pressure on it. Shifting on the bed she realized that she wore her bikini and a cover up. Remembering her ordeal, she sat up carefully. She wondered if anyone would miss her on Gillien's Island, then remembering the minimal communication there, she relaxed. She would find David and use his phone or computer to check in with her boyfriend and her agent. Retrieving the crutches, she maneuvered herself off the bed.

Outside the bedroom, the house was spacious and quiet. Delicious smells drifted from the kitchen where Loni was apparently making dinner. Alexis checked the area out by the pool. It was empty. Finally she acknowledged that she had been looking for David Anthony. It caught her off guard since she barely knew him and had no right to be wandering around his home uninvited. Turning her thoughts to her unfinished book, she headed back to the bedroom to look for paper and pencils.

Alexis propped her foot up on a stool and sat at the dresser to work on her novel. Without her synopsis and character sheets, she had to use what she remembered of the plot. For several minutes she stared at the blank page. Then she managed to start a scene that featured the hero's partner.

A soft tapping noise interrupted her thoughts. Alexis called out a greeting. The door pushed inward and David stood in the opening. The signature blond hair was mussed, much as it appeared in the movies. He even had the five o'clock shadow, but this time he was dressed in a white golf shirt and shorts. Legs! Lord the man had the legs of an underwear model! And what else? She didn't dare let her gaze stray any further. Alexis momentarily averted gaze to keep from staring.

"Thought I'd check on you. Are you feeling better?"

"Oh yes." Alexis smiled gratefully. It still surprised her that David Anthony was such a pleasant person. What amazed her even more was that he already felt like a friend. And something in his smile told her that he could be more. This wasn't like Alexis. She didn't make friends easily. And she couldn't remember looking at another man since she'd been with Michael. So why were things so different with David?

"I had an ulterior motive for coming in here," he confessed, looking extremely handsome in a slightly scruffy sort of way. "I had to make sure you weren't in here writhing in pain or hiding out until someone came to look for you."

"No, none of the above." Alexis eyed him with amusement. "I was actually trying to write."

He eyed the pencil and paper she was using. "Wouldn't that be easier on a laptop?"

"Yes. Do you have one that connects to the Internet?"

"Sure. Hold on and let me get it."

Minutes later he was back with the laptop. "I can set it up in here or under one of the umbrellas by the pool, or you can join me under the cabana on the beach. I've been out there reading scripts."

Kicking herself for going with what would probably be another distraction, Alexis joined him in the cabana on the beach. He was quick and efficient as he opened the word processor for her and got her on the Internet. Then he went back to reading from a stack of scripts.

Quickly checking her email, she discovered that her boyfriend, Michael had gone out of town on business, but would be checking his email. She emailed him and her agent that she was doing fine. Then she opened the word processor and entered the three paragraphs she'd handwritten. After that her creative muse quit. The nearly blank screen seemed to mock her.

A little frustrated, her ankle throbbing, Alexis stared out at the surf. She spared David a careful glance. He was deep into his script. She wished she could get into her manuscript. The sounds of the water and the birds chirping and playing soothed her. Gradually, she relaxed, and the words began to flow.

At one point she looked up to find David watching her. "What?" She asked, trying to read his expression.

"Nothing. Just watching your face. You make faces when you write."

"I do?" This was first time anyone had told her that.

"Yep. You're writing something sad now. I can see it on your face."

Alexis inclined her head. She had been writing a sad scene. Was it possible that she was hearing this for the first time because she couldn't relax enough to write around most of the people she knew? "Is that script any good?" she asked, changing the subject.

He rotated one hand from side to side. "So-so."

"Why don't you have one of the writers you like develop a script just for you?"

He flashed his trademark grin. "You offering?"

Liking the implied compliment, she considered the idea. She might have hit the best-selling lists a few times, but none of her books had made it to a movie. "When I finish this book, yeah."

"Why not finish the book with me in mind? Blake Moran could be the other lead. We've been planning to do a movie together."

Alexis tilted her head. Blake Moran would fit as the other lead. In fact, she'd been using his picture when she wrote a lot of the scenes. "It could work."

"Let's be positive. It will work." He placed the script he'd been reading on the table. "So when can I take a look at it?"

Alexis shook her head. "You can look at the promotional stuff on my website, but I've got to finish it first. If all goes well, I could be finished by the end of the month. If it doesn't, it'll take every bit of the next two months, maybe more. I can't even consider an effort with you unless you agree to wait till I finish. The pressure would be too much."

He raised both his hands. "No pressure."

Alexis found herself staring at him. "Have you ever even read one of my books?"

"I've read all of them. I was going to ask you to autograph the collection before you left."

With that settled, they both went back to work. For Alexis, the words kept flowing for a change and when the book she was writing played as a movie in her mind, she saw David Anthony and Blake Moran's faces. New questions slipped between her thoughts as she wrote. Would David and his people see her book as a good effort for David? And could her story provide the vehicle he needed to win that academy award?

Since David's girlfriend, Rena was not back by the time dinner was ready, David and Alexis dined alone on the terrace overlooking the ocean. It was so romantic that Alexis felt almost envious of what Rena had in David. Alexis couldn't remember the last time she'd shared a romantic dinner with Michael. Most of the problem was her fault, since she had a crazy writing schedule, but then Michael spent a lot of time working too. Sighing, she wet her lips. A girl could dream, couldn't she?

The mood changed as they prepared to eat desert. A beautiful, dark-haired woman with exotic features strolled onto the terrace in a nude colored slip dress that left little to the imagination. "David darling, instead waiting to travel in the morning, I flew in tonight to surprise you."

"Rena!" Standing, David went to her and enfolded her in an

enthusiastic embrace. Latching on to him, Rena kissed him deeply, her hands all over him. When he failed to show the proper enthusiasm, she pushed back. "What's wrong? Aren't you glad to see me?" Then she followed the direction of his gaze and found Alexis. Her tone took on a negative note. "You were having dinner with another woman?"

"This is my new friend and author, Alexis Calhoun," David said quickly. "She's staying at Miranda's alone, but she sprained her ankle and can't get around much, so I invited her to stay for a couple of days."

"Oh hi, I'm Rena Roulet." Phony toothpaste smile in place, the woman approached Alexis with a limp hand. Alexis shook it, not missing the stark enmity in Rena's eyes. She'd already made an enemy and she didn't even know the woman. Of course, she did know that the woman was an up and coming actress on one of the daytime soaps.

"You don't have a boyfriend or someone who could come up and take care of you?" Rena asked in a soft, innocuous tone.

Alexis ground her teeth. "I'm at Miranda's to finish my book without distractions," Alexis explained, not giving Rena the satisfaction of knowing that she did have a boyfriend.

"Really?" Rena's glance touched on Alexis and David.

David moved to stand between the two women. "Why don't you put your things in the room while I tell Loni that you're back and needing dinner?"

"That would be wonderful." With a dewy look, Rena pressed her lips to David's. This time he discreetly covered her hands so that they stayed in place.

David released Rena and headed for the kitchen. Rena lingered. As soon as David was gone she glared at Alexis. "I hope you really do have a boyfriend because David is mine. You're not even his type."

"I think you're jumping to the wrong conclusion," Alexis began.

"Really? I can see the way you two are looking at each other."

Alexis stared incredulously, realizing that nothing she said would impact what this woman thought. "You've got some mental issues. I just met him."

"Did you?" Rena glared at her.

David strode back into the room. "Rena, your food's coming. I took your suitcase to the room. Why don't you take the rest of your things there and get ready for dinner?"

"Sure honey. Good idea." Tossing Alexis a baleful look, Rena turned and left the room.

Going back to his chair facing Alexis at the table, David tightened his jaw. "Alexis, I'm sorry. She's not usually like this. I think it's the shock of seeing someone else here. Here I stop being David Anthony, the actor and become just David. No fans, no press, no paparazzi, just us."

His words hit Alexis like a klunk on the head. For the first time since she'd met him she felt like an outsider, an unwelcome guest. What am I doing here? She wondered, lifting a hand to rub the sudden ache on side of her neck. "I'm feeling much better. I can go back to Gillen's."

"No. You're feeling better thanks to lots of pain medicine. You're in no condition to be by yourself."

"I can get someone to come and stay with me."

"This is my home. I invited to you. My invitation stands. I'll talk to Rena. She's a very special, giving person when you get to know her."

Thoughts churning, Alexis met his green gaze. You had to know Rena before you saw her special, giving nature? "I don't want to be the cause of any problems between you and your girlfriend."

Shaking his head, David smiled grimly. "You won't. I'll straighten things out."

"Okay." She didn't believe he could fix this with her in his home, but she wanted to give him the benefit of the doubt. "I'm going back to my room to write." She removed the ice pack from her ankle and placed it on one of the empty chairs. Pushing her chair back, she reached for her crutches.

He placed them in her hands and came around the table to help her up. "So how much did you get done today?"

"Four pages." Alexis stood and maneuvered past the chair.

"Is that good?"

She nodded. "It's a good four pages and the best I've done in weeks."

He pushed her chair back in place. "Good. Let me or Loni know if you need anything and don't treat that room like a prison. Make yourself at home here."

"Thanks." She started the awkward journey back to her room. At the door she paused to say good night.

David was staring out at the moonlight on the water, his expression thoughtful. He said good night.

Alexis reached her room, grateful to have been spared another session with the bitchy Rena. The first thing she saw in her room was one of her suitcases by the bed. As she went to examine it, someone tapped on the door. "Come in."

The door moved inward. Loni stood in the opening. "Everything okay?"

"Yeah, I just saw my suitcases," Alexis began.

"I hope you don't mind. You were asleep and I understood that you would be here a couple of days, so on my way to the market I stopped by Miranda's to grab some of your clothes. There's nothing like wearing your own clothes."

"Did you open it?" Alexis asked, trying to remember what she'd packed in each case.

"Yes, I did, just to make sure you had at least two outfits, a nightgown, personal toiletries, and another swimsuit. I hope you don't mind," Loni said, looking a bit uncomfortable. "I don't make a habit of invading people's privacy."

"I don't mind." Alexis smiled. "I appreciate you being so thoughtful."

"Good. By the way, David had me leave a chest with a couple of those ice packs by the bed. I slipped in some soda and a couple of small bottles of wine too. See you in the morning." Loni moved out of the opening and gently closed the door.

Alexis moved one of the sodas and an ice pack to the desk where she'd left the borrowed laptop. With her ankle propped up on a small file cabinet and the ice pack in place, she settled down to write.

Again, the words poured out of her and onto the laptop in a literary torrent. When she finally made it to bed, she dreamed about the book. David Anthony was the hero, moving her plot past all that she'd written. She got a chuckle out of that, especially since she played the heroine.

Chapter Four

The next morning Alexis awakened early and wrote to the accompaniment of bright sunlight, singing birds, and the soothing sound of the ocean. Using the crutches she managed a shower, but her ankle throbbed painfully. Some of the swelling had gone down, but David had warned her not to put any weight on the foot.

Dressing as quickly as she could, she left the room in search of pain medication. The house seemed unnaturally quiet except for slow, occasional movement in the kitchen.

On the way, Alexis went past one of the tropical print couches in the Florida room. David was sprawled there, asleep in nothing but a pair of shorts. Prime beefcake! Yes, she had a boyfriend, but she wasn't dead. Her mouth watered. If David Anthony was her man, she knew she'd have a hard time letting him out of the bedroom.

Alexis pried her eyes from the vision of male beauty and forced herself to keep moving. Somehow she didn't think he'd like knowing that she'd spotted him on the couch and drooled. Apparently David had talked to Rena and succeeded in getting himself kicked out the bedroom.

Loni was making coffee in the kitchen. "You're up early," she remarked when she saw Alexis.

Alexis checked the clock above the breakfast table. It was only seven-thirty. "My ankle's hurting." She dropped into one of the chairs.

"Legal drugs coming right up." Loni reached into an overhead cabinet, drew out a white bottle, and placed it on the table in front of Alexis. She followed that up with a glass of orange juice, a plate with sliced pineapple, orange, and strawberries, and wheat toast.

Alexis opened the bottle and tilted it to let two of the tablets fall into her palm.

"This is decaffeinated." Loni placed a cup of coffee by Alexis' plate. "Three of those pills equal a Motrin six hundred."

Alexis shook another tablet into her palm. Popping all three into her mouth, she washed it down with coffee.

"You saw David," Loni remarked as she placed cream, sugar, and utensils on the table.

"Yes." Alexis fixed her coffee. "I'll keep it to myself."

"Good idea." Loni took the chair across from her. "He really likes you, you know."

"I really like him too." Alexis realized that she was smiling. "As a friend," she added quickly. Much as she thought the woman didn't deserve him, she had no intentions of making things any worse than they already were between David and Rena.

"Oh course." Loni flashed an amused smile.

Ignoring the smile, Alexis nibbled on the pineapple slices. "How long have you been working for David Anthony?"

"Eight years. He used to work at the hospital with my son before he got discovered."

"What's your son up to these days?"

Sadness washed over Loni's face, hardening her pleasant features. "He's dead. He died in an accident seven years ago."

"I'm sorry," Alexis gasped.

Loni shook her head. "No problem. How could you know?"

"Is this a private party or can anyone join?" David stood in the kitchen doorway. He'd thrown on a muscle shirt with the shorts, but was still barefoot.

"Come on in and join us, boss." Loni got up to get another plate and cup of coffee.

David visually checked Alexis' leg. "That ankle wake you up this morning?"

"No, I got up early and wrote for a while, but it's really throbbing now. I just took some pain medication."

He pointed to one of the chairs. "You need to prop that up."

Alexis carefully lifted the leg and placed it on the chair.

"Where's your ice pack?"

Alexis expelled a puff of air. She'd left it in the room.

David fixed her an ice pack, wrapped it in paper towels, and placed it on her ankle. They sat at the table talking and nibbling on the fruit slices while Loni made banana walnut pancakes.

"How's Rena this morning?" Alexis asked after a while.

"Still sleeping." He scrubbed a hand across his forehead. "She may be heading back out today. Something's come up."

Like having an incredible case of jealousy over another woman enjoying an innocent dinner with her man? Alexis left the lie uncontested. She didn't like the way things were turning out. She didn't like being the cause of romantic problems for the man who'd rescued her yesterday, but she thought Rena was going overboard. "So what's up for today?"

David shrugged. "More time on the beach, reading scripts, riding the Jetski, and going for a swim. Did I mention that I was on vacation?"

"Yes, you did. Loni and I are the only ones working around here." Alexis watched Loni set a plate full of banana nut pancakes and bacon in front of David. Sensing movement at the entrance to the kitchen, she checked.

Rena stood there with her big breasts spilling out of a tiny white halter-top and a long knotted sari emphasizing her small waist and riding low on her curvy hips. "Good morning David, everyone."

Loni and Alexis returned the greeting. David gave Rena a slow, thorough perusal that was pointedly devoid of masculine appreciation. He stopped at Rena's face, with a cold, harsh glance. "Morning."

Blinking quickly, Rena's eyes grew shiny. "Can I talk to you alone for a few minutes?"

David's head dipped in acknowledgement. "When I get done."

Rena turned to Alexis and Loni. "I want to apologize to both of you for my behavior yesterday. I was tired and not feeling well, so… I wasn't at my best."

Both women graciously accepted her apology. Alexis saw the gesture for what it was, a ploy to ease some of David's anger.

Ignoring them now, Rena watched David for a few moments with pleading eyes. "Could you at least have breakfast with me by the pool? I'd like to talk to you in private."

David stood, gathering his plate, utensils, and coffee. "Tell Loni what you want for breakfast. I'll be waiting by the pool." He strode out of the room and headed outdoors.

With David out of the room, Rena turned challenging eyes on Alexis and Loni. "I'll have one of those banana nut pancakes, a slice of pineapple, and black coffee."

Loni washed her hands, prepared the items, and put them on a tray. "I can bring this out for you," she offered.

"I can manage." Rena took the tray. "Thanks."

"That's some piece of work," Loni remarked under her breath.

Alexis didn't bother asking Loni to elaborate. Her writer's imagination and the few juicy tidbits she'd read about Rena Roulet while standing in line at the grocery store were enough to fill in the blanks. Rena Roulet was the type of actress who made the bulk of her movie money off her sex kitten looks and voluptuous body. She went for the big name actors, gaining extra prestige and press off her relationships.

Chapter Five

David ate his banana pancakes and bacon beneath the poolside umbrella. The last thing he needed was a lot of drama and Rena was a drama queen. He needed someone beautiful, artistic, and calm that he could talk to. Someone like Alexis. He'd been thinking about her too much.

So what did he see in Rena besides the beautiful face, nice body, good sex? Come to think of it, she'd been feeling that way a lot lately.

In the past he'd liked her quick smile and her engaging personality. Neither was evident as she sashayed out to the pool in an outfit guaranteed to make him drool. This time it wasn't working. He couldn't believe that he'd actually missed her.

Rena flashed him a brilliant smile. It wasn't his favorite, but close. Still, inside he didn't trust what he saw. It didn't inspire any tender feelings this time. What was bothering him?

Artfully arranging herself on the chair, she gave him a look filled with apology and placed a hand on his. "I'm so sorry about last night, David. I-I thought I was coming home to you, only you. When I saw that you were having dinner with that writer lady, something just snapped and I couldn't handle it."

Scanning her face, he looked for the truth. "I have dinner with a lot of people. So do you. I haven't slept with anyone but you. Don't you trust me?"

"Of course I trust you. I was just…jealous."

"So you pick a fight and push me out of my own bedroom to the couch last night because you were jealous?"

Coloring, Rena looked down at her plate. "I said I was sorry. I apologized to Loni and Alexis too." A tear washed down her tawny cheek. "What can I do to make it up to you?" When he said nothing, she added, "I'll do anything."

That got his attention. After all he was a healthy man with needs and she was still his girlfriend. He didn't let those needs control him, but he indulged himself when he could under controlled circumstances. "Anything?"

Beneath her lengthy eyelashes, her eyes took on a sly glint. "Yes, anything," she replied softly.

"Come here," he said, his voice going deeper.

In less time than it took to notice the sudden tightening in his pants, she was in his lap, pressing her lush curves to his hard body, and offering her mouth. Her mouth tasted of pineapple as he filled his hands and his thoughts with those curves, touching, tracing, squeezing.

She laughed as the chair tilted back precariously. "Take me to bed?" she whispered with another sultry giggle.

David stood with his arms full of Rena and headed for the bedroom.

****

Finished with breakfast, Alexis was making her way back to her room when she caught sight of David carrying Rena. The couple made a romantic picture, she thought as she flattened herself against the curve of the wall to give them some privacy. Still, Rena's triumphant gaze sought her out from the sensual haven of David's arms as the couple passed. She looked like a self-satisfied cat.

The childish action disturbed Alexis and made her wonder if Rena had any real feelings for David. She knew that if her man were carrying her off to bed like that, she'd have been too wrapped up in him to worry about showing off to anyone.

Alexis waited until she heard the bedroom door close on Rena's calculatingly sexy laughter. Then she continued on to her room. From a spot at the desk, she sat at the computer and wrote for hours. From time to time she looked up and wondered. Was it her imagination? Or did she actually hear them. She chalked it up to envy since she hadn't enjoyed afternoon delight with Michael in some time. After all, David's bedroom was in a different wing of the house.

When she realized that it was time for lunch, she hobbled out of the room on her crutches.

Loni was in the fragrant kitchen putting the finishing touches on pita sandwiches and home made chicken noodle soup. "I don't think David and Rena will be joining you for lunch," Loni said, looking up from the tray she was fixing. Where would like me to serve your lunch?"

Alexis shrugged. "If you don't mind the company, I'll have it here with you."

"I love company," Loni replied with a smile. "Let me take this to them first."

While Loni took off with the tray, Alexis found the plates and began to fix her own. Bright sunlight beamed in from the large windows. The view of the beach and the water was breathtaking. She broke into a big smile at the thought that despite the fact that she'd hurt her ankle, she was enjoying her stay on this island and had rediscovered her writing muse.

Loni came back as Alexis was sitting down with her plate. "Not used to being waited on, are you?"

"No." Alexis poured herself a glass of sweet tea. "I kind of like to do for myself."

"Me too." Loni began to fix her own plate. "And so does David, of course she has a way of distracting him."

Alexis laughed. "Isn't that a woman's prerogative?"

Loni snorted. "Hopefully that's not all the woman's got going for her. When he stops being distracted, he's going to realize that he really does not like her."

"What makes you say that?" Alexis bit into her sandwich.

"In case you haven't noticed, he's a nice man."

Alexis nodded. "I noticed."

"Well in case you haven't noticed, she is not a nice woman."

"Hmmm, is that a requirement?"

Loni tossed her a sage glance. "For David it is. Trust me on this."

After lunch, Alexis hobbled out to the cabana on the beach to write. It was hot outside, but the water made it bearable and she was tired of the air-conditioned cool of the house. Time and pages flew by. Around three in the afternoon she realized that she was a little lonely.

Going back inside, she decided to call her boyfriend. The phone rang several times, but Michael didn't answer. Refusing to talk to his voicemail, she tried his private emergency line.

After several rings, he answered the phone. "Hello?" His voice was slurred with sleep.

"Hi Babe, It's Alexis. Did I wake you?"

"Yeah. I must have fallen asleep. It's been a hard week."

"What's going on? Tell me. I want to help."

He cleared his throat. "I told you. Mason is trying to take credit for my work. He's trying to convince the boss that they can do without me. You know how hard I work for them. I brought more clients than anyone this quarter."

"That's why I can't understand why they would listen to Mason," she said sympathetically. "Where are you?"

He hesitated for a moment. "Uh, at home. I was so exhausted I took off early. How's your ankle?"

"Throbbing. Painful if I put any weight on it. I'm hobbling around on crutches."

"Want me to send somebody down to take care of you?"

"No. No, I'm all right," she insisted, wondering why his offer bothered her. She remembered when they'd first started dating and she'd come down with a severe case of bronchitis. He'd camped out at her place and taken care of her until she'd recovered enough to care for herself. After a couple of years together, she almost felt hurt that he hadn't hopped a plane to take care of her at the first sign of trouble. Maybe she expected too much.

"So how's the writing coming?" he asked, changing the subject.

"Really good. I've written a couple of chapters since I got here."

"Fantastic!" he declared. An uncomfortable silence followed. "Uh, look Alexis, can I call you back a little later? There's something I've got to do."

"Sure," she agreed, feeling as though he was getting rid of her. Quit feeling so insecure! She chided herself.

"Okay. Love you, baby." He ended the call on an abrupt, automatic note.

Hearing the dial tone, Alexis replaced the receiver. It didn't take a covert intelligence to know that something was going on with Michael, something he wasn't sharing with her. And why hadn't he offered to come and take care of her?

Alexis rubbed her forehead. She and Michael had been together for two years and for a long time she'd been sure he was the one. Now, she didn't know. Now she felt sad and more alone than ever.

Chapter Six

Morning sun forced its way into the room, making everything look sunny and bright, but the beauty was lost in the red haze of anger surrounding David as he ended a call with his agent and a man who had hoped to produce David's next picture. He turned on Rena. "Did you think I wouldn't find out?"

"I don't know what you're talking about." She gazed at him with innocent eyes, but the silk sheet that had been artfully draped around her nude body slipped. How long had she been distracting him with sex?

He held her gaze, searching for signs of a lie and hoping what he'd heard was wrong. "I'm talking about the money you took to convince me to read Morrison's trashy script and the money they've promised for you to help convince me to sign with them. And what about the role they promised you?"

Rena tugged at the covers, gaining a marginal amount of modesty. "David, you're wrong. It's not like that. Why do you always think the worst of me?"

He gave her a sharp glance. "Why don't you tell me how it is?"

She scooted across the bed to enfold him in a hug. "Darling…"

Retrieving her frilly robe from the bedside table, he tossed it to her. "Here. Put this on."

"Don't you want to look at me?" she asked, sounding hurt.

"I want to hear the truth," he insisted.

"I didn't do anything wrong," she said shrugging into the robe and pulling it closed. "It was just business."

"What kind of business?"

"You know I told you that I was toying with the idea of becoming an agent."

David shook his head. "I didn't think you were serious about that. How many clients do you have?"

Her lids lowered. Then she glanced back at him. "Well I was just getting started, so just the one."

"Okay. Who else did you shop the script to?"

She ran a hand down his cheek. "David, you're the best. Why wouldn't I start with you first?"

He shot to his feet. "I don't believe this shit. Do you really think you've screwed out all my brains? You're supposed to be my girlfriend. Since when did I become business?"

"David, you're taking this the wrong way," she insisted, coming after him with open arms.

The woman thought she had him by the balls. With an incredulous stare, he moved away. "Get dressed."

"David!" With a tearful look she ran into the bathroom and slammed the door.

Suddenly the cloying scent of sex and her perfume were more than he could stand. He hadn't been in love, but he'd had real feelings for Rena. Now he wondered if she'd ever seen him as anything but another way to make money.

Rummaging through his drawers, he found fresh clothing and headed to one of the guestrooms to shower.

*****

After getting up early to hobble along the beach and dip her unfettered foot in the water, Alexis heard other signs of life coming from the house. Then a limo pulled up and an angry-looking David stalked out to talk to the driver.

"Trouble in paradise," Alexis sighed from her vantage point on the beach. Was Rena going back to Hollywood to work a new movie or had David finally taken a good look at his girlfriend? "Do da-da-da-da" she sang, mocking the melody used on her favorite soap opera. "Tune in tomorrow folks for Days in the Life of David Anthony…"

The driver mounted the stairs and went into the house. He came out with several floral patterned bags. After a while, Rena came out, begging David to let her explain.

He faced her with disbelief and anger in his expression. "I've heard more than enough to know it's over."

"Please?" she begged, touching his face, touching his broad shoulders.

He stopped her with a hard look. "No. Enjoy your new career and get yourself a new boyfriend." With that he turned and went back into the house.

&&&&

Later, David found Alexis writing on the laptop in the Cabana on the far side of the beach.

She stopped typing on the keyboard to look at him. "You all right?"

He slid down into a chair. "Yeah."

"I'm sorry you're not having a good day."

Bending his elbows to pillow his golden head on his hands, he shot her a good-natured grin. "Who said I wasn't having a good day? I just dumped a girlfriend who wasn't who I thought she was. I can't believe that I had been looking forward to her getting back from the shoot."

Alexis turned to him, looking somewhat guilty. "My being here seemed to have a lot to do with it. I'm really sorry, David. If it would make things better…"

He cut her off. "Alexis, it's over. I'm getting so tired of women attaching themselves to me for who I am, how much I make, or how I look."

She flashed him a frank grin. "It is a nice package."

His teeth flashed and for just a few seconds the potent heat of his gaze sizzled on her flesh. "Hey, you're no slouch either."

Dry mouthed, Alexis felt herself melting. If she could have spoken, it would have been a bunch of gibberish.

David shook his head from side to side and lifted one hand in the universal gesture for stop. "Friends?" he asked. "You're one of the few women friends I have and I don't want to mess this up."

That cooled her down. Alexis smiled back at him. "Believe me, you haven't."

He relaxed back into his chair. "Take it from me; there's more to the mess with Rena than you know. Let's talk about something more interesting, like your book. How's it coming?"

"Good." Her smile widened, her caramel brown eyes sparkling. "Very good. I've gotten over the slump and the words are flowing. The only downside is that you've jinxed me."

"Huh? What do you mean?" He asked slowly stretching his legs and arms.

"Since yesterday, when I write, and even when I dream about my characters, I see you and Blake Moran as my lead characters."

David chuckled. "I know you're not expecting me to apologize for putting that in your mind. I need a good story written just for me. I'm looking forward to reading yours."

"I hope you like it," she replied modestly. "I've tried to make the characters unique and exciting know, but sometimes I'm not sure I can accomplish it until somehow I actually mange it. Do you know what I mean?"

"You're talking to an actor," he reminded her. "I have goals that I want to accomplish with each picture. I'm never sure how successful I am until I see the book on the shelf. We have that in common."

Alexis nodded and turned her attention back to the screen.

Later, David checked her ankle and thought it was starting to heal. Alexis was quiet and she didn't jerk or cry out, but he said he could tell that it still hurt. She insisted on not taking anything stronger than Ibuprofen for the pain.

They ate lunch beneath the canopy on the beach. An hour later, it was too hot and humid to stay on the beach. Because they were also tired of the sterile air-conditioned cool of the house, David taped a plastic bag over the cast and persuaded Alexis to put on her swimsuit and get into the pool.

The cool water felt heavenly against Alexis' overheated skin. She bounced on her good foot, letting the water keep her upright as she held onto the metal railing near the steps. She wanted to swim laps too, but the pain meds weren't that strong. Her body needed time to heal.

Watching longingly while David's sun-kissed body that had inspired many a fantasy glided through the water in several laps, Alexis tilted herself in the water and proceeded to exercise everything except her injured ankle. She pushed herself in a tapped down version of the water aerobics she often used to stay in shape.

Tired, she pulled herself to the steps and sat down to rest. She panted as dark spots danced in front of her eyes. Had she overdone it? Alexis clung to the railing, trying to get her bearings as she waited for her strength to come back.

She heard the sounds of movement in the water and felt the splash of David standing up in the water beside her. "You all right?"

Alexis shook her head. "I think I overdid it. Just give me a moment, I'll be all right."

David shoved an arm beneath her legs and lifted her into his arms. "I'm definitely getting my exercise these days," he muttered good-naturedly as he waded to the steps and climbed out of the pool.

As he carried her into the house, the buzz of a low flying helicopter added to the ambient noise. Someone coming home to their island, Alexis reasoned.

Her cheek rested against the silky softness of the hair sprinkling his muscular chest. Alexis fought the dark spots eating at her vision and tried not to think about the heat inspired by the feel of his bare skin on hers. She and Michael had been so busy with their work that she was physically vulnerable. Behind her closed lids, her overactive imagination painted erotic pictures. She could see herself in David's arms. This strong, ultra virile male was looking at her with enough heat in his eyes to melt her bikini. And he was carrying her to bed. Her imagination went on overload.

Alexis trembled. Only she knew that it had nothing to do with the cold water in the pool and everything to do with David Anthony. He'd starred ina several of her hot fantasies.

His arms tightened around her. "Hey, you okay?" David's deep voice, sounded close to her ears. "C'mon, talk to me Alexis."

"I just need to rest," she answered without opening her eyes. "And I need something to eat. It's too hot to exercise and I didn't eat much today."

"Trying to break the other ankle?" David cracked.

"I guess so."

Minutes later Alexis lay on the bed in the guest room. Loni had helped with her wet suit and rubbed her vigorously with a soft, fluffy towel. Then she helped Alexis into a clean nightgown and covered her shoulders with a lounging jacket.

"You don't have to prove anything to anyone and you're very welcome here," Loni said as Alexis sipped cocoa and ate a sandwich. "So what were you trying to do out there?"

"Trying to get myself back into shape," Alexis admitted between sips of the hot liquid. "Sooner or later I have to go back to Gillien's and I want to be able to take care of myself."

"Oh honey…" Loni came over and gave her a hug. "You get better for you. Is it so awful to let us care for you?" Loni asked softly. "David and I enjoy your company."

Alexis' head dipped. "I enjoy your company too."

Loni flashed hera bright smile. David came in later and they chatted about old movies until Alexis got sleepy.

After he'd gone, she tried to explain away the fantasy she'd had when he'd carried her in from the pool. Was she falling in love or lust with David Anthony? It didn't make sense. He'd just dumped his girlfriend and Alexis was still involved with Michael. She sighed. She liked David a lot. He may not have noticed, but she had been attracted to him from the moment they'd met. Couldn't a girl entertain a few good fantasies about an ultra handsome and sexy movie star?

Chapter Seven

Feeling much better, the next morning, Alexis hobbled into the kitchen. Loni was at the table with a stack of gossip magazines and the morning paper. Staring down at an article, Loni shook her head and muttered, "No, she didn't!"

"Didn't what?" Alexis came closer.

Loni jumped guiltily and hurriedly closed the magazine. "You scared me!"

"Sorry." Wondering how someone on crutches could sneak up on anyone, Alexis eased down into one of the kitchen chairs. "What are you reading?"

Loni looked embarrassed. "The gossip magazines are my guilty pleasure. I usually wait till I'm off to read them, but something caught my eye and I simply forgot about everything else. What do you want for breakfast?"

Alexis shrugged. "I'll get myself some cereal in a moment. Do you mind if I look at your magazines?"

"No." Loni opened a cabinet and snagged a bowl and a couple of boxes of cereal.

"What were you reading?" Alexis glanced up at Loni's silence; suddenly certain that there was something she needed to see in the magazine. "Loni?"

Loni looked much too serious. Placing a carton of milk on the table, she sat down in one of the padded chairs. "Page twenty-nine."

All but holding her breath, Alexis flipped to page twenty-nine. The block-lettered headline screamed, "Alexis Calhoun Stole My Boyfriend." Alexis tore her gaze away from the headline to take in the gorgeous studio shot of Rena Roulet. "That bitch!" she gasped. When her gaze dropped to the picture underneath, she gritted her teeth, but a screech of pure rage escaped her. Her hands balled into fists.

Someone had snapped a shot of David carrying Alexis in from the pool. In her bikini, she looked nearly naked and both their facial expressions lent a lot of emotion to the photo. Anyone viewing the photo would think that he was carrying her to bed.

She'd enjoyed a few fantasies, but nothing happened. She and David

34

were innocent. Alexis scrubbed a fist across her forehead. She was going to have to call Michael, her mother, and her sister and explain the photo, explain what she was doing in David's home. It wouldn't be easy. Being grown and responsible for herself didn't mean that the opinions of her friends and family mattered less. Angry tears pricked her eyelids.

Going to the window to wave off the approaching security guys, Loni patted her hand. "I warned you that she wasn't a nice person."

"Yes, you did. And that hussy didn't waste any time spreading her poison." Knowing that she was going to have to defend herself against an avalanche of gossip, Alexis forced herself to read the rest of the article. It was crammed full of blatant lies and innuendo.

Looking far too gorgeous for a man who had just woke up, David hurried into the kitchen dressed in nothing but a pair of shorts.

Alexis tore her gaze away from him. Was she being punished for fantasizing about him?

"I heard a scream." He visually checked both women. "Is everyone all right? Where's security?"

"Security's outside doing their thing. We're okay. Physically speaking that is," Loni amended. She tilted her head meaningfully towards the open gossip magazine on the table.

Glancing at it, David's eyes narrowed. "Can I take a look at that?"

Alexis mutely handed it over.

Scanning the pages quickly, his expression went from questioning to downright furious. Tossing the magazine onto the table he turned to Alexis. "I'm sorry about this. I've only recently discovered how predatory and materialistic Rena is. She probably made a bundle on this trash. Hopefully something good, like increased sales on your new book or a good television appearance will come out of this for you."

Alexis nodded. "Hopefully. Right now I've got to find a way to explain this to Michael, my agent, and my family."

"If I can help, let me know," he said gruffly. "I'm going to call my lawyer and my publicist to see if there is anything I can do."

Hours later Alexis packed her things and prepared for Michael's arrival. Somehow Michael, who hadn't thought of coming when she broke her ankle, was now coming to take care of her after reading articles in several gossip magazines and seeing the story on a Hollywood gossip show.

In a convoluted way, Alexis supposed she should almost thank Rena for giving Michael a wake up call, but she couldn't summon any real conviction for that thought. Maybe Michael spending time with her would be the good that would come out of the ugly thing Rena did.

Finished with the packing, Alexis thought of how Michael had sounded on the phone. He seemed to accept her explanation, but didn't say much. She wasn't sure he believed her. Her family and her agent had been more vocal with their outrage and positive that the articles were based on a pack of lies.

*****

Late in the afternoon, Michael showed up in a rented boat. Dynamically handsome, he hugged and kissed Alexis passionately. Alexis kissed him back, reminding herself of all the reasons why he was still the man for her. She still loved Michael. So why did his kisses fail to move her?

David and Michael were cordial. Michael thanked David for rescuing Alexis and taking care of her. David told him that it was the least he could do for someone who had become a good friend.

Soon afterward, Michael went to the boat and came back with a wheel chair. While he wheeled Alexis to the boat, she fought wistful thoughts of being carried by David. As the crew carefully handed her into the boat, she glanced back at David.

David waved, giving her a warm, encouraging smile. "Let me know if you need anything," he called.

"I will," she promised, returning the smile. "And thanks again. It meant a lot to me."

"You won't need his help," Michael assured her. Her turned her chair, blocking her view of David as they pulled away from the shore.

"You sound as if you're jealous," she said, locking gazes with Michael.

"Of course I'm jealous! He's a big time actor, you've been staying in his house, and he obviously likes you."

"Yes, but his housekeeper's been there the entire time, his girlfriend some of the time, and I've been hobbling around on crutches. There's no reason to be jealous," she countered. "Nothing's going on and nothing happened."

Michael snorted running a hand over his short afro. "Maybe it's just a matter of my getting here in time."

Alexis frowned. She didn't appreciate his cynical view of things. "Maybe it's really a matter of you believing those lies they printed. If you do, why'd you bother coming for me?"

Michael knelt down and drew her into a hug. "You know I love you, sweetheart. I've just been crazy with all the stress at work."

It had been a long time since they'd had time to enjoy each other. Alexis tried to lose herself in his solid strength and clean scent. She let him comfort her.

Back on Gillian's, Alexis quickly settled into a pattern of rising early to write, lunching and spending time with Michael, taking a few hours nap, and then rising to write until bedtime.

Although they didn't sleep together, Michael proved to be wonderful company. He arranged for a doctor and someone to cook and clean for them. The doctor confirmed that Alexis had received excellent care and that her ankle was healing nicely. The cook was competent, but she wasn't Loni. Knuckling down, Alexis spent more time writing.

At the end of the first week Michael grew restless. Alexis caught him whispering into the phone or going outside to talk on more than one occasion. It made her feel that he was hiding something. Angry, because she'd always been a secure person when it came to her relationships, she called him on it.

Michael flashed her a look so innocent that it had the opposite effect. "Sweetheart, I was trying not to disturb you."

Alexis slanted him a cynical glance. "Let's be honest with each other. "Do you have someone else?"

The innocent expression on his nut brown face faded. A detached coldness in his brown eyes captured her breath. "I haven't replaced you unless you want to be replaced."

"But you've been screwing around with someone else?"

He blinked, the chill in his eyes taking on frost. "I was lonely and stressed. You were busy. It didn't mean anything."

Hurt, Alexis ground the end of a balled fist into her eye. "It means something to me. Being committed means not getting a little extra on the side."

Scooting his chair closer, he put his face close to hers. "The way you've been carrying on with David Anthony, you need to get off the high horse."

"As I've been telling you all along, I wasn't having an affair with him. He rescued me, took care of my ankle, and we became friends."

He snickered. "C'mon Alexis, this is me you're talking to. Admit to having the affair. We can forgive each other."

She stared at the man she'd once thought of marrying and realized that the man she'd given her heart to didn't really exist. "Michael!" Something inside Alexis tensed and shattered. Her head dipped and she closed her eyes, willing herself not to cry, not to show weakness. It hurt

Chapter Eight

A month after she'd gotten rid of Michael, Alexis sat under a tree near the beach with her laptop. In the distance she heard a familiar buzzing sound. As it got louder, she gazed out over the water and began to smile.

David had come to see her a few times while Michael had been on the island and it had been awkward. Despite their innocent conversations, something lingered between them, something neither dared acknowledge. She'd missed David when he stopped coming, but she'd understood.

Looking like the ultra masculine bad boy out of a television ad with tousled blond hair, dark sunglasses, swim trunks, and muscle shirt, a figure on a jet ski rode into view. Minutes later he was walking towards her spot on the beach. The sight sent electric current-like energy coursing through her.

Sun-kissed, and looking as gorgeous as ever, David Anthony, greeted her. She was so happy to see him, she could have jumped up to give him a hug. Instead, she took a deep breath, greeted him calmly, and worked at appearing relaxed.

"I've been thinking about you, wondering how you were doing," he said, dropping down on a large rock beside her. Blond hair glinting in the sun, his emerald eyes twinkled.

"I'm great, thanks to you." Lifting the previously injured leg, Alexis rotated the ankle slowly. "I did see a doctor and he said that you provided excellent care, but I didn't need him to tell me that. I owe you."

David shifted closer. "You don't owe me because I didn't do anything I didn't want to. I enjoyed every minute you spent with me."

Alexis smiled. "I enjoyed it too, except for the stuff with Rena and the lies in the gossip rags."

His glance held hers, making it impossible to look away. "We know what really happened, right? The rest was just a lot of noise and misunderstandings."

She was glad that he had such a balanced view of the things that had happened. "I've been trying to view it that way too," she admitted.

"So are you and Michael still seeing each other? I want to be prepared if he's going to come down here and try to kick me off the island."

Alexis' fingers closed on handful of sand. "Michael and I split up almost a month ago. He's gone for good. I found out he was cheating." She winced. Why did I have to go and tell him everything?

"Sorry that he hurt you," David murmured softly, taking her hand and clasping it warmly. "You deserve a lot better."

"Thanks." Alexis blinked intent on keeping herself from trembling. The pure havoc on her body from just a little hand-holding with David made it hard to talk. "You know, I've been thinking about how it was between us and yes, I was hurt, but not the deep down, I'll-never-get-over-it kind of pain. I—I guess he wasn't the one."

David's fingers caressed her hand. "We're going to have to make a toast to finding the right one," he said.

"Now?" Alexis scanned the items she'd lugged to the beach. Her only beverages were lemonade and water.

"No, let's make our toast over lunch. I'm inviting you over to the island. Can you come? Have you done your writing for the day?" David stared hard, as if he couldn't get enough of looking at her.

She felt the blood rush her face. Pleased that he'd come to see her and was considerate of the work she had to do, she started gathering her things. "I'm ahead on my writing. I can take a break."

"Good." He began to help her. "I missed you."

Turning to look at him, she spoke from the heart. "I missed you too. I've been lonely these past few weeks."

David flashed a smile full of his unique masculine charm. Somehow it had a lot more impact in person. "You should have called me."

"And said what?"

"That you wanted some company."

Flattered, she felt something inside her start to warm. "How was I to know you'd come?"

"You knew." He shifted closer. "We're friends. We have a connection."

Enjoying his presence and the excitement it inspired, she wondered about the depth of that connection. "Yes, we do have a connection. I'm glad you're here."

They finished gathering her things and deposited them in the house. Then Alexis put a change of clothes in a backpack and hopped on the back of the Jet Ski, and wrapped her arms around David's waist. The water was warm near the shore, but much cooler farther out. Still, the cold water spray felt good since it was so hot.

They arrived on his island and David tied up the Jet Ski and helped her off. As they approached the house, Loni came out and gave Alexis a hug. "I'm glad to see you," she said, "I've been thinking about you and hoping you were okay."

"I'm fine," Alexis assured her. "And my ankle has healed."

Alexis and David had lunch on the shaded terrace. Loni outdid herself with a tasty seafood linguini and Caesar salad.

True to his word, David produced a bottle of Cristal champagne and filled two glasses. His gem-like eyes mesmerized her as they lifted their glasses. "To finding the one."

Repeating the toast, she couldn't help wishing for the chance to see if he was the one for her. She didn't know how to interpret his expectations of their friendship and she didn't want to ruin things by going after him like some little groupie. Touching her glass to his, she drank the fizzy liquid.

When she had finished, he took her glass. "Wanna go for a little walk?"

"Sure." Returning his smile, she stood, and followed him to the beach.

Although similar to the beach on Gilliens island, Pepper Island's beach had added touches that made it unique such as the white sand on his beach, the landscaped palms and plants, his boathouse, and the canopied area on the beach. David took her hand and they walked from one end of the beach to the other. Finally they stopped to sit on the covered sand beneath the shade of the canopy.

"Good?" he asked as they made themselves comfortable.

Alexis shifted so that she was lying on her stomach with her face supported on her elbows and hands. "Good."

His eyes glinted with humor. "You look too comfortable. If you hadn't just gotten over a bad ankle, I'd challenge you to swim back to Sailor's Island."

She broke into laughter. "If I hadn't just healed this ankle I'd take you on. Give me another couple of weeks."

Their shoulders bumped. "Alexis!" he said softly. Suddenly she was in his arms and his wonderful mouth was on hers in a gentle, tentative kiss.

Eyes closed, Alexis realized that the kiss wasn't nearly enough. Her hands shook as they latched onto his muscular arms and slid around his broad shoulders to lock. Groaning, he drew her closer, kissing her lips, caressing the interior of her mouth with his tongue, and tasting her like she was the most amazing ambrosia. Tilting her head up, she leaned into the delicious taste of him. He kissed her like a man, dying of thirst.

The kiss ended much too soon. Still, David didn't move away. His hands cupped her face as his lips brushed hers. "I swear you've been on my mind. You don't know how hard it was for me to keeping acting like I just wanted to be friends. I haven't known you long, sometimes you just know. I want a lot more. We didn't do anything wrong, but doesn't mean I didn't think about it, fantasize about it."

Alexis eyed him in amazement. "Me too, but I wasn't going to say anything. You had a girlfriend and I was still with Michael. When I make commitments, I stick to them."

Chuckling, David drew her closer. "Do you think Rena sensed something? They say women have radar when it comes to that sort of thing."

"Those lies she told came from somewhere," Alexis observed.

"Vindictiveness and spite." David kissed her again, drinking her in and filling her mouth with his wild and wonderful taste. They lay together on the covered sand, breathing hard and touching each other. He showered her face and neck with warm, exhilarating kisses that had Alexis trembling beneath him.

"Is it too soon?" he murmured against her skin. "I don't want to wait. All I can think about is kissing you, touching you, and making love to you, but if you want to wait, I'll find a way to do it."

His words sent threads of heat melting the very core of her. Alexis' fingers traced his angular cheekbones and circled his sensual mouth. She was living the best of her dreams and hoping it would come to more than a memory of good sex. Her voice grew husky. "I want you too. All this time I've been thinking that the heat between us was all in my mind."

Shifting, he pulled her down on top of him. His hands slid down to cup her butt and squeeze the firm globes. "Mmmmm, you feel better than any dream I've ever had. Still think you're imagining this?"

"No," she sighed, gazing into his green eyes and reveling in the sensation of his stiff erection pressing against the crotch of her bikini. Rotating her hips, she let her fingers caress and explore the muscled planes of his chest, twirl around the hard nipples, and slid down to his trim waist.

His fingers whizzed through the buttons on her swimsuit cover up and eased it off her shoulders. Then his hot mouth pushed aside her top to cover the sensitive tip of one breast with his mouth. Alexis moaned, tangling her fingers in his golden hair.

A wild, high-pitched cry escaped her as he shoved his hands into her bikini bottom to touch and cup her intimately. She collapsed against him, her body spasming.

"Alexis," he groaned. Gathering the side edges of her bikini bottom, he smoothed it down her legs and off.

David shucked off the rest of his clothes. Golden hair sprinkled his chest and trailed down his flat stomach to his impressive sex. Alexis stared at his pert, model worthy rear, strong, athletic thighs, and well-shaped legs. "Condom?"

"Left pocket." Heat rushed to her face. Clearing her throat, Alexis reached for her discarded cover up. "I didn't know what to think, but I hoped."

"I'm glad you did." He pulled her close for another mind-altering kiss. Then he opened the pack and she enjoyed the task of applying the protection to his thick, hard, length. "I can't take much more of this," he growled.

Straddling him, she eased down on his rigid sex as he thrust upward. Alexis rode him like he was a wild stallion. They moved together in an aching, pumping mass of overheated flesh. There was nothing but the sound of her sighs, his groans, and the wet sucking sounds of skin slapping against skin.

Alexis breathed in the sultry scent of sex. David's skin was warm and wet against hers. Her legs were trembling with building excitement. David rolled with her so that he was on top with her legs locked around his waist. The erotic sensations grew stronger as David pushed into her with piston precision. He arced suddenly, gasping, and they both dissolved into the mother of all orgasms.

Afterward, they lay together on the covered sand and he spent a lot of time just looking at her. "You are so beautiful," he whispered, licking and stroking her damp skin until most of it was dry. Then they made slow, exquisite love that was so wonderful Alexis cried. She'd never experienced anything like it. David assured her there was a lot more where that came from.

Holding each other beneath a humongous beach towel, they drowsed in the afternoon heat. "Stay with me?" he asked when she awakened from a short nap. "I promise to let you sleep. If you want to that is."

Alexis giggled. She spent a glorious night in David's bed. The next day she forced herself to go back to Gillien's Island.

Chapter Nine

Over the next few days, the words flowed in their emails to each other and her book. Although she thought of David often and wondered if their being together had been a fluke, Alexis made fantastic progress with her book. As the book moved closer to completion, she became more certain than ever that David was the core of the hero in her novel.

On the morning of the last day of the week she heard the sound of the Jet Ski again. This time she ran down the beach to meet David. Meeting each other halfway, they embraced and kissed passionately. Then he took her inside the house and they had hot sex in nearly every room. Alexis knew she would never view any of the rooms in the same way again. Afterward, they showered and dressed and David took Alexis to Sailor's Island for lunch.

The fact that she remembered every detail of the island surprised Alexis. Despite the ordeal with her broken ankle, it was a beautiful place. Being there with David forced her to make new memories.

They had lunch in the shade of a large tree. When they were done, they sat and talked on a quilt beneath a tree.

"I spent the past few days missing you almost all the time," he said shifting closer to her.

Alexis took his hand. "I missed you too, but it's not as if you couldn't get over to the island to see me."

His green eyes studied her. "I know how much your work means to you. I'd never want to be the cause of you missing out on anything related to that, so I've been trying to pace myself."

"But?"

"It's hard. Very hard. We—we need to come to some sort of arrangement."

Excitement and anticipation choked off Alexis' air supply. Was David asking her to stay on his island with him or something more? She'd secretly envied Rena, but more time with David had shown Alexis just how vulnerable she was to him. David had her heart and it terrified her to think he might not feel the same way. She needed more than a live in lover, but did she have the strength to hold out for it?

Opening her mouth, she forced fresh air into her lungs, aware that he was watching her intently.

"You're tense," he said, looking concerned. "What's wrong? Do you want to discuss this later?"

"I couldn't stand the wait," she admitted, gripping his hand tighter.

"Then what is it? Tell me now, cause I don't take rejection well."

Gathering herself, she let the words tumble out in a rush. "It's too soon, but I love you and I can't be with you the way Rena was… The more I see you, the more I'm into us and—"

David stopped the flow of words with a finger to her lips. His mouth followed with a gentle, caressing kiss that deepened and went on for several moments. "I've got you, sweetheart and I've got more for you."

He reached for his swim trunks. Alexis saw him pull a zipper and remove something from the pocket. "I love you Alexis. When I think of you, I know that you're mine. Nothing's ever felt like this. Every bit of me is yours if you want it. I can't stand the thought of being away from you. Will you marry me?"

Not believing her ears, she froze in amazement.

He slid something sparkling on her finger.

"You—you're asking me to marry you?" she trilled breathlessly.

"Yes." Tense, he waited.

Studying the emerald cut diamond that had to be at least four carats, she gasped. "David, it's beautiful!" She drew his head down for a kiss. "Yes, I'll marry you! Oh David I'm so happy!"

"Me too." Embracing her, he stole another kiss.

"Do you mind if we wait a year?" She added anxiously. "I don't want there to be any surprises. Besides, we've got to plan a wedding."

"Whatever you want." David grinned at her. "You know people will talk, but I don't care."

"Me either," she echoed. "And when you win the academy award for staring in my movie, I'll be there with you."

"Always."

"Always," she echoed.

The End

Baby It's Cold Outside

By
Karen White-Owens

Chapter One

I can't get used to this Michigan winter. It's wet, icy, slippery, and snowy. How can anyone enjoy this type of weather? Resa Warren wondered, pulling the edges of her copper-colored, fur-lined coat together as she crossed the lobby of St. James Ski Lodge.

At the bank of elevators, Resa took a gander at the large, open lobby. A huge fire crackled in the stone hearth located in the center of the room. Guests congregated around the fireplace, sipping mugs of liquid pleasure while swapping tales of navigating difficult slopes and skiing exploits.

Turning back to the elevators, Resa shook her head sorrowfully. After three months of living in Michigan, she felt no closer to acclimating herself to the move or the weather than when she first arrived. The promotion to financial director had been a good thing – one of the best moves in her accounting career, but living in the cold weather state of Michigan – not so much.

Sighing longingly, Resa thought of her parents and big brothers. She missed them all. Most of all she longed for her neat little apartment in Las Vegas and the warmth of Nevada days and nights.

The ding of the elevator roused Resa from her pity party. Like sheep, Resa and a group of guests filed into the elevator and she settled into a spot at the back of the car. Resa shoved her hands inside the pockets of her coat and leaned back against the steel panels.

Eyes shut; Resa did a mental checklist of her audio-visual equipment needs for her upcoming presentation. She planned to amaze the small investment group with her financial knowledge and cement her role as financial director for the Detroit regional office.

Something cold and wet smacked her face and slithered down her cheek. Her eyes popped open. What in the world? She wiped the cold slush from her skin and studied it. Confused, she glanced up, searching for answers.

Resa found them in the form of a tall, broad-shouldered man standing in front of her. Snow dangled from the edges of his shoulder length blond locks. He ran a large hand through his hair, slinging snow all over the place.

"Hey!" she protested.

The man pivoted on his heels. He stared in Resa's face. His eyes focused on the snow sliding down her face. Red color filled his cheeks. "Sorry," he whispered in a velvet-edged voice.

Resa's heart seemed to stop in her chest. He had the greenest eyes she'd ever seen. Those eyes seemed to see straight into her.

Snow clung to his jacket, ski pants and boots. The man looked like a blond, drowned rat. "I'm sorry," came his deep baritone apology. The tremor of his voice sent her senses into overdrive. He reached out and brushed the wetness from her cheek. "I'm so sorry."

Resa's breath caught in her throat. Although his fingertips were cold, something warm and invitingly sensual swirled and settled between them. Gasping softly, Resa took a step away, bumping into the back panel.

"I'm o-o-kay," she stammered, brushing her knuckles across her cheek to extinguish the feel of his touch.

The elevator dinged, dragging her from her trance, Resa reached for her leather bag and noticed a wet spot spreading across the expensive leather. Peeved, she gritted her teeth and cut him to pieces with her eyes.

If possible, he turned even redder. "Sorry."

"Hmm." She pushed her way through the group, leaving the elevator. As the doors shut, she caught sight of the man one final time. He stood in the center of the car, watching her with an unreadable expression. Something about that look rooted Resa to the spot.

Resa shook off the weird connection. Forget him. She grabbed the handle on her luggage and rolled it down the hallway to her room.

As Resa stuck her hotel room card in the slot, she glanced down the hallway to the elevator. Is he staying the weekend? Hopefully not. I've had enough of him.

Chapter Two

Late that evening Resa navigated her way out of the elevator, through the hotel toward the row of restaurants. *I really shouldn't take a break right now. There's too much work to do. I should have dinner sent to my room and keep working. I still need to finish the projections for Thursday's meeting.*

But after three hours of Excel spreadsheets, Word documents, and PowerPoint presentations, she needed to chill out. This was the perfect opportunity to unwind and check out the hotel's amenities. A glass of wine or two, a great dinner, and a delicious dessert completed Resa's agenda before she returned to her room to get back to work.

Resa stopped outside the restaurant entrance, watching guests mill around. Couples stood close together, talking in intimate tones. At the arched doorway, a young woman dressed in a black vest, slacks and white shirt stood at a podium. She quickly spied Resa waiting near the doorway,. "Good evening. Welcome to Maxie's. One for dinner?"

"Yes." Resa gnawed on her bottom lip, taking a quick peek at the couples gathering near the doorway. She felt so conspicuous. Did the hostess have to make her sound so pitiful because she was here alone?

The hostess pulled a black leather menu and wine list with gold writing from a pocket on the side of the podium. "This way, please."

Good! Get away from this crowd, Resa thought. *Alone, I feel like an oddity.* "Can I get a booth in the back?"

"Certainly."

Hardwood floors and tan suede booths were the restaurant's trademark decor. As they passed the bar, a group of guests were sipping cocktails. One familiar blond head towered above the rest.

Resa's heart danced in her chest. *I hope he didn't see me. I don't want to be bothered with him,* she thought, ducking her head. That idea quickly went up in smoke when his gaze found and held hers. Resa ignored him, but his piercing gaze shot needles into her back as she made her way through the restaurant behind the hostess. The hostess stopped beside a booth with a spectacular view of the slopes.

"Your server will be with you shortly." The hostess placed the menu and wine list in the center of the table before leaving.

Resa scooted into the booth, opened the menu and studied the entrees. The sound of approaching footsteps drew her attention. Assuming the server had arrived, she glanced up with a smile on her lips. She was wrong.

"May I join you?" he asked in a deep baritone voice.

Her heart lurched. Stunned, she stared.

The man wore a green cashmere sweater that complimented the striking green of his eyes. His powerful legs and thighs were encased in denims and white leather running shoes covered his feet. He provided the second most spectacular view for the night.

My, my. He is a pretty specimen, Resa thought. If she did white boys, he would definitely be on her program. But she never had.

"Hello?" He waved a hand in front of her face. "May I sit down?"

Snapped back to the present, she asked, "Why?"

"Because I feel bad about what happened earlier. I want to make it up."

She smiled. "A new piece of luggage would do the trick."

He grimaced, playfully adding, "I don't want to go that far. Will a drink do instead?"

Resa considered the situation for a moment and then made an executive decision. Why not? It's not as if he asked you to go to bed with him. That thought conjured images of him stripped naked. The idea sent her spirits soaring. Her body went all warm as blood pumped hard and fast through her veins. Calm down, Resa. This is a drink or two and a little company to pass the time while you eat your dinner. Don't go beyond that.

"Sure." Resa felt her pulses suddenly leap with excitement and waved a hand at the booth.

A pleased grin spread across his face. His perfect smile caused a tingling in the pit of her stomach.

Staring intently at him, Resa found herself questioning what she'd gotten herself into. He slipped into the booth beside her and placed his drink on the table. Her interest stirred as a delicate thread began to form between them. His nearness made her senses spin.

"Clay Shire," he said with an outstretched hand.

"Resa Warren." She offered hers. The moment his fingers touched hers an electric jolt shot through her.

Grinning, he shook her hand. "Nice to meet you, Resa."

Her heart thumped erratically when he said her name.

"That's an unusual name. Is it short for something?"

She grunted and then admitted, "Yeah. Resanna. It's my grandmother's name."

"Resa for short."

Nodding, she answered, "Pretty much. Is Clay short for Clayton?"

"You've got me." Clay noticed the approaching server and asked, "What would you like to drink?"

The server stopped at their booth and removed a spiral pad from his pocket. "I'm Eric and I'll be your server this evening. Can I start you off with a cocktail and an appetizer?"

If he's buying, I'm drinking, she thought. Without hesitating, she stated, "Long Island Ice Tea."

"Excellent," Eric stated, turning to Clay. "And for you, sir?"

"Scotch."

After placing an order for shrimp cocktail, Clay turned to Resa and asked, "I'm a regular at St. James. I've never seen you here before. Is this your first vacation here?"

"Actually, yes."

"I know the lodge and town pretty well. I can show you around if you'd like. Do you ski? We could do the slopes together."

"Thanks, but I'm actually here for work."

"You've got to have some fun. Maybe I can talk you into a ride on my snowmobile. I store it up here during the winter. What do you think?"

"Mmm," Resa shrugged. "That sounds nice but I'm not much of a winter sports girl."

Surprised, he stared at her and then chuckled. "Then what are you doing here?"

Resa nodded a silent thanks to the server as he placed their drinks on the table and moved away. "My job. They chose the lodge." She picked up her drink and sipped from the glass. The alcohol warmed her belly. "I'm conducting a seminar next Thursday and Friday."

"What do you do?" Clay asked.

"Financial analyst," she answered.

"Even if you're here to work, there's still a lot of stuff to do. Make sure you take time to check out the sites. The slopes are beautiful when they're covered with snow."

"I can't guarantee it. But I'll think about it."

Frowning, Clay studied her over the rim of his glass. "You don't sound like you're from Michigan. Am I right?"

"Correct. I'm not into the cold weather."

He laughed out loud. "Wrong place for your conference."

"It wasn't a choice," she answered. "I moved here from Las Vegas when I got a promotion."

Clay wiped an imaginary streak of sweat from his forehead. "Vegas is way too hot for me. Nice place to blow my money, but I wouldn't want to live there."

"I could say something similar about Michigan. It's too cold for me. Nice place to visit, but I wouldn't want to live here," she taunted, taking a long swallow of her drink.

Saluting her with his drink, Clay chuckled. "You've got me on that one. Although I have to add, given a little time, I believe I can change your mind."

Resa watched him. He probably could. But she didn't want to stay in Michigan and she didn't intend to get involved with anyone. Her plans didn't include staying in Michigan for more than time needed to get a bigger promotion. Resa's gaze slid over him as she contemplated having a little fun.

Clay picked up the menu and gave it a cursory study before laying it on the edge of the table. "Here comes Eric. I can recommend the grilled salmon or filet mignon. They do them perfectly here. What's your preference?"

"Salmon."

After placing their dinner orders, Resa leaned back in her chair with her Manhattan Long Island Ice Tea in her hands. "So Clay Shire. What do you do for a living?"

Clay sipped from his glass and answered, "I'm a psychiatrist."

Interested and a bit surprised, Resa leaned forward. "Really. That must be interesting." She expected him to be some sort of ski bum or personal trainer. Her eyes slid along his body, admiring the slick lines and muscles before returning to his face in time to listen to his response to her question. Her body hummed in response to his purely male aura. The man was becoming more intriguing by the minute.

"Some days," Clay said with a hint of pain he couldn't hide in his voice. "Incredibly stressful on others."

"I can imagine." She took a cool swallow of her drink. "Do you have a practice somewhere close?"

"My partners and I have an office in Birmingham." Noting a lack of recognition on Resa's face, Clay elaborated, "It's a suburban community of Oakland County."

"Oh. So you deal with neurotic housewives and stressed out executives?" Resa asked, imagining men in thousand dollar business suits tearing out their hair as they talked about their days in the corporate jungle. Or women in expensive linen suits, perfectly styled hair and overpriced handbags stretched out on a leather sofa, telling Clay of their daily trials in suburbia.

"My practice deals with teens."

Oh wow! Resa thought. Clay had surprised her a second time. He went up a notch on her Resa meter. She expected him to be the type that charged huge hourly rates instead of working with troubled teens. "That's got to be difficult at times."

"It can be. Today's kids are under a great deal of pressure and stress. They're expected to succeed in school, work and life. Most of them haven't decided who they are, let alone made a choice on the career they plan to pursue. It's a cruel cycle that doesn't seem to be getting any better."

Highly impressed, she listened intently, nodding occasionally. Her impression of him was changing as she realized how effective she felt he could be as a psychiatrist. His baritone voice lured her into an immediate sense of security.

"Well, Ms. Resa Warren. I know you're here to work, but how come you're here without a husband?" Clay asked.

Shrugging, she responded, "Because I don't have one. What about you?"

"No husband," he answered solemnly.

She laughed but the question still lingered.

He grinned back and answered, "I'm single. No kids. No wife."

Pleased, Resa drew her tongue across her lips and then asked, "So you're here for fun?"

"Partly. During the winter months I bring some of my teens up here to ski. They get some one-on-one time with me and I get a chance to spend a little extra time with them. It works on a lot of levels. You could join us if you'd like."

Resa shook her head. "I'm not one of your patients."

"No, you're not, but you're a very attractive woman that I'd like to spend time with. Skiing is a way for us to do that."

Clay sure knew how to turn on the charm. But, she still didn't want to ski. "No thank you. Skiing doesn't appeal to me. During the winter months I prefer my activities indoors." Heat flew along the back of Resa's neck. Oh wow! Did I really say that? Clay might think she meant something very different and very personal.

Their server placed chilled cups of shrimp cocktail in front of them. Clay dragged a shrimp through the red sauce as he questioned, "You sure?"

"Oh yeah," Resa muttered back, chewing on a shrimp. The seafood tasted heavenly. She relaxed and decided to let the evening flow, refusing to acknowledge how Clay's presence really affected her. She wanted to share her evening with him and learn more about this intriguing man.

"If you change your mind, I'm here all week."

After finishing her Long Island Ice Tea, Resa switched to Chardonnay to keep a clear head.

Chapter Three

"I'm stuffed," Resa announced, pushing the empty dessert plate from her. The flaky pastry filled with vanilla bean ice cream covered in dark chocolate had been down right sinful.

Clay leaned close, scooped up the melted ice cream from the plate. "Oh, come on. You only ate half of it. I'll finish it for you."

Resa inhaled the subtle mixture of Clay's aftershave and soap. The scent of sandalwood and musk swirled under her nose creating an olfactory bouquet of unique scents. She liked the aroma and inched closer to enjoy more.

"True. But it's more than I'm used to eating. I'll have to work out on the treadmill for hours to get rid of all of this rich food." Resa's pink tongue darted out and licked away the last crumbs from her lips.

Clay's warm gaze followed the gesture and then did a slow perusal of her form. His heated green gaze journeyed down the slim slope of her milk chocolate-colored neck and settled for a moment on the curve of her breasts before taking in the rest of her frame. Clay focused on her almond-shaped brown eyes and smiled. "You're a tiny thing. I don't think one ice cream puff, half a cream puff," he amended, "will add an ounce of fat to your figure. You're perfect just the way you are."

The compliment hit its mark. It spiraled through Resa's veins like warm cognac. But she didn't feel quite ready to let Clay knew she liked all of his attention. "Right," she drawled. "This from the man who stays in shape by skiing, snowboarding, and snowmobiling and Lord knows what other snow sports. Oh yeah, let's not forget teaching troubled teens how to navigate the slopes and life."

Clay grinned. "We're not talking about me. I'm more attracted to women with some meat on their bones. A curve or two is a good thing. And your curves are all in the right places."

He knew what to say to a woman to make her feel attractive. Resa decided to hold the compliment close and worry about the consequences later. Although she'd had her reservations regarding sharing a meal with Clay, it had been a wonderful, exciting and fun adventure. She found him easy on the eyes and fun to be with. Yes, indeed. She'd had a great time. But like all good things, it was time to call an end to the evening.

Their server silently approached, placed the bill in the center of the table and quickly moved away. Resa reached for the leather folder. Clay got to it first. He whipped the bill off the table and immediately removed his American Express gold card from his wallet. Before she could protest, the server returned, scooped the folder off the table and headed to the back of the restaurant.

"No. No." She raised a hand to summon the server. "Our deal didn't include dinner. Drinks. That's all."

"Relax." He placed his hand on top of hers, gently stroking his thumb back and forth across her tender skin. "I owed you and I enjoyed my evening. If you're really concerned about the cost, you can buy me dinner tomorrow night. What do you say?"

The word "yes" puckered on Resa's lips. But her "be careful" radar warned her against letting this man get too close to her. "We'll see."

Unfazed, Clay added a hearty tip to the bill and signed his name at the bottom of the receipt. He rose and recaptured her hand, helping her from the booth. "Come on. I'll walk you to your room."

Hand-in-hand, they strolled from the restaurant to the elevator. All the while, the tantalizing aura of Clay surrounded her, drawing her further into his web. His touch stirred something deep and primal within her and she found it hard to deal with it. Were things going too fast between them? Should she put a stop to anything more?

They entered the elevator and settled in the back of the car. Clay draped an arm around Resa's shoulders and drew her against his side. Her head rested on his shoulder and nestled against the strong column of his neck. They stayed that way until they reached her floor. He led her down the corridor to her room. Resa removed her card key from her purse, stuck it into the slot, and waited for the blinking green light before turning to Clay.

When she glanced into his eyes, her heart fluttered in her chest. The same emotions she'd tried to hide were clearly and plainly visible on his face. She felt like a school girl on her first date. *Resa Warren, you are a director of finance and an excellent judge of character. Pull yourself together, girl. Say good night and go into your room.* What came out was, "I had a really nice time. Thank you for dinner."

"You're welcome." Clay reached out and pushed a renegade lock of hair behind her ear. His large hand settled on her shoulder. He leaned down and gently brushed his lips against hers. The light caress set off a riot of sensations within Resa. Clay drew back and smiled down at her. Resa smiled back.

Clay's head dipped a second time. She lifted her chin, meeting him.

This kiss was different. He nibbled her bottom lip, requesting entry. She complied, allowing his tongue to slip past her lips. He swept the interior of her mouth, using a gentle pressure. Clay tasted wonderful. He tasted of cognac, ice cream, and the essence of him. Her arms found their way around his neck as she pressed herself closer while threading her fingers through his blond hair. She fitted perfectly against the hard planes of his body and lost count of the time they spent discovering the textures and nuances of each other.

The sound of voices growing closer barely penetrated Resa's lust intoxicated brain. Clay broke off the kiss and reached behind her to turn the door handle. He gathered her into his arms and whisked her inside, slamming the door behind them. Wrapped in Clay's arms, they waited quietly as the hotel guests strolled by the room, exchanging jokes and suggestions regarding dinner. Somewhat subdued, Resa ran her fingers through her hair and straightened her clothes. Boy, had she allowed things to get too hot too quickly.

Remnants of passion still lingered in the depths of Clay's green eyes. Heat pooled between her legs, responding to the question in his eyes.

"Well." He swallowed, running a shaky hand through his hair. "I think it's time for me to go." Contrary to his words, Clay moved closer, lightly leaning into her body. His heat and the tangy aroma of his cologne swirled around her, capturing her in his web. Clay caressed her cheek with the pads of his fingers, setting off a riot of sensations and emotions. His slight touch made blood surge through her veins.

"Yeah, well." Resa stopped, not sure what to say next.

He took a step toward the door and then halted, returning to her for one more kiss, whispering, "Good night."

"Good night. Thanks for dinner."

"Any time." Clay turned and smiled. The effect was devastating and shattered her resistance. Resa felt as if she were privy to a private showing of something very unique. Something so special that she refused to let him go without exploring its depths.

She didn't know what to say. The closeness of his body made her almost forget decorum and proper manners. She felt the need to be with him and to hell with the rest. Welcome him into her room and do whatever came naturally and then some.

Resa considered her options, debating the merits of the situation. In her twenty-eight years, she'd never considered having mindless sex with a stranger and never with a white man. She studied his sculptured frame for a beat. No one needed to know. *I can definitely have this particular piece of white cake and eat it too.* She smiled. This could be a night of exploration and then back to sanity tomorrow. Why not?

For the second time that evening, Resa Warren made an executive decision. "Clay!"

"Hmm."

"Don't go."

A question formed in his eyes. "Are you sure?"

Resa wasn't certain about anything. She was scared as hell. But she wanted to be with Clay. "No. But, I don't want you to leave."

The door shut with a decisive click. Clay added the latch for good measure before returning to her side. "For the record, I don't want to leave," he admitted, taking her face between his hands and gently touching her lips with his.

Resa didn't know what this thing was between them. Maybe it was just physical attraction that could be remedied with a few hours together. But she sure planned to find out.

They kissed over and over. Clay's slow, drugging kisses made her hungry for more. Her tongue intertwined with his, licking, sucking and tasting.

Clay's fingers worked open the buttons on her blouse, exposing her heated flesh to the coolness of the room. He caressed the fullness of her breasts through her black lacy bra, drawing tiny circles as his fingers approached her nipples. Resa moaned her approval when his hands cupped her breasts. Skimming the edges of the lace, he popped the front snap and her breasts spilled into his hands. Clay hooked his fingers inside the bra straps and pushed the bra and blouse off her shoulders. The garments fell into a heap on the floor. His gaze focused on her flesh warm and golden brown in front of him. "You are so beautiful," he murmured.

"You're not so bad yourself." She lifted his sweater off his flat belly, over his broad shoulders and off his head. Resa feasted her eyes on the broad expanse of muscled chest covered by pale skin. Wanting a taste of him, she licked his nipple like an ice cream cone. Instantly, the pebble hardened. Resa alternated between licking and suckling the hard nub while her free hand explored the flat planes of his chest and stomach before moving lower.

Clay cupped her face and kissed her deeply. Resa drank in the sweetness of Clay's kiss while she stroked him through the fabric of his denims. Her hand rubbed up and down his stiff shaft, enjoying the feel of him as he stretched and grew in her palm. Not satisfied with touching him through his pants, Resa unzipped his trousers, hooked her thumbs inside the waistband and pushed them down his legs. He stood before her completely nude. Clay was a beautiful specimen. His heavy rod sprang free, proud, stiff and thick.

Resa felt as if she'd nearly died and gone to heaven. She loved the feel of his hard stiff erection twitching in her hand.

Now it was Clay's turn. His large hands circled her waist and pushed her Dockers over her hips, down her legs and off her feet. A little embarrassed, Resa tried to cover herself with her hands.

"Stop. Don't," Clay said, pulling her into his embrace. "Don't ever hide yourself from me. You're beautiful."

He peppered the long slope of her neck with tiny kisses, making his way to her breast. He leaned down and drew a nub into his mouth. Resa pumped his shaft as his lips sucked her nipple with tantalizing possessiveness.

Gently Clay eased her to the floor. His tongue caressed her sensitive, swollen nipples while his hand slid across her silken belly. Clay's hand slid down her taut stomach to her heated core. Clay traced the slit with his finger. Then his fingers slipped between the folds and caressed the tender nub with his thumbs. She buckled against this intimate invasion.

Resa picked up the rhythm of Clay's fingers and moved her hips, swaying back and forth. The tension built as her orgasm drew closer. Her internal walls begin to quiver. Instinctively, her body arched toward him as his tongue sucked strongly on the brown peaks of her breasts. Suddenly, a powerful wave of sensations hit her, shattering into a million pieces around his fingers. Sated, Resa lay panting, her chest heaving as she tried to recover. "Thank you."

Sucking on his finger, Clay leaned over her, kissed her tenderly and replied, "You're welcome."

It was his turn. She sat up. A thought crossed her mind. "Do you have any protection?"

He nodded, reaching for his pants. Clay removed a foil package for his back pocket. "I'm like the Boy Scouts. I always come prepared."

"I want you to come," she whispered, taking the foil wrapper from his hands and tearing it open. Straddling Clay on the floor, she removed the latex from the wrapper. With the gentlest of touches, she stroked his shaft several times before rolling the latex over the tip and down his length.

Using her hand to hold him in place, she positioned his rod at her entrance and pushed down as he surged up, taking his length into her body in one swift movement. She gasped in sweet agony. He felt wonderful. Clay filled her completely. The pleasure was intense and explosive. With her palms planted on his chest, she slowly rose above him and then lowered herself onto his shaft, taking him deeper into her canal. Eyes shut, Clay rode out the pleasure, moaning with each stroke. His hands rested on her hips, guiding each movement.

As she moved, her breasts swung in front of Clay. He took one taut nipple into his mouth, lapping the bud and rousing her passion. A moan of ecstasy slipped from her lips. Resa felt the sensation to her core.

Resa felt Clay's finger move down her belly and settle in the hair covering her heat core. His fingers dipped inside, stroking her nub as she rose and fell on his shaft. The dual sensations were taking them both higher. She writhed over him, seeking fulfillment.

Clay reached for her, bringing her close for his kiss. Passion pounded through her veins. Their bodies moved in perfect harmony, striving for completeness. Her body hummed as it grew closer to her release.

For the second time that evening, Resa felt the world spin and she exploded. She cried out his name while riding out her orgasm. Seconds later, Clay called out her name.

Deeply satisfied, Resa rolled off him and nestled at his side. "That was good."

Clay got to his knees, scooped Resa into his arms and started toward the bed. "Yes, it was. Give me a minute and let's do it again."

"I'm ready when you are."

Chapter Four

The sun scurried into the room through a small slit between the closed drapes. Resa slowly opened her eyes and shut them immediately against the harsh morning light. "My head hurts." She moaned, running a hand through her rumpled hair.

Resa turned on her side and her foot accidently brushed against the hairy, muscular leg of a man. Shocked, her eyes flew open. She found herself gazing into the handsome, but sleeping face of Clay Shire.

This is not good. I need to get out of here. Thinking hard and fast, Resa considered and discarded several ways out of this mess. She could wake Clay and tell him to go to his own room. Or she could ease out of this bed, get dressed and leave. If Resa could just ease away without waking him, everything would be good.

Resa watched Clay as she softly planted her feet on the floor. She gently tossed the bedding aside and gasped when she realized that she was completely naked. Wake up and smell the spreadsheet. What do you expect when you spend the night with a man? Clothes are the least of your concerns.

Images of them together played in her head like a slideshow. Her flush deepened to crimson. Each picture slowed and then halted, lingering in her head for far too long. In her mind's eye Resa saw them, kissing, touching, stroking, and making love.

I've got to get out of here. Resa scanned the room for her clothes. She stood, tiptoeing across the room after spotting her bra and panties on the floor near the front door. Resa shook her clothes from the garments mixed with Clay's. After retrieving her underwear, she searched for her sweater, slacks, and boots.

Unable to resist, she took a quick peek at the bed. Resa nearly wet herself at what she found. No longer asleep, Clay sat silently, warm and inviting, watching her. His gaze was as soft as a caress. She focused on his face. Clay's beautiful green eyes were heavy with sexual satisfaction and slumber. Something deep within her trembled in response to what she saw.

He plumped his pillow and anchored it against the headboard, smiling back at her. "Morning," he said in a low, husky tone.

Naked, embarrassed and confused, Resa stood with her underwear barely shielding her breasts and the juncture between her legs. She glanced at him, lingering a moment too long on the broad expanse of sculptured chest as her nipples hardened to tight pebbles. Swallowing hard, Resa answered shyly, "Hello."

His gaze slid over her and momentarily rested on the curve of her breasts before moving lower. It was so easy, too easy to get lost in the way he looked at her. When his gaze returned to her face, his head tilted toward the empty spot next to him, beckoning her to return to the bed. Strains of scarlet appeared in both sets of her cheeks. Resa fought the urge to run back and snuggle at Clay's side. That wasn't possible. She needed to take control of the situation and put everything back into its proper prospective.

"What ya doing?" He folded his arms.

"Umm." Resa swallowed a second time. "Getting my clothes."

Clay drew back the bedding, patted the sheet and suggested in a deep, sensual rumble, "Forget them. Come back to bed."

Heat surged through her, settling between her legs. Her inner walls quivered in response. Resa took a step to the bed and then halted. This man was too enticing. She wanted to climb back into that bed with him. Resa wanted to continue where they left off last night. Could they? She shook the thoughts from her head. That wasn't possible.

Wetting her dry lips with her tongue, Resa said, "It's late. There are things I need to do." Spying her clothes, she shook her slacks from the pile of clothes. His shorts fell out of the mess. Red faced and wide-eyed, Resa stared at Clay.

He shrugged. "It's early. There's plenty of time."

Resa nibbled on her bottom lip. What did she want to do? She studied the clock for a heartbeat. 5:43 blinked back at her. Maybe there was time for a bit more fun. What harm would it do? Resa could enjoy being with him just a little longer before they went their separate ways for good. She took another step closer to the bed.

Palm up, Clay raised a hand toward her. "Come here, Resa."

She knew that she couldn't leave. She had to be with him one more time. Resigned, she dropped her clothes in a heap on the floor, stepped over them and headed back to the bed.

Resa took Clay's hand. He tugged gently on her hand and gathered her into the circle of his arms. She fell against him as he wrapped his arms around her, hugging her against his chest. Clay rolled Resa onto her back and leaned over her, peppering sweet kisses along her cheek.

Eyes shut, Resa caressed his back, moving her hands over the smooth skin to his round derriere. She massaged the firm mounds and then squeezed. Clay moaned, capturing her lips in an erotic tangle of tongues. His kisses ignited a gentle heat within her.

This was an equal opportunity sport and she definitely planned to play. Resa cupped his face and deepened the kiss. He tasted so wonderful. She wanted to devour him. Her fingers crept into his shoulder length blonde hair.

Chuckling, Clay's hand moved between their bodies, capturing a breast in his hand. Her nipple blossomed under his palm. He massaged the flesh and then took her nipple between his forefinger and thumb, rolling the button back and forth. The mere touch of his hand sent a warming shiver through her. Wanting more, he suckled the nub with rising enthusiasm, alternating between sucking and lapping the button while his other hand moved lower, searching out a different sensitive area.

Lifting his head, Clay gazed into her eyes while fingering her nub. Resa rubbed herself against his fingers, creating greater pleasure.

He smiled, "Welcome back, sweetheart," he whispered, his breath hot against her ear.

At least for the moment, Resa was definitely at home.

Anticipation nibbled at Resa's belly as she waited behind the hotel room door. Clay would be back from his morning slope trip any minute now. As soon as he entered the room, Resa planned to jump his bones.

She slid out of her navy business jacket and hiked her matching skirt up her thighs, preparing for Clay to enter the room. Giddy like a kid receiving Halloween treats, she waited. Boy, was he in for a surprise.

It hadn't taken them long to establish a routine. Each morning Clay woke Resa with a kiss and invited her to accompany him to the slopes, offering to teach her the basics. She returned his kiss and politely declined the offer, instead choosing to remain in bed or work on the PowerPoint documents for her presentation. The days breezed by and before Resa realized it, Thursday had arrived and it was time for her to present her findings.

Although they had spent much of the night making love, Resa craved a personal, intimate celebration between her and Clay. A giggle rose from the pit of her stomach. She'd never been so amorous in her entire life. Even when she had been madly in love, her former boyfriends had never gotten her as hot with desire as Clay did with one of his dazzling smiles or tell-tale expressions that told her exactly what he wanted to do to and with her. She never got enough of him. With Clay, a great deal of the excitement came from pleasing and being pleased by him. Who would have thought a one-night fling would provide so much fun and pleasure? Fortunately, their fling had been going strong for five days.

It must be that pale white skin. A second belly laugh rose from the pit of her gut. If she'd known it would be this good, she'd had tried a white boy a long time ago.

She heard a sound outside the door. The key card slid home and the lock clicked seconds before the door opened. Clay entered the room and hit the wall switch, instantly illuminating the hallway.

Resa stepped from behind the wooden entrance and jumped into Clay's arms. Surprised, he grunted, dropping his timberwolf-gray ski jacket and boots as he caught her.

Smiling down at him, Resa said, "Hey, you."

"Hello to you, too." Grinning, he pulled her tighter against the hard planes of his body.

Arms linked securely around his neck, Resa leaned closer and trailed her lips across Clay's. Instantly, he responded, opening his mouth and sucking the tip of her tongue between his lips. Clay's touch, firm and persuasive, invited more.

After hours on the slopes, his face felt cold. That was okay. She had big plans for Dr. Clay Shire.

"How did it go?" he asked.

Concentrating on warming him up, it took Resa a moment to realize that Clay had asked her a question. She draped her legs around his waist, linked them at the ankles and responded, "Excellent! I wowed them."

"And why wouldn't you? After all you are Resa Warren, Financial Wizard Extraordinaire. a.k.a. my reesie cup."

"And don't you forget it," she teased.

Eager to get down to business, Resa slid one hand between their bodies. While exploring the sweet tasting recesses of his mouth, she took a moment to swipe a quick feel of his tight muscular chest. It was hard to believe this man spent hours in an office chair talking to anyone, let alone a bunch of teens. From everything she'd learned about him so far, he loved participating in sports like skiing, snowmobiling and snowboarding. Her hand moved lower, finding Clay hard and ready. Breaking off the kiss, she leaned back, gazing into his eyes. "Ohh! Somebody's eager to get busy."

"Yeah, you are," he teased, stealing a quick kiss. "You didn't even let me get through the door."

She giggled, tracing his stiff shaft with her fingertips. The flesh pulsated, stretched and if possible grew harder as she worked him through the rough denim fabric. "What happened to your ski pants?"

He grinned. "I knew you'd want to get to me as soon as possible, so I decided to help you out."

"Good idea." Resa squeezed his cock through his pants.

Clay sucked in a sharp breath.

Seriously involved in arousing the man as much as possible, Resa focused on nibbling his ear as he caressed her back through her silk blouse.

Without warning, Clay spun her around. The cold wall provided support. She drew down his zipper and quickly released his rod. His flesh fell into her hand heavy and erect.

At the same time Clay's hands were busy with work of their own. His fingers brushed the string from her thong away from her hot moist opening. He lowered it to her to her feet and quickly pushed the scrap of delicate fabric down her legs and off her feet. Next came the blouse. Clay opted to pull the blouse over her head. He made quick work of her bra. Within minutes she stood nude in front of him.

This was a partnership, so Resa went to work on his clothes. She pushed the sweatshirt over his head and off his body. Clay's denim hung loosely around his hips. Resa hooked her thumbs inside his shorts and pushed both garments down. He stepped out of them and kicked their clothes out from underfoot.

"Where were we?" he asked with a devilish smile.

"Right here," Resa answered, rubbing her breasts against his bare chest.

He grabbed her butt cheeks and lifted her against his body as she wrapped her arms around his neck and jumped into his arms, locking her ankles around his waist. Using one hand, Clay guided the head of his erection to her wet opening. He rubbed the smooth head of his penis against her wet opening, coating it in her juices.

She fought the primal urge to push down and impale him. Instead she eased him inside her opening and then rotated her hips on the head of his penis. She took another inch into her canal, but this time she rotated her hips in the opposite direction.

The feelings were exquisite. She could stay like this for hours. Or maybe not. The itch to take all of him warred with the need to make this time more memorable then the last. If she could handle it. It took every ounce of will power she possessed to keep from ramming down on his rod and riding him until they both were sated. She wanted to prolong the sensations and heighten the pleasure as she, inch by incredible inch, took his entire length into her body.

With his face hidden in her shoulder, Clay groaned. "You're killing me."

She laughed, littering his face with tiny, quick kisses. "No, I'm not. You love it."

"Yeah, I do."

Resa sucked more of his shaft inside of her, wiggling on him as she adjusted to his size. She rose, allowing all but the head of his flesh to slip out of her canal and then slid down on him, this time taking more of him into her quivering walls.

Moaning, Clay gripped her cheeks and shoved into her. Resa gasped, fighting to take air into her lungs. He felt absolutely perfect. Still connected, Clay turned and pinned her against the wall and then pulled out to the head of his penis.

Resa cried. "Clay!"

"Want some more?"

"Oh yes." She panted, pushing upward to meet his downward thrust.

Clay complied, giving her exactly what they both wanted. He rammed into her over and over, taking them higher with each stroke of his cock. She took everything, meeting his downward thrust with her hips, drawing Clay as far inside her as she could.

"That's it. Don't stop," she demanded, focused on taking every ounce of pleasure Clay had to give.

They danced the dance of lovers. Resa knew she couldn't hold out much longer. Her interior walls quivered and shook with each thrust of his hips. Resa's interior walls sucked him deep into her, squeezing every drop of ecstasy from him. She shattered into a downpour of fiery sensations as waves of ecstasy throbbed through her.

"Resa," he shouted, releasing his seed inside her.

Completely spent and breathing hard, Clay and Resa broke apart, sliding to the floor.

Sated, Resa leaned over and kissed Clay gently on the lips. "Welcome home, baby."

Chapter Five

Sleep eluded Resa for much of the night. Although she and Clay had made love several times before slipping into a light doze, she still found herself wide awake, studying the light patterns under the door.

"What's wrong, sweetheart?" Clay inched closer and caressed her arm in a slow, tender motion. "You've been quiet all evening."

True, she'd been very reserved throughout dinner and dancing at the hotel's best restaurant. The fact that it was their last night at St. John's Lodge kept her from enjoying the wonderful evening Clay planned. Her emotions were in an uproar at saying goodbye and walking away from Clay tomorrow morning. She didn't want to say goodbye. She wanted to continue their relationship.

Resa realized that Clay was waiting for an answer. She hunched her shoulders, but remained silent.

"Reesie cup?"

Her heart contracted at the endearment. There were times when Clay made her feel so cherished, so special.

There was a lot wrong. Things she didn't know how to say to him. There was so much going on in her head and heart. Resa didn't have the right words to explain her feelings.

Uncertainty chewed at her insides. She was out of her element. In the business world, she was the expert. It was her job to ask the questions and make the final decisions. If the situation took a negative turn, she'd use her considerable negotiating and persuasive skills to get the answer she wanted. In matters of the heart, Resa was a novice, lacking the skills to navigate the romantic waters.

What do you say to a man that you've barely known a week? Yes, I know we agreed to a fling, but I want to change the rules. Do you think we can continue to see each other after tomorrow?

"Come on," Clay coaxed, kissing the side of her neck before nibbling his way to her shoulder. "Tell me."

Resa shook her head and shifted on the bed, turning away. A lone tear slid down her cheek and she quickly wiped it away.

Clay scooted closer and wrapped an arm around her waist, drawing her against the warmth of his body. "Do you want to talk about it?"

Despite the severity of the situation, she laughed softly. Clay was such a sweetie.

"What?" Frowning, Clay turned her to face him, trying to read her expression in the darkened room.

She laid her cheek against Clay's chest. The steady beat of his heart comforted and reassured her. "Nothing."

He nudged her with his leg. "Something."

"You sound like a psychiatrist when you asked me that."

"I am a psychiatrist."

"I know. But your question conjured up this image of you sitting in a chair next to the couch taking notes while I'm revealing all of my deepest, darkest secrets and childhood traumas."

Clay chuckled, hugging her closer. "You can tell me anything and it has nothing to do with being a psychiatrist. Besides, my area of expertise is teens. Adults are off my radar. But I want to help." His voice turned soft, seductive and persuasive. "Tell me what's going on in your head."

"Tonight is our last night together."

With her cheek against his chest, she instantly felt the increase of his heart rate. "I know."

"We're leaving tomorrow," Resa added, hoping he'd pick up the hint.

"And? Are you worried about driving home alone?"

So much for picking up on the hint. She'd have to go all the way with this boy. "No. I'm worried about being alone."

Clay cupped her face in his large hands. "You're not alone. I know you have family. Parents and brothers," he paused and then added quietly, "And me."

"Do I?" she asked in a skeptical tone, leaning back to gaze in his face. "Can I depend on you? Are you really part of my life?"

Instantly, Clay tensed against hers. The threat of tears exploded inside her. Resa shut her eyes against the pain. She'd just received her answer.

Pain made it impossible for her to speak. Her heart ached. Clay didn't care. A fling was all he wanted and had gotten. Clay didn't plan to see her once they returned to the real world. Maybe this wasn't the right conversation to have.

She shook her head and pushed her way out of his embrace, turning back to the light patterns under the door. How do people make situations like this work out? Were they supposed to ignore their feelings and go on about their business? She wasn't that cosmopolitan or cavalier after sharing so much of herself with this man.

Gathering her back into his arms, Clay answered, "Absolutely."

Tired of pussyfooting around the subject she asked, "Just how do you plan to be part of my life?"

"What?"

"I think I've been pretty clear. Sunday morning you and I will go our separate ways. We won't be seeing each other again. How do you plan to be part of my life with that scenario in place?"

Groaning, Clay leaned across Resa and switched on the light. His brows were furrowed into a frown. "Where did you get that idea?"

"Remember? This is a fling." Resa scooted into a sitting position and folded her arms across her chest. "We've spent time together at the lodge. You haven't suggested anything about seeing me after we get home."

"Oh." He massaged his forehead. "Sorry. This is my fault. I thought once we get back to town we'd go out and have fun. Get to know each other better."

"Well, that's news to me," she replied. "You haven't asked for my phone number or anything. How am I suppose to feel? What am I suppose to think?"

"I'm sorry. I just assumed we'd go out."

"You haven't said a word. You know what they say about assuming."

He grimaced. "Yeah. Yeah. Don't repeat it. Let's get our relationship on track and put any doubts to rest." He cleared his throat and said, "Resa Warren, will you have dinner with me next Friday night?"

Finally, he'd said the R word that she longed to hear. Relationship! Yes! Her heart did a flip-flop and happiness surged through her veins like electricity through the wires. She flung herself into Clay's arms and asked, "Where?"

Kissing her forehead, he leaned against the headboard. "You work downtown, right?"

Resa nodded.

"On Fridays I counsel teens at the Children's Center in Detroit. Why don't we meet at Fishbone's?"

"Fishbone's?"

"Yeah. It's in Greektown."

"Okay. I'm sure I can find it. What time?"

"I'm normally done between five and six, closer to six. Look for me about 6:15."

Pleased, she said, "Okay."

Grinning, Clay's gaze slid seductively along her nude body, asking.

"Am I off that list?"

"What list?"

"You know. The 'you don't get any' list."

She laughed, returning to her place in his arms and planting a kiss on his lips. "Yes."

"Excellent."

Clay teased her lips with his, licking the moisture from her bottom lip. "We've still got a few hours before checkout." He reached across her and switched off the light, easing them down among the bedding. "We shouldn't waste any opportunity."

"You're right." Resa leaned over his, threading her fingers through his hair. "We better get busy."

"I'm ready when you are, Reesie cup."

Friday didn't come fast enough. Resa returned to work on Monday and quickly found herself immersed in several major projects. Although she kept busy at work, her evenings were quiet and lonely. She missed Clay.

It was odd how comfortable they had become with each other while staying at the lodge and staying in a room. Within a day or two they had established a routine that worked for them. Each morning after Clay left for the slopes, Resa powered up her laptop and worked on her presentation. Once Clay returned, showered and changed clothes, they spent the day doing tourist things, like visiting the surrounding towns and shopping or hanging out in the lobby with some of Clay's friends.

Now that she was back to her regular life, Resa missed the time they spent doing ordinary things, having fun and getting to know each other. Before leaving the lodge, they had agreed to stay focused on their work so that when they got together on Friday, work would not interfere with their time together.

Friday afternoon Resa Googled Fishbone's Rhythm Kitchen Cafe, took a look at the menu and then asked her administrative assistant for directions. She had brought a separate set of clothes to work so that she could change into something less formal before heading to the restaurant.

At five o'clock, Resa bade her staff a good weekend and watched them leave the office before changing. She hung around the desk until about six. Dressed in a black crepe pantsuit and crème silk blouse with a deep v-neckline, she completed the outfit with a gold necklace with a lone tear shaped pearl that rested between her breasts. Resa put on her coat and left the building, stopping on the sidewalk to get her bearings.

Resa opted to walk, expecting Clay to take her back to her car after dinner. If the evening worked out the way she hoped, she wouldn't be going home alone. Clay would return to her place, stay the night and they could retrieve her car from the company parking lot sometime Saturday.

The brisk air pushed her along the street toward Greektown. Resa wrapped her coat closer, trying to keep warm. She still hadn't got use to the chill of Michigan winters. Clay loves this weather, she thought, remembering how his rosy red cheeks and cold hands were all over her when he'd return to the room after skiing.

The whole week they had stayed together at the lodge, Clay had tried to persuade her to try out the slopes. She always declined, preferring the warmth of their room to the frigid temperatures of snow and ice. She'd barely adapted to the cold weather and sub-zero temperatures.

Her thoughts turned to Las Vega and the contrast in climates. Would Clay be able to handle the warmth of Nevada nights? Or enjoy hiking the mountain paths, instead of flying down the slopes on his ski board? Maybe she'd find out someday, if Clay could handle her world. Although there were mountains and skiing outside of Las Vegas, she'd really hadn't been interested in exploring them.

The musical notes of New Orleans guided her to the restaurant. She stopped outside Fishbone's and peeked through the window. The cabinet style layout was a throwback to 1920s Bourbon Street.

Jammed with customers, Resa watched people continue to pile into the restaurant. From where she stood, customers were packed into every crook and cranny. The Friday night after work crowd dominated the place as they gathered around the hostess, jockeying for tables and spots at the bar.

Resa continued down Brush to the corner of Monroe and entered the building. The jazzy trumpet that led her to the building was now incredibly loud. She moved between the couples, heading to the hostess. A green dish sat on the table next to the reservation book, filled with beaded necklaces of every color. She slid between couples, silently searching for Clay. Nibbling on her bottom lip, she stopped at the bar, checking the patrons. He wasn't there. A quick glance at her watch told her that it was six-twenty. He said he might be a little late. Resa decided to freshen up and give Clay a little more time to arrive.

Ten minutes later she emerged to find the after work crowd had grown. Customers piled into the restaurant, tripping over each other. To avoid being trampled, Resa decided to wait in the foyer. This move gave her a clear view of anyone that entered the building.

For the next hour Resa stood, waiting and watching. Customers came and went. But, Clay wasn't one of them.

When seven o'clock arrived, Resa pulled out her cell phone and dialed his number. Her call immediately went to voicemail. Swallowing her nervousness, she said, "Hi Clay. It's me. I'm at Fishbone's. Where are you?"

At seven-thirty, she gathered her courage and asked the hostess, "I'm meeting a friend. Did a Dr. Clay Shire call to say that he was going to be late?"

The woman examined an array of multicolored sticky notes with names and messages on them. "Shire. Shire." The hostess shook her head and then gave Resa a pitying look. "No. Sorry. There's nothing here."

Embarrassed, Resa tried to smile but her lips felt stiff and glued together. She felt as if her face would crack into a million pieces. Where was he? "Thank you." She returned to her point in the foyer and studied her watch. She'd give him another half hour before calling his office. Clay wouldn't disappoint her, Resa knew this. They'd made these plans together.

After standing for more than an hour, the chill creeping into Resa's heart also penetrated her limbs. Her feet were numb from the cold winter evening and the opening and closing of the door. When she called his office, she got the same thing. Her call was instantly transferred to his voice mail. Determined to see things through, Resa decided to give Clay a little more time. He'd been here. Something had just slowed him down. She returned to the hostess desk and asked, "I'm sorry to keep bothering you, if I'm going to wait I might as well be seated. Do you have a reservation for Dr. Shire?"

"Let me look." This time the hostess opened a computer file on her laptop and scrolled through a series of files. She shook her head, offering a second pitying smile. "I'm sorry. There's nothing here."

Why hadn't Clay reserved a table? They had agreed to meet here. She knew why. He didn't plan to be here. No. That's not it. Clay just assumed there would be a table available. Resa swallowed her disappointment and put on a smile. "Do you have a table?"

"For two?"

Resa nodded.

"The crowd is thinning out a bit, so there may be room." She glanced at the restaurant seating arrangement and said, "I can seat you in nonsmoking."

"That would be perfect." Resa took a pen from her purse and added her name to one of the colored sticky notes. "I'll leave my name so when my date shows up, he'll know where I am."

Resa sat for an additional forty minutes. During that time she had a glass of wine that she barely touched. She ordered an appetizer of Alligator Voodoo that stuck in her throat and watched singles hook up and break up while she searched for Clay's blonde head. She dialed his cell phone three more times, but hung up when the call went to voicemail, no reason to keep leaving the same message.

With each passing minute, pain and ice gripped her heart, squeezing until she wanted to scream. By nine-thirty, hope and pretense had ended. Clay was not coming. She'd spent more than three hours in the restaurant waiting for him. Obviously, he had other plans that didn't include her. Humiliated, she rose from the table dropped enough money for the bill and tip on table and made her way to the hostess station. The woman ordered a cab and Resa returned to the company parking lot to get her car.

On the way home, the tears began to fall. By the time Resa reached her apartment, her makeup was ruined and her eyes burned from crying. She had such high hopes for this evening and possible relationship. She wanted it to work. She wanted Clay in her life.

One thing she'd learned tonight, a fling was a fling and nothing more. She'd never confuse a fling and a relationship again.

Chapter Six

For Resa, Monday was the day from hell. Twenty minutes into her work day, she wanted to run from the building, screaming in frustration.

Everyone on her floor knew about her dinner date at Fishbone's on Friday. Several of her colleagues stopped by her office to chat, inquiring about her weekend. It took every ounce of willpower she had to stay in her chair and reply pleasantly. Dropping a pleasant mask into place, Resa smiled and told the curious visitors how much she had enjoyed Alligator Voodoo and the restaurant's New Orleans French Quarter decor. By mid-morning, Resa's face felt like fine porcelain ready to shatter from the constant smiling and gentle ribbing from her co-workers.

Resa understood their interest. Since arriving in Michigan, she'd turned down all after work and dinner invitations and hadn't shown the least bit of interest in what went on around her. If it didn't involve work, she hadn't cared.

Her questions about Fishbone's had fueled their curiosity. Resa's career was her life. She focused exclusively on her work at the office, took financial files home in the evenings and stopped in the office most weekends.

At noon, her secretary, China, poked her head inside Resa's office. "I'm going to lunch. Do you want me to bring you back anything?"

Resa's stomach almost heaved at the thought of food and she doubted she could get anything to stay down even if she wanted to. She produced the same smile she'd produced all morning and answered, "No thanks. I'm good."

"Don't forget I'm stopping at the Jefferson office to pick up the Ford documents. That'll probably take me an additional twenty minutes."

"Take your time. Have Tamika pick up the phones," Resa suggested, tipping the mouse and switching on her calculator. "I'm working on a project that needs my complete attention."

"Will do." China waved goodbye and shut the door.

Now that most of the staff had left for lunch, Resa relaxed, dismissing the happy façade and let sadness overtake her. Miserable, she dropped her head on the desk and sighed. She was so tired. Thoughts of Clay and their last conversation swirled in her head, keeping Resa from getting any rest over the weekend. She refused to call again. After all, if he checked his messages, he'd know she'd called.

How had she been so wrong about Clay? She rubbed a palm across her forehead. Truthfully, it didn't matter. Everything was out of her hands. Get your act together, Resa Warren. You can't change what happened. Move on.

Resa shook her head and retrieved the Anderson file from her in-basket and mentally calculated different methods to establish a solid financial background for the family. After a few minutes, she became absorbed in the work and placed her troubles on the back burner.

Several hours later, Resa heard raised voices outside her office. Listening more intently, she stopped, catching a word here and there. One distinctive voice soared above the rest.

Shocked, Resa's mouth dropped open. It couldn't be. She rose from her desk and headed for the outer office.

In a heated discussion with China, Clay stood stiff and angry. Resa almost didn't recognize him. Gone were the ski pants, sweaters and sneakers, replaced by an olive-green business suit, spring-green button down shirt, geometric designed multi-colored tie, tan hand-crafted leather shoes and a tan cashmere top coat. A bouquet of red, yellow and pink roses filled his left hand.

Resa gasped. Was this a mirage? She wondered, amazed to find him in her office when he'd been so prominent in her thoughts for days. He'd been on her mind so much this weekend had she conjured up his image?

"Clay?" she whispered, expecting his image to disappear before her eyes. Why was he here? Correction, why was he here now? Anger filled her. Where had he been on Friday night when she made such a fool of herself at Fishbone's?

At the sound of her voice, he turned and took a step toward her. "Resa."

"What are you doing here?" she asked, noticing the curious gazes of several passersby. She didn't want speculations about her personal business floating around the office. There was enough from her Friday night catastrophe.

China stood, dropping the telephone in its cradle. Annoyed, she pointed a finger in Clay's direction. "I'm sorry we were making so much noise, Ms. Warren. This gentleman insisted on seeing you. I told him that you couldn't be disturbed. He refused to listen or leave. I was calling security."

"It's fine. I'll handle this." Moving to Clay's side, she took his arm and

75

led him to her office. Once he entered the room, she shut the door and slowly headed across the floor. The large expanse of her desk provided a needed barrier between them. I need a minute, she thought, staring, unseeing, out the window before turning to face her former lover.

When she first saw him, she wanted to throw herself into his arms. Common sense and his betrayal cut that idea short. Plus, her workplace was an inappropriate location for a rant. Enough of her personal life had been revealed last Friday. She didn't want to expose any more of her private life to the company employees. Clay was welcome to make his explanations before she'd ask him to leave.

Her gaze fell on the bouquet in his hand. She snorted, folding her arms across her breasts. A bunch of flowers wouldn't change her opinion, nor would it erase the embarrassment and humiliation she'd felt last Friday.

Silently, the seconds ticked by. Clay waited calmly until she looked at him and then said, "I'm sorry."

Whatever she might have said was instantly cut off. He'd surprised her. Resa expected him to go into some elaborate explanation followed by some psychobabble to get back into her good graces and panties. She needed to understand what he was saying.

"For what exactly?" she asked in a sarcastic tone. "For letting me wait for more than three hours for you to show up on Friday? For standing me up? Leaving me at Fishbone's without a call? Which items are you sorry for?"

"All of it. Everything."

She looked away, fighting the urge to believe Clay. She wanted to accept the sincerity in his voice and the sorrowful expression on his face. No Resa, you can't trust him. He let you down and hurt you deeply. Letting Clay off the hook so easily didn't seem like the right thing to do. "That's not enough."

He sighed and hung his head. "I didn't want to go into this. But, it looks as if I'll have to. You already know that I sometimes work at a crisis center in Detroit." He paused for a moment gathering his thoughts. "On Friday one of my colleague's sons called the center. He'd swallowed a bunch of pills. Aaron knew I was there and called me to say goodbye. Years before I helped him over a difficult time while he was in high school. We always kept in touch. I thought he was back on track. We spent most of the evening on the phone. I tried to convince him to tell me where he was. But he wouldn't. While I kept him on the phone, two of the workers called his parents and the police. We tried to track the call, but couldn't because he used his cell phone. We got nothing. I couldn't leave. We had to find him." Clay's voice broke. He cleared his throat and tugged at his tie. "Saturday afternoon his aunt found the body in her basement when she got home from Traverse City."

Resa's hardened her heart against the sympathy she felt. Not this time. There were still questions that needed to be answered.

"This was not the way I wanted to talk with you. What happened to Aaron took me down and I spent the weekend trying to help his family work through the pain of this tragedy. Please understand. I planned to meet you on Friday. Nothing short of what happened would have kept me away. I'm sorry."

Through the window pane in her door, Resa saw several of her colleagues stroll by. Her conversation with Clay needed a different venue. "Let me close out what I'm working on and then we can go to Starbucks for coffee.

Resa placed her order and took a seat near the window, watching the traffic move along Jefferson Avenue while Clay waited at the register for their drinks. Nervously, her foot tapped against the leg of the chair. So many questions swirled around in her head. When Clay told her about Aaron, sympathy had floored her.

Clay arrived with a tray filled with coffee and baked goods. He smiled sheepishly at her questioning gaze. "Sorry. I couldn't help myself."

A slice of marble cake was the last thing Resa wanted. Her stomach cramped into knots at the thought of eating anything sweet.

He placed a cup of green tea and sugar packets in front of her. Coffee and a donut were placed at his spot. Clay sat, sliding the empty tray on the vacant table next to theirs.

Silence reigned as they prepared their drinks. Finally, Clay faced Resa. She wrapped her arms around her waist and asked, "I don't completely buy your explanation. You couldn't take five minutes to call?"

Instantly, his cheeks flushed red. "No. I couldn't. It was critical that I keep Aaron on the line. The night crew was working with other cases and my secretary was on the line with the police. We were trying to trace his call. The longer I kept him talking the better the polices' chances of locating him."

"That took a complete weekend? Why didn't you call me Saturday or Sunday."

Unconsciously, Clay began to break the donut into little pieces.

I'm not the only one who's nervous, she thought.

"I was exhausted after being up with Aaron most of the night. I went home and fell into bed. I didn't wake up until the phone rang. It was Aaron's father telling me that they had found him. I'm sorry if what I'm saying sounds cold, I don't mean to disrespect you. But, I wasn't thinking beyond finding that boy."

She understood that. But, why hadn't he called later?

"You know, you could have called me," Clay reminded. "You're always telling me that this is an equal opportunity relationship. It shouldn't have all been on me."

"I did. But every time I called your cell, it went to voicemail."

"Did you try my number?" he asked.

"Once. Voicemail again." She didn't want him to think she was pitiful. "I didn't call again."

"Well, you should have," he stated with a firm edge to his voice. "Things were so out of control, I needed the reminder."

"I figured you didn't want to be bothered."

"Then the fault is all mine," he replied. "Besides, my secretary told me she called the restaurant. You got that message, right?"

"No."

Frowning, Clay shot back, "No? What do you mean no?"

"I never got the message."

"I don't understand that. I gave her the name of the restaurant and she told me she called."

"Didn't happen."

Clay leaned closer. His voice carried a touch of puzzlement. "Are you sure?"

His tone bugged her. Resa felt as if he were trying weasel of out of his responsibility. "Yes. I went up to the hostess more times then I want to admit to. There wasn't anything for me."

Wrinkles marred his forehead. Clay leaned deeply into his chair and twisted the paper cup around on the tabletop. "Everything went crazy that night. I told her to call Fishbone's. Maybe she called the wrong one. There's one in St. Clair Shores and Southfield." He shook his head, dismissing the notion. "I know I told her downtown."

Thinking back, Resa remember seeing an array of colored notes. "I remember seeing sticky notes with the names Adrian, Horace, Corzetta, Georgia and Beverly."

A sharp gleam filled his eyes and a spark of excitement entered his voice. "Wait a minute. Did you say Corzetta?"

"Yes. Why? I thought it was an unusual name that's why it stuck in my head."

Clay chuckled unpleasantly. "That's my secretary's name."

"Yeah, right," Resa stated. A note of disbelief filled her voice.

"Really." He pulled his cell phone from his pocket and then glanced at his watch. "Corzetta should be back from lunch. Call the office and ask for me. You'll see."

It was time to call his bluff. If Corzetta answered, then they could put this ugly incident behind them. If things didn't work out, then she could move on and know the truth. Resa took the phone and dialed his number, amazed and a bit embarrassed by the fact that she knew the number by heart. The automated attendant quickly switched her to Clay's office.

"Good afternoon, Dr. Shire's office, Corzetta speaking. How may I help you?"

A barrage of emotions stuck her at once, relief, happiness, even pain were on hand. Clay hadn't been lying. She felt pain because they had to go through this and relief because she still wanted him in her life.

"I'm sorry. I have the wrong number," Resa replied and quickly hung up.

A pleading light entered his eyes. Clay took her hand and kissed it, stroking his thumb back and forth over her knuckles. "I would never not call you. If Fishbone's was packed as it normally is on a Friday night, then anything is possible. The hostess probably got the names confused."

With a mixture of relief and pleasure from his touch, Resa answered, "True. There were a million people in that place."

Clay hadn't left her. He'd tried to reach her. He hadn't dumped her like rotten food. The tight knot in her chest began to unwind. One question remained. "What's next?"

"Can you get past this?" His voice shook and he grabbed her hand tightly. "Forgive and give me another chance?"

The hope in Clay's eyes was mirrored in her heart. "I don't know. Maybe."

"Can you try?"

"Yes. But there's got to be rules if we're going to be together."

"What kind of rules? Name them," he asked persuasively. "I'm willing to do whatever it takes. I don't want to lose you.""You hurt me, Clay. I was so embarrassed. People walking by and looking, wondering what kind of fool I was." Her voice turned strong and she held his gaze with a determined one of her own. "I won't go through that again. Ever."

"You won't have to. I promise," he said, "If anything like that happens again, I'll call and keep calling until I reach you."

Perplexed, Resa considered how they would handle a situation like the one that came up on Friday. After a moment, she reached for her purse and removed her cell phone. "I'm going put all of your numbers in right now. That's will I'll have them when I need them. You should do the same."

"Perfect!" Clay pulled the Blackberry from his jacket inner pocket and began keying in the numbers Resa rattled off to him. "That'll work."

"Clay," Resa called. The embarrassed and pain-filled note in her voice refused to be erased. "Don't do that to me again. Keep calling until you reach me."

"I will." He swallowed loudly and then smiled gently at her. "Am I off the list?"Smiling softly, she asked, "What list?"

"The 'you don't get any' list," he offered with a grin.

"No. You're not. I need some pampering before you get any."

"Anything you need, baby. I'm up to the challenge."

Chapter Seven

How did I get myself into this mess? Laughing softly, Resa shook her head. You know why?

After the Fishbone's debacle, Clay and Resa had talked for hours about what they wanted from this relationship. They established some rules and were working together to make things better between them.

Resa mentally rehashed the conversation that had landed her at Belle Isle on a Sunday afternoon. When Clay came to her with idea of snowmobiling, she'd tried to be fair.

Clay slid into the place at her side on the sofa. He wrapped an arm around her shoulders and drew her against his side. "Okay, I know you're not interested in skiing. Would you try snowmobiling with me?"

She folded the Wall Street Journal and gave Clay her full attention. "What do you mean? Like driving down a hill on a bike?"

Grinning, he shrugged. "Sort of. It is and it isn't like a motorcycle. You'd ride with me. We could go over the snowy terrain on the snowmobile."

Actually, she wasn't too sure about this, but she planned to keep an open mind and listen. "Tell me more."

"I thought we'd go to Belle Isle and give you a chance to see the park. It's on the Detroit River. You'll be able to see Windsor's downtown area. Besides, there is a beautiful wooded area that works best with a snowmobile. I think you'll love it."

"Do you have snowmobiles?"Nodding, Clay answered, "Mmm-hmm."

"What would I need to bring or do?"

He leaned close and kissed her lips. "Bring yourself, dress warmly and hold on tight to me on the snowmobile."

Resa leaned deeper into the sofa while considering the matter. After a long moment of contemplation, she said, "I can do that. When do you want to do it?"

The expression of surprise on Clay's face tickled her. He opened his mouth to speak, but halted before a word left his lips. Clay cocked his head to one side and stared back at her. He shook his head as if he didn't believe his ears. "Are you sure?"

She nodded, smiling back at him.

The most beautiful, engaging smile spread across his face. "Thank you!" He took her face between his hands and kissed her. He kissed her again and again. "Thank you!"

From that moment forward, Clay had done nothing but assure her about how much she'd love snowmobiling. Excited, Clay talked non-stop about the different sites in Michigan they could visit for snowmobiling. Resa listened, but didn't have the heart to tell him that she had no true interest in pursuing snowmobiling or any of the vacation spots he mentioned.

Now here she was, out in the cold on Belle Isle. Resa climbed out of the Jeep and stood on the snow covered ground while Clay prepared the snowmobile. Standing next to the SUV, Resa pulled her pink mittens from the pockets of her red jacket and covered her head and ears with a red and pink striped cap.

Cold weather didn't appeal to Resa. But, there were a couple of important reasons she'd agreed to this activity. Clay was her priority. She wanted to please him. In addition, Resa wanted to understand Clay's love of winter sport.

During her youth, her mother had always preached cooperation. To make a relationship work, couples needed to give as well as receive. Resa had always tuned her mother out when she'd gone into this particular rant. But things had changed. She cared for and about Clay. He was important to her.

Besides, she couldn't say no to him forever. After turning down his invitation to go skiing, hiking and/or snowmobiling, she'd chosen what she believed to be the lesser of the three evils. At least with the snowmobiling all she had to do was sit and ride. She could do that.

Resa glanced around the park while Clay puttered around the Jeep. Belle Isle was indeed an island that sat on the shore of the Detroit River. Clay had shown her information about the island from the Internet. The 900 acre park included a children's zoo, conservatory, golf course, and a view of Canada's shoreline. Curious, Resa strolled across the street to the huge fountain and climbed the stairs, examining the cement structure. Although it didn't run during the winter, Scott Fountain dominated this section of the park.

"Reesie cup. I'm ready," he called from the back of the Jeep.

She hurried down the stone steps and crossed the street to where Clay stood next to the snowmobile. He took her hand and drew her to the bike.

"We're all set. Normally, you'd ride your own. For today, I want you with me while I show you how to use it." Clay swung a long leg over the seat, settled behind the handles and patted the black leather spot behind him. He turned the key in the ignition and the engine sprang to life, purring softly. "Hop on. It's going to be a little tight. But we'll survive," he explained with a devilish grin.

Resa slipped into the place behind him and snuggled close. She wrapped her arms around his waist and leaned her cheek against his back. Hmm, she thought, this snowmobiling stuff has potential. Smiling, Resa slipped her hand under his jacket and stroked her fingers across his stomach through the wool of his sweater.

"Hey, you," he admonished good-naturedly, holding her hands against his belly with his. "Keep your hands to yourself."

"You'll regret those words later tonight," Resa promised.

Chuckling, Clay squeezed her hand. "I probably will."

"Hold on tight, Reesie Cup," he called over his shoulder.

"Will do."

Resa held on and squeezed her knees into his thighs for support. Clay accelerated slowly, deliberately keeping the snowmobile at a moderate pace. They rode along the one way street, around the fountain and made their way along the edge of the park on the Detroit River side, following a large group of snowmobilers. Clay and Resa rode deeper into the park's wooded area. The deeper they went, the faster the snowmobile moved.

Wind whipped across her exposed cheeks. Resa ducked her head and held on to Clay. This isn't so bad, she thought, studying the trees free of leaves but full of snow.

She gasped. Oh wow! A family of deer stood on the edge of the pathway leading into the deepest portion of the park.

Clay sped by the animals and took the next turn with lightning speed. A gush of wind slapped her in the face, sending her hat flying in the wind. Instinctively, Resa grabbed for the wool cap and lost her hold on Clay. She felt herself slipping off the edge off the seat as the snowmobile raced around the corner and cried, "Clay!"

One hand on the snowmobile, the other reached for Resa. He caught hold of her jacket, but the weight of her body and the movement of the bike conspired against him. The buttons popped on the jacket and Clay lost his hold. The jacket slipped between her fingers and Resa hit the ground with a heavy thump. The fall knocked the wind out of her. She opened her eyes in time to see the tail lights from the snowmobile.

"Hold on. I have to circle around. I'll be back in a minute," Clay yelled over his shoulder.

"Great!" she muttered, struggling to her knees. That's what you get.

You should have kept your butt at home.

Cold began to settle in her hands and joints. Resa stood, brushing snow from her denims and jackets. She shoved her hands into the pockets of her jacket and glanced around, trying to determine what to do. It was way to cold to wait here for him. Maybe she should start back and make her way to the Jeep.

Standing here wasn't doing any good. It was cold. Resa hobbled to the road, looking both ways. She wasn't sure where to go. Cars crept along the icy road, passing her. She got a few curious and confused looks for her trouble. Moving slowly, she followed the cars, hoping it would take her back to the SUV.

Fifteen minutes into her walk, a SUV pulled alongside her. Resa glanced up and found Clay sitting in the Jeep. The snowmobile was in the cab. He jumped out of the driver's seat, gathered her into his arms and hugged her tightly.

"Thank God!" he muttered into her hair. Clay drew back, examined Resa for injuries. "Are you hurt?"

She shook her head. Just my pride, she thought.

"Good. I was so scared. I had visions of you with broken bone or a head injury." Clay let out a relieved sigh.

"I'm cold."

"Come on. Let me get you in the car." He wrapped an arm around her shoulders and drew her to the passenger side of the car. After helping her into the Jeep, he climbed into the driver's seat and switched the heat to its highest point before speeding off. "You've got to get warm. When we get home, I'll make you some soup and tea to warm you up."

Resa snuggled into the seat and wrapped the edges of her coat snugly around her. She was chilled to the bone.

Clay kept snatching quick glances her way. "You warm enough? Are you sure you're all right?"

"Yeah."

"Any pain?" he asked in a worried tone.

Again she answered, "No. Just cold." She shut her eyes and tried to relax, allowing the warmth from the heater to swirl around her and fight off the cold. Today's adventure had taught her a thing or two. Number one, snowmobiling wasn't for her. And two, she didn't plan to repeat the experience ever again.

Chapter Eight

Clay and Resa traveled through the downtown neighborhood as he searched for a parking space. The neighborhood was clean, neat and attractive. This was the kind of community Resa dreamed of residing. She could easily see herself settling down here. Except, snow was part of the package. If she didn't find a way back to Nevada soon, she might look for a home in this area.

"There's a lot." Resa pointed at a parking structure on the left hand side of the street. Immediately, Clay hit the left turn signal and waited for the traffic to clear. He turned onto the side street and pulled up to the entrance gate. Instantly, she dug inside her purse and produced a dollar bill, handing the bill to Clay. "Here. It says they charge a dollar to park."

"Thanks, sweetheart." Clay stuffed the bill into the machine. It sucked in the bill, spit out a ticket and the gate lifted, allowing them access to the structure. He parked the silver Mercedes on the fifth floor and they left the car, following the boisterous crowds along Main Street to the center of town.

In a second attempt to show Resa the beauty of a Michigan winter, Clay had insisted they attend The Plymouth Township International Ice Sculpture Spectacular. The township of Plymouth played host to the largest and oldest ice carving festival in North America.

For the second time in as many weeks, Resa had agreed to attend a cold weather activity. When Clay suggested going to the festival, the idea appealed to Resa. News of the festival reached as far away as Nevada. She had heard good things about the event and wanted to see the ice sculptures.

As they waited at the corner for the light to change, Resa stamped her feet, trying to bring the circulation back into her toes. They were numb from the cold.

I'm freezing, Resa thought, zipping her coat to the neck and pulling the hood over her knit cap. Two minutes later, she was on fire. She unzipped the jacket and fanned herself with her hands. Beads of perspiration dotted her forehead. Resa wondered if she were fighting the effects of a cold or the flu.

As usual, the cold didn't bother Clay. No matter how far the temperature dropped, he handled it without a hitch. Dressed comfortably in denims, a turtleneck sweater, boots and a wool jacket, he waited at her side. His blond head was bare.

"Come on." He steered her down the street. "We passed a concession stand on our way to the parking structure." His eyebrows rose suggestively. "I'll buy you something to drink if you treat me right."

Resa laughed out loud. Clay acted so goofy sometimes. "And what do I have to do?"

A sensual fire stirred in the depths of his green gaze as he did a slow perusal of her body.

Clay's eagerness excited Resa. Her body quivered in response to the flame in his eyes.

He took her gloved hand and squeezed it significantly. "I'll tell you later. But I think you'll like it."

Laughing, she shook her head and patted his chest through his sweater. "You are so bad."

In a fake innocent tone, Clay asked, placing a hand on his chest, "Moi?"

Teeth chattering, Resa poked a finger at Clay's chest. "Yeah. You."

Frowning, he studied her. "You alright?"

"Yeah." She wrapped her arms around her middle. "But I'm cold."

The hum of a generator drew them to a white truck sitting on the corner, selling goodies to the festival goers. Clay purchased hot chocolate and kettle corn. Resa passed on the popcorn, but the hot chocolate soothed the raw ache in her throat.

"Let's duck inside the bookstore for a moment," he suggested. "That should warm you up before we go to check out the ice sculptures."

"Sure." Anything to get out of the cold. She took his hand and ran across Main Street to the store. They spent the next hour browsing the shelves, snuggling on an old sofa while sifting through current issues of magazines and listening to soft melody of Mozart playing through the speakers mounted on the walls.

Reaching for his coat, Clay faced her on the sofa and brushed a lock of dark hair behind her ear with a gentle finger. A sensuous light passed between them. "We've been here a while. Are you ready to check out the sculpture?"

Resa nodded.

He rose from the couch, pulled a yellow and black knit scarf from his coat sleeve and wrapped the scarf around Resa's neck. "This should keep you warm. You look like you need this."

Touched by his thoughtfulness, Resa gazed into Clay's eyes and couldn't resist the urge to get closer. She stood on her toes and softly kissed his lips. "Thank you."

Hand-in-hand, they exited the bookstore and crossed the street. The oval shaped park area housed ice sculptures of all shapes and sizes, covering the fringes of the park. Resa and Clay strolled through the area, stopping at each sculpture to admire the frozen art work. Ignoring her queasy stomach and throbbing head, Resa enjoyed the exhibits.

"These are really good," she said, admiring a life size sculpture of a Clydesdale horse. "Look at the intricate work. The mane and facial features are exquisite."

Clay moved closer, pointing to the horse's tail. "Look at this. Every hair on the mane looks real. The artist put every detail into place."

Despite how unwell she felt, Resa was having a good time. Smiling at him, she linked her fingers with his and leaned against him, inhaling Clay's clean, fresh scent. "Thank you for inviting me. This is wonderful."

He kissed the palm of her gloved hand, through her glove she felt the familiar tingling in the pit of her stomach his touch always brought. "You're welcome."

As the day progressed, the pain in the back of Resa's head shifted to the front. She gritted her teeth and tried to focus. She didn't want a repeat of last weekend's embarrassing events. Determined, she strolled through the park, studying the ice sculptures.

"I'm hungry," Clay announced, examining the downtown eateries for an appropriate place.

She shrugged. "What's new? You're always hungry."

He pointed toward a row of restaurants. "Not all the time," he countered. "How about something over there?"

Resa hunched her shoulders. "Fine."

"Would a burger be okay with you?"

"That sounds good," she answered, feeling her stomach churn at the thought of consuming anything more than a cracker.

Cupping her elbow, Clay led her across the street and into a local pub called Blast From the Past. Madonna's Crazy For You blared through the speakers. Dark wood floors and booths filled the restaurant and stained glass provided the bar's ambience. Crowded with visitors here for the festival, it took a few minutes for Clay and Resa to get a booth.

Within minutes, the waiter appeared, took their drink requests and provided menus. Clay ordered a cheeseburger, fries and a beer. Resa selected a turkey wrap and hot tea. Once the server delivered their drinks, Clay asked, "Did you enjoy yourself?"

Smiling she answered, "Yeah, I did."

"Enough to try something else?"

The smile dropped from her lips and her heart rate raced. What did he want to do now? "Like what?" she asked cautiously.

"Next week I'm headed back to the lodge." Clay smiled at their server when the man slid plates of food before them. The aroma of fried beef made her want to toss her cookies.

Clay doctored his burger, adding mustard, mayonnaise and sauce before biting into his cheeseburger and wiping his mouth with a paper napkin. Swallowing the mouthful, he leaned forward and whispered seductively. "Do you want to come along?"

She'd had her fill of cold weather sports for a while, especially after her fall from the snowmobile last week. But she still wanted to spend as much time with Clay as possible. "Sure. When are you planning on going?" Resa stretched a hand across the table and stole a French fry.

"Thursday. Can you get off a little early?" He dipped a French fry in a mountain of ketchup before popping the red painted potato into his mouth. He swallowed and said, "I'd like to get there before night fall."

Sitting straighter, Resa stated indignantly, "Of course I can. I'm the boss. Seriously, let me check my schedule and I'll let you know."

Working his way through his meal, Clay watched Resa nibble on her plate of food. Clay's lips puckered as if he were sucking on a sourball as he swallowed the last of his beer and glanced at Resa's plate. "Sweetheart, is everything alright? You've hardly touched anything on your plate."

She managed to shrug and say offhandedly, "I'm fine. Just a little tired."

His blond eyebrows slanted into a frown. "You sure that's all?"

"Yeah."

"Ready to go?"

"Whenever you are," she replied, reaching for her coat.

Clay grabbed his wallet from his back pocket and tossed some bills on the table. "Let's get out of here." He slid out of the booth, reached for her coat hanging on a hook, and held it up for Resa to slip into. His fingers brushed against her neck when he dropped the coat on her shoulders. Surprised, Clay's green eyes widened. He came closer, looking at her intently. "Hold on a minute." He placed the palm of his hand on her forehead. "Resa, you're burning up!"

Her heart banged like a jack-hammer against her breast. "Little bit."

"A lot. Why didn't you tell me?"

Close to tears, Resa licked her dry lips. "I didn't want to spoil the day."

"To hell with the day," Clay barked. "You're more important than anything else. Don't ever hesitate to tell me what's the matter with you." He pulled Resa into his arms, rocking her back and forth. Releasing her, Clay zipped up her coat, placed the wool cap on her head and tied the hood over it. "Warm enough?"

She nodded.

"Good." He pulled her against his side and led her from the restaurant. "Come on. You're coming home with me."

Chapter Nine

"Baby come back. You can blame it all on me. I was wrong."

The off-key lyrics nudged Resa from her dosing state back into the land of the awake. Groaning, Resa peeked out the slit of one eye and immediately shut it against the bright morning light shining through the windows.

Man, I feel bad. She ached all over and her mouth tasted like hot garbage. Resa flipped on her back, running her fingers through her damp, sweaty hair. Pain shot through her body and she bit down hard on her lips to keep from crying out.

The bathroom door swung open and Clay stepped into the bedroom followed by a dense fog of stream. Wrapped in a brown terrycloth robe, he opened a dresser drawer, retrieved fresh underwear and reached for a hair brush. Clay's green gaze met her in the mirror and noticed that she was awake. Smiling, he greeted, "Welcome back, sweetheart."

The warmth of his smile made her feel so special although she knew she looked like a mouse trying to wiggle free of a trap. "Hi," she muttered weakly, wallowing in a pile of pillows.

Clay crossed the room, scooped her into his arms, stacked the pillows behind her and then laid her tenderly among the pillows. He sat on the edge of the mattress next to Resa, drawing the bedding around her. He reached for a slim yellow case on the nightstand and shook out a thermometer. "Open up."

She complied.

Clay stuck the thermometer under her tongue and then focused on the clock. "Hold that under your tongue." Three minutes later, he studied the mercury level and then said, "Your temperature is in the normal range. Looks like you're on the mend."

"I feel better," Resa croaked and shook her head. "Except I sound like a frog and I ache all over."

"You will for a while."

She tried to clear her throat.

"Throat dry?" He ran a finger down her neck.

Resa nodded.

"You need water." Clay rose from the bed and headed for the door.

"I'll be right back."

With nothing else to do but wait, Resa curiously glanced around his bedroom. Although they had been seeing each for a little over a month, she'd never been to his house in Troy. They always ended up at her apartment.

Clay's bedroom ran the length of the back of the house. High navy walls and crème cathedral ceilings dominated the room. She laid in his custom made king size bed covered by a navy and crème comforter, dark blue sheets and crème-colored pillows. Clay owned all the man toys, including a 50 inch flat screen television mounted to the wall and surround sound speakers. A mahogany dresser, armoire and dual nightstands rounded out the furnishings.

Clay returned with a glass of ice water in one hand and orange juice in the other. He set the glasses on the nightstand, helped Resa into a sitting position and then retrieved the water, holding it to her lips. He warned, "Be careful. Take small sips."

Thirsty beyond belief, Resa resisted the urge to snatch the glass from his hand and swallow the water in one big gulp. Besides, she barely had the strength to hold a glass.

Shaking his head, Clay said, "Take it easy. I don't want you to choke." After swallowing several sips, he switched the glass of water for juice. "Okay?"

She nodded, taking the glass from his hand and sipping the cool drink. "Clay?"

"Yeah?"

"How long have I been here?" she asked.

"Since Saturday."

"What's today?"

"Wednesday." Clay reached for a brown prescription bottle, shook a pink pill into a small paper cup and handed it to her. "Antibiotics."

"Thanks." She took the pill and swallowed it with a sip of water. A thought hit her. "Oh no!" With shaky hands she grabbed the telephone and tried to dial. Her fingers refused to cooperate and she ended up with a wrong number. Frustrated, she muttered low and ugly words as she tried again.

Smiling sympathetically, Clay removed the phone from her hands and returned it to the cradle. "Relax. I took care of your job."

"What? How?"

"I called China."

Resa smiled. "Thank you."

"Anyway, I told her that you had the flu and wouldn't be in for a few

91

days. China was very concerned, but promised to hold down the fort until you were better. Everything is under control."

"She was probably wondering who you were."

He laughed, folding his arms across his chest. Blond chest hair winked at her from the deep vee of his robe. "China remembered me."

"What about your job? How did you juggle that and me?"

"Easy. One of the partners in the practice picked up my patients for a few days. I'll do the same for him when he goes on vacation next month."

Resa leaned more comfortably into the pillows and watched Clay for a moment. "It looks as if you've got both of our lives under control."

He grinned, leaned forward and gently kissed her lips. "I tried, sweetheart. You needed me."

Shocked, she leaned away. "Don't do that. You'll get sick."

Laughing, Clay kissed her. "I don't get sick like that."

Resa pulled the sheet closer as a thought struck her. Curious about what she had worn to bed, she lifted the bedding and found herself dressed in one of Clay's white button down shirt. She turned to him with a question in her eyes.

He hunched his shoulders. "It worked when I needed to sponge you down."

Resa's skin went hot all over. Her thoughts went to Clay sponging her down. "I need a shower."

"Nope. You're too weak to stand up in the shower. It's a bath for you."

Smiling seductively, she suggested, "You can come in the shower with me. Help me wash all over."

He laughed, examining her body. "I'd love to. But you are not ready for anything like that. Maybe in a few days."

She pouted prettily. "You're no fun."

"That's not true. We have lots of fun. Just not right now." Clay brushed a lock of sweaty hair from her forehead and kissed the spot. "Once you're better, I'll show you."

The next morning Resa felt better. After breakfast and a bath, she persuaded Clay to let her use his laptop. Propped against a pile of pillows in the center of his bed, she placed the computer in her lap and logged into the company's Intranet. She got into her e-mail and reviewed comments on several of her current projects. "Oh wow! Clay, you must have been wrong about how long I've been sick? You won't believe this. There are 376 new messages in my e-mail inbox."

Exiting the bathroom, Clay hopped onto the bed beside her and glanced at the laptop computer screen. "See, Reesie Cup, you're a very important lady. You've been missed." He kissed her shoulder while caressing her arm. "But I got you," he said in a seductive and tantalizing tone.

Resa did a quick perusal of Clay's body clad in a robe. He stretched his long legs out in front of him and crossed them at the ankle on the bed. She grinned. "Actually, I think we've got each other."

"I hope so."

"I know so," she answered, picking up his hand and kissing it.

"Okay Ms. Workacholic. Do your thing. I know you plan to read all of your e-mail, aren't you," Clay stated with certainty.

"No, Dr. Psychiatrist man, just the ones from work, my family or marked urgent. Like this one." She clicked on the e-mail and began to read. Lips pursed, Resa leaned back against the headboard as her heart began to race. "Clay, hand me the phone."

A puzzled expression spread across his face, but he handed her the phone anyway. "What's up? Everything all right?"

Nodding, she raised a halting finger in Clay's direction as she spoke into the receiver. "Hi, China."

"Hey Resa. How are you feeling?"

"Yeah, I'm better. Listen, I need you to check on something for me."

"Sure. What do you need?" China asked.

Resa continued, studying the computer screen. "I got an e-mail from corporate about a position for an assistant vice president of corporate accounts. Find out if that position is still open. It's located in Nevada."

"Will do," China answered. "Where are you going to be?"

"In bed, but you can reach me on my cell." Pleased with herself, Resa hung up, turned to Clay and pointed to her purse sitting on the dresser. "Can you hand me my purse?"

She expected him to be curious, interested in what he'd overheard. Instead, anger, tense and palpitating glared back at her from his green eyes. Jaw tight and stiff, Clay rolled off the bed and moved away. Shocked by his expression, Resa froze. It almost frightened her. Clay could never do anything to hurt her, right? She reached for his hand, but he shook her off. Clay had never rejected her, no matter what happened between them. Resa felt as if he'd slapped her. "What's wrong?"

He stiffened at the question. "What was that all about?"

"There's the possibility of a position back home. I want to find out more about it."

"In Nevada?"

Annoyed by his tone, she snapped, "Yes. Las Vegas to be exact. What's that got to do with you?" she asked.

"I'd say everything. There's you and me. Us to be exact. Or have you forgotten?" Anger lit up Clay's green eyes as he stood next to the bed, glaring down at her. "How do we fit into this job? Las Vegas to be exact? Or are you making plans for us to continue our relationship, long distance?"

Embarrassed, she dropped her gaze. Okay, the truth was she hadn't been thinking about anything but the job. The prospect of moving home pushed all other coherent thoughts out of her head. "Oh." She pushed a lock of hair behind her ear. "I wasn't thinking. I'm sorry."

"Sorry is not going to cut it this time. How do you think it made me feel? You were discussing leaving Michigan without a second thought. Actually, I didn't enter into your thoughts, did I?"

"Clay! Stop. Think logically. Why are you working yourself up this way?" Resa folded and refolded the edge of the sheet. "It's only an inquiry. Nothing is set in stone. I haven't sent a resume or anything, let alone gotten an interview for the job."

"That's not the point. You didn't hesitate one iota." Clay tapped his chest. "What about me? Don't I count for anything? Other than a good screw?"

Resa rose onto her knees, shouting, "That's not fair."

"Guess what? Life isn't fair. You should know that."

His tone infuriated her and she fired back, "You're right. I didn't. But Clay, I've never lied to you about how I feel about living in Michigan. I don't like the cold weather." She linked her hands. "Of course I want to go home. That's where my family is. It warm and I have friends who I miss me and they miss me."

"Don't I have a place in your life?"

In the face of Clay's pointed questions and anger, Resa stopped, feeling weak and vulnerable. She wanted to appease him. "Yes, of course you matter. But Clay, we're pretty new. Anything could happen between us. Remember the Fishbone's incident. I thought we were done then. All I'm doing now is checking out my options."

His stance became defensive. "I explained that. We talked it through."

"Yes, we did," she answered quickly. "But it doesn't mean that we'll stay together. You could have a fiancé that I don't know about."

"That's ridiculous. And another thing we're far from new. Resa, we're involved in a love affair. We love and take care of each other." He hunched his shoulders. "What do you think I've been doing for the last four days? I've been taking care of you because I love you."

Hearing those words brought pleasure to her and she instantly wanted to respond. But, there were issues that needed to be addressed.

"Not your job or family. Me. Your boyfriend, lover, man friend. Whatever." He tossed his hand in the air. His voice was heavy with sarcasm. "You lived in my house. I was there for you."

Hoping to defuse the situation, she softened her voice and answered, "Of course it does. I appreciate everything you've done for me. The job thing is nothing to get upset about. Please, calm down."

"You don't get it, do you?"

Puzzled why he was getting so upset, Resa stared back at Clay as he moved around the room, removing clothes from the closet and tossing them in a chair.

"I thought we had more than that. I thought you cared, maybe even loved me. That we were headed toward something special."

"I do care."

"Not enough apparently. I think the only person you care about is yourself. I'm sorry. This is just too much for me to handle right now." He stormed across the room and jerked open a dresser drawer, tossing items on the dresser surface. "I'm going up to the lodge. You can stay here for a couple of days until you feel better. I'll be back Sunday evening. I'd appreciate it if you weren't here when I get back."

Shocked, a hot tear rolled down Resa's cheek. All she could do was watch him leave the room. What in the world was wrong with him?

For the next hour Resa trailed around the house behind Clay, trying to make him see reason. Ignoring her, Clay gathered his stuff and packed. Once he was done, he grabbed the keys off the kitchen counter, tossed his bag over his shoulder and headed for the back door.

With a hand on the doorknob, he turned to her. The expression on his face broke her heart. Clay had lost that edge of laughter that always seemed to be part of him. His eyes were dull and lifeless.

"Go back to bed. You need your rest. When you leave, shut the door. I'll have a neighbor lock up later." He drew in a deep breath. "Goodbye Resa." Clay said and closed the door after him.

How had they gotten here? Aching to be in his arms, Resa prayed this was the moment that Clay realized that he didn't want to do this.

Chapter Ten

With a sense of déjà vu, Resa stepped through the doors of St. James' Lodge. As she marched through the lobby, her gaze systematically scanned the area for Clay's blond head.

Things are still the same here, she thought, searching for Clay among the guests gathered around the fireplace, telling tales of their accomplishments on the slopes. Had it been less than two months ago that she'd strolled into this building and allowed Clay into her life?

Was she making a huge mistake by coming to the Lodge and confronting Clay? Would she be able to persuade him? Of course, Resa considered herself the great negotiator. Would Clay listen? Had she hurt him so much that he wouldn't be able to get past the pain? These were all good questions. Unfortunately, she didn't have any answers.

Heart racing, Resa headed for Maxie's. She stood for a moment, adjusting to the darkened lighting before heading to the bar. Sure enough, Clay sat, holding court with a group of his ski cronies.

Telling her shaky limbs to calm down, Resa moved to the bar. She stopped next to him and waited for the flow of conversation to die down. One of the men nodded toward Resa. Noting the expression on the man's face, Clay turned. His green eyes grew round as Granny Smith apples. He made a move to turn away, but Resa touched his shoulder and said, "Clay. Please. We need to talk."

Instantly, Clay shook off her hand. Without saying a word, he turned his back and brought the tumbler to his lips, sipping the amber liquid. "Not going to happen," he offered with heavy sarcasm.

Suddenly all of the frustration, worry and pain she'd felt sprung to the surface and without thinking she grabbed his arm, turned him to face her and said with equal sarcasm, "Going to happen. Either now in front of your friends or in private." She shrugged. "Your choice."

Aware of the interested gazes watching them, he slammed the glass against the bar's surface. It surprised Resa that the glass didn't splinter into a thousand pieces. "Okay. You've got this round. But not here." He fished in his pocket, drew out a twenty dollar bill and tossed it on the counter top. "Gentlemen, I'll see you later."

"This way." Cupping her elbow, he led her from the restaurant. Once they were out of ear range of his buddies, Clay spun her to face him. "What are you doing here? I thought I told you to get some rest."

"I need to talk to you."

He shook his head. "No. We're done. No more talking."

Fury filled her like a volcano ready to explode. "No, we're not. You are going to listen to me."

Lips pursued, he grabbed her arm and marched her toward the elevator. "Fine. We'll go to my room." Dead silence filled the elevator as they entered and rode to his floor. Once they stepped inside his room, Clay switched on a light, took a sit in the chair next to the bed and waited. "Say what you've got to say and then leave."

The ice in his voice chilled her soul. Not for the first time, Resa questioned the wisdom of this trip. "I don't think you've been fair to me."

His stoic expression turned to incredulous. "What? Bullshit!" he jumped to his feet and stalked to within inches of where Resa stood.

Shaking in her boots, she met his furious gaze without flinching and continued in a false bravado tone, "You heard me. Since we met, all we've done is play at a relationship. We tiptoe around each other, never really sharing our true feelings."

"I'm not buying that. You and I have been as close as any two people can be."

"Yes, we have. Physically. But we don't talk. Clay, we don't trust each other. Not completely. The closest we came to a true intimate conversation happened after the Fishbone's incident."

"I disagree." He paced the room. "I told you I loved you. Those were my true feelings. That's as intimate as it gets."

"True. You said it and then you left. There was no discussion. No talk. You wouldn't have told me if the situation hadn't turned out so badly."

"I-I-I," he stuttered and then stopped. He shoved his hands insides his pockets and studied the floor.

She took a sharp breath. "Guess what? I love you. But, we didn't get there the right way. The way we should."

He gazed up at her with hope and longing in his eyes. "Why are you telling me this now? Are you saying this to get me back?"

"No. Our time together has been spent making love and trying to convince each other about the weather."

Clay was silent as he considered what she'd just said. She pushed a little harder. "We never talked about dreams. Expectations. Aspirations. Do you have family in Michigan? Brothers and sisters? Are your parents alive? Where do they live?"

A crimson stain crept up Clay's neck and settled in his cheeks. Digging the toes of his sneakers into the carpet, Clay answered, "Yes. They live in Bloomfield."

Good. Maybe her words were sinking in. "Do they?" She asked.

He nodded.

"Did you know that I had two older brothers and that I'm the youngest of three?"

"No," he mumbled, slowly moving around the room.

"That's my point. We don't know enough about each other. We have feelings for each other and they're wonderful. But, the truth is I haven't trusted you with any of my deepest, darkest secrets and I don't know yours."

Brows knitted together, Clay asked, "So what should we have done?"

The look on his face made her want to laugh. The all-knowing psychiatrist was as confused as any other person. But the situation was far too dire for her to do that. He needed to understand what was going on in her head when she requested info about that job. Clay should understand how she felt. That was the only way they were going to make it. They had to find a way to get past this latest roadblock.

"Clay, if we really want this relationship, its time for you to let me see the real you and for me to do the same."

That's not right, Resa thought, wringing her hands together as she searched for the correct words. "Let me rephrase. I've only shown you the good stuff. It's sort of like being on a first date where you're trying to make a good impression. You don't let them see much beyond that. You only know the surface stuff about me, but not the things that make me tick, besides you. In fact, you didn't try to find out. It's time to move past politeness to the real deal."

"Okay." Clay sat on the edge of the bureau. "I'll buy a little of that."

"You're the psychiatrist. If you take a moment to think about it, why do you think you exploded this afternoon? Because I had never told you that I wasn't completely happy here. I've mentioned that I don't like the cold. But you just chucked it off. I didn't want to disappoint you. And come on, Clay. There were things about you that you never told me. We don't talk about your job. I would love to know some of the experiences you have with the kids. I'm interested in you. You didn't know that I wanted to go home. I assumed you understood. But you didn't. Maybe things did happen to quickly between us. But I do love you."

"And I love you," he stated.

His declaration of love made her body sing with happiness. Sensing that they were headed toward true communication, she moved to him.

"How do we fix us?"

"Are you busy tomorrow night?"

"What?" He asked, gazing at her with a question in his eyes. "No. Why?"

Please God! Let this be the right thing for us, Resa prayed. "I'd like to take you to dinner."

His eyes lit up.

"Just dinner." She placed her hands on top of his. "Clay, the upshot to this situation is we've got the love already. We can have more than great sex and love. We can share trust."

Chapter Eleven

"Girl, that white boy is hot! Where did you find him?" Kendra Phillips, Resa's cousin asked as she zipped up the back of Resa's dress. "And does he have any brothers?"

Grinning, Resa shook her head. "You don't like white boys."

Kendra planted a hand on her hip and her head swayed from side-to-side as she spoke, "Neither did you before you moved to Michigan. Now look at you."

Resa nodded meekly. Kendra had a point. Things definitely had changed in the last few months. Not only was she dating a white boy, but she was very much in love with him.

"How did Aunt Helen and Uncle Nick take the news?" Kendra smoothed the imaginary wrinkles from the front of Resa's dress.

"Shocked at first," Resa admitted. "But they could see how much we loved each other. So they gave their approval."

"Even if they didn't, I could tell that you weren't giving him up and he wouldn't let you go. Clay's signed on for a lifetime."

Resa examined herself in the mirror, admiring her knee-length strapless dress. Yes, they'd both signed on for the long haul. Although it was scary to place her life in someone else's hands, Resa truly believed she was in the best hands.

Fussing around Resa, Kendra continued, "You know. This is not what we talked about growing up. You wanted the huge wedding with everybody there. Here you are at the Little White Chapel in Las Vegas. What's up with that?"

"It's what Clay and I wanted. We don't need a big wedding. That's all for show. Weddings should be about the couple in love. At least this one will be."

"Where are you guys going for your honeymoon?" Kendra asked, picking up the bride's bouquet.

"We're taking a month to explore. We're going to Alaska for fifteen days."

Grunting, Kendra shivered. "Too cold for me."

"I once said something similar," laughing, Resa admitted. "Clay will keep me warm. Then we're going on a cruise to the Caribbean."

"Ohh! That's more like it. Why don't you skip the cold stuff and head straight for the tropics?"

"No." Resa shook her head. "I have to share and that means traveling to both locations. Besides, I'm looking forward to seeing Alaska." This is what sharing truly means. You give and take.

There was a tap and then the door opened. Resa's mother poked her head into the room. "Is everything all right?"

"Come on in, Mom," Resa invited. "We're just talking."

Mom hurried across the room and took her daughter's hands. Resa smiled. Her mother always seemed to be in motion. Her hands and body were always moving, doing things.

Kendra moved to the door. "It looks as if you need a minute. I'm going to round up everybody.

"Resanne," Mom sat in front of her. "We expected something very different for you. But now that you've made your choice, I want you to know that we're behind you one hundred percent. You have our support and will always have our love. You've never disappointed us and I know you never will. We love you. Always remember that we are here for you." She unwrapped a tissue, revealing a gold necklace with one tear shaped diamond in the center. "I want you to have it."

She gasped. Grandma's necklace. Tears filled Resa's eyes. Her heart filled with such love for her mother. "Thank you, Mom."

"No tears. You'll ruin your pretty face. Mom would want you to have it." Mom dabbed at her daughter's eyes with the same tissue and then hung the necklace around Resa's neck. "There, you look perfect. Come on. It's time to get married. That man of yours has been pacing the floor."

They stood. Resa drew her mother into a big bear hug. "I love you, Mom."

"I know you do. And I love you, Resanne. It's time to go. Your dad and Clay are waiting."

Kendra poked her head inside the room. "Hey ladies, we're waiting for you."

Laughing, Resa answered, "We're coming."

"Good, because if you don't hurry, I'm going to snatch that cutie-pie for myself."

"I'm not worried," Resa stated confidently. "He'd never leave me. We're in this for life."

Resa, Kendra and Mom moved down the hall and found Dad waiting near the doorway, leading to the chapel.

"All set?" he asked, eyeing the women.

Nodding, Resa said, "I'm ready. Let's do this."

Dad extended his arm as the first chords of the wedding march began to play. Together, they made their way to the front door to the chapel.

Mom stepped into the chapel first on the arm of one of the ushers. She kissed Resa on the cheek. Kendra followed. "Remember, if you don't treat that honey right, I'm coming after him."

"I'll remember."

Resa and Dad rounded out the wedding party. Tall and handsome, Clay stood at the altar next to the minister and Jim, his best man. Clay winked at her and she broke into a smile.

As they moved down the aisle, she considered all that she and Clay had gone through to get to this point. None of that mattered now. They were here and she planned to work hard at her marriage, to never take Clay for granted or assume anything. Clay deserved all of her love and she intended to give it to him.

When they reached the altar, Dad placed Resa's hand in Clay's and stated softly, "You'd better take good care of my girl. Hear me? Treat her right."

"I will," Clay promised, holding Resa's hand securely in his.

"Are you ready?" she asked.

"I'm ready when you are," Clay answered, turning to the altar.

The minister stepped up and began the speech known all over the world. "We are gathered together . . ."

The End

Rode Hard

By
Seressia Glass

Chapter One

It was high-school reunion time again. Not that he'd go. He hadn't gone to Lassiter High School's tenth reunion five years ago or any other memory-lane trips because some idiot liked to schedule them during Bike Week, the most profitable time for his custom bike business. Then again, he'd never received an invitation before, since technically he'd never actually graduated. Getting a G.E.D. ten years down the road meant you weren't invited to any of the reindeer games, but donating the funds to build a new vocational shop had made him a Very Important Alumnus.

Still, he'd accept an invitation now, if it meant seeing her again.

Matt Ryan stared at the photo on his laptop. Regina Maria Lourdes Lieberman, the most unforgettable girl of his high school years. With a Black and Cuban mother and a Jewish father, she'd been a 5'5" bundle of contradictory human dynamite. Even then she'd been gorgeous, with her caramel brown skin and wild black hair. Way too much for his fourteen year-old hormones to handle.

His thirty-three year-old hormones thought he could handle her just fine, if he had the opportunity. This was why he intended to make one.

Angel DeVine entered his office. At 6'1" with arms full of tats and a taste for low slung jeans and leather, Angel was every bit the biker domme she looked. God knows she tortured him by making him sit in the office and handle business before going to the shop and lighting up a torch.

"Matt, we need to work on the plans for Biketoberfest," she said, pulling her PDA out of a back pocket. He wondered how it actually fit, the jeans were so tight. "I know we're still months away, but—"

"But we need to start planning now," he finished. "I understand. I already have an idea for a caterer."

He turned the laptop around so that Angel could look through Gina's site. The blood red tank top emblazoned in gold with the words, "I Feel A Sin Coming On" strained against her generous copper cleavage and showed off her sleeves of Egyptian tats to their advantage. More than a few of the guys thought Matt was nuts to not want a piece of her, but Angel was too valuable to his company to ruin things with sex. Besides, both her boyfriend and her girlfriend were bigger than he was.

"Come on, Matt—she ain't our kind of people," Angel said as she straightened, tossing her braids back over her shoulder. "We're Daytona Beach. She's Miami Beach."

"I know." He didn't have any illusions. Gina hadn't gone for the scrawny geeky kid who'd been her lab partner in biology class or shop. He doubted she'd go for the tattooed grease monkey that he'd become. The highly successful bike designer to the stars, however, probably had a shot. Either way, he intended to find out.

"I don't care if she's not our kind of people. If she's worth half her rep, she'll make it work. Call her up and get her to cater our party. Keep mentioning dollar amounts until she says yes."

"Dammit, Matt." Angel pierced him with her tortoise-shell gaze. "You used to do her, didn't you?"

"No." Unless you counted a healthy imagination and a five-fingered salute as doing Gina by proxy.

"But you want to."

Matt looked at his manager. "Wouldn't you?"

"Hell yeah, I would," Angel told him, entering notes on her Blackberry. She was a tech-head of the first order, which she wouldn't admit to enjoying even if caught smiling in the act. "I could do her and be done, but there's more to this for you than a memory-lane hookup."

He opened his mouth to protest, but she threw up a hand. "Unh-unh. Back to business. Do you have any sort of theme in mind for the party?"

"We've got some reps from Japan coming in to talk about a possible partnership," Matt said, pulling up a file on his laptop. Business was definitely a safer topic with Angel. "A few members of Young Hollywood are coming, and we're doing the usual bike donation for the Foster Parents' Foundation auction, so we'll want major press for that. Given everything we have riding on the show, I want first class food. We'll keep with our regular beer and barbecue menu for the other days."

"And you want this woman to cater all of that?" Angel's skepticism shone through loud and clear. "Woman's probably never had a baby back rib in her life."

"Considering that her dad's Jewish, you're probably right," Matt said. "But I bet she'd get familiar real quick if the price is right. No, we'll do our usual for the open house, and have Gina handle the big show. Feel free to name drop. I'm expecting that chick from Apocalyptic Angel to put in an appearance."

Angel smiled. "Emma Rose, the one that had the hots for you?"

"Don't remind me." Matt groaned. The starlet was pretty in a negative-body-fat kind of way. Supplying a couple of custom bikes for her blockbuster movie had been a nice coup.

"I thought y'all looked good together," Angel said with a sly smile.

She was baiting him. He knew it, and he bit anyway. "I'm a decade older than her," Matt retorted. "Old enough to be her older brother. We were both in it for a good time, not a long haul. After a while, wild and crazy sex can get old. Thank God she's got a short attention span. I was never so happy to come back to Daytona in my life."

He glared at Angel. "This'd better not get around the shop. I got a rep to maintain."

"You remember that when it's contract renewal time."

Matt groaned. "I should have never asked you to pose with my bikes all those years ago."

"Dylan asked me to pose with the bikes. You asked me to run the ad campaign."

"That's because you laid Dylan out with a single punch. I'm a quick learner."

"That you are. Amazing how the business took off once you got rid off that lazy excuse of a partner."

Dylan had wanted the glamour of having a custom business, but not the hard work it entailed. Matt hadn't had breakups go as bad as kicking Dylan out, even if you added in psychotic actresses. Thank God Angel had a killer business sense and MBA to go along with her killer bod.

"Yeah, business is booming, which means we can afford Gina's services."

"Depends on the services," Angel murmured. "Fine, I'll snag your lady friend, but it's gonna cost you."

Matt smirked. "I have no doubt of that."

Regina Maria Lourdes Lieberman discovered that being drunk in a bridesmaid's dress had its disadvantages.

Cursing loud enough to curl her mother's hair, Gina kicked off her strappy sandals and managed to pick them up while maintaining a hold of her turquoise hem, the bridal bouquet and half a magnum of champagne. Carefully balancing her bridal burden, Gina teetered over to one of the last tables then flopped into a tulle-wrapped chair.

The wedding had been beautifully emotional, the reception—her wedding gift to Kat and Pietro—fabulous and filling. The bride and groom were probably even now screwing themselves silly on the way to the airport for an undoubtedly raucous celebration with Pietro's family in Sicily before moving on to the Amalfi Coast for their honeymoon.

Gina sighed, then gulped an unhealthy swallow of the champagne. She didn't want to feel jealous of her friend, but had given up trying to fight the emotion several hours ago. Kat deserved her happiness, but Gina couldn't help wondering when her second chance would happen. Maybe the imminent relocation back to Miami would kick start things.

Her cleavage vibrated. Gina pulled her Bluetooth out of her hair ornament and clipped it to her ear. "Regina Lieberman here."

"Is this All Ways Catering?" a feminine voice asked.

Gina sat up. "Yes it is. How may I help you?"

"I'm Angel DeVine with Oceanside Choppers in Daytona. We'd like to hire you to cater our Biketoberfest event."

The bubbly buzz vanished. "Biketoberfest?"

"It's a motorcycle festival here in Daytona," Angel clarified. "We have an open house and a Custom Chopper show, but our main event is saved for the end of the week. It's partly a bike show, partly a charity event that's going to be attended by some Hollywood types, investors, and industry professionals."

Why the hell hadn't she stuck a notepad and pen down in her freakin' cleavage? "How many people are you talking, exactly?"

"About a hundred people, and we're looking to go upscale. How much would it cost to bring you on board?"

Gina rubbed at her forehead. Sure, she had some contacts in Daytona, but Biketoberfest sounded a little out of her element. What the hell did you feed to bikers that would also please Hollywood stars and business people?

"Ms. Lieberman?"

Oh, right. "I'm wrapping up a wedding right now, Ms. DeVine," she said into the phone, wondering if she was speaking to a former stripper or something. A drag queen probably didn't last long with a bunch of bikers. "I'd really like to create a few sample menus, research the event in question and meet my potential clients face-to-face before I agree. We should see if we're the right fit for each other."

"Would you be able to come to Daytona next week?"

"Next week." It was ten o'clock on a Saturday night. Next week started in twenty-six hours.

Do something spontaneous, Kat had advised. Look what it had gotten her—a gorgeous Italian man who loved her to death. Gina had already planned to drive down next week anyway, to meet with her realtor and maybe or maybe not attend her high school reunion. Of course, hopping a plane to Daytona at the last minute was expensive. Sometimes being spontaneous wasn't cheap.

"We would, of course, reimburse your travel expenses," the woman said.

That sealed it. "I'll come down Monday afternoon," she answered, deciding that would give her plenty of time to recover from the torture of being matron of honor, and wrap up last-minutes business. "Where should I meet you?"

"I'll book you into the Hilton, right on the beach," the woman said briskly, then rattled off her contact information. "Take the day to soak up the atmosphere of our town. We can meet you in the hotel's lobby at eleven Tuesday morning. We look forward to working with you, Ms. Lieberman."

"I look forward to meeting you."

She disconnected. She very much doubted there was anyone in Daytona who could sweep her off her feet and make the luck of the bridal bouquet come her way, but there was no reason to thumb her nose at fate

Chapter Two

Hot damn.

Gina looked at the biker lounging on the chopper in front of her hotel, and forgot how to walk. The opening riff from AC/DC's Back in Black pounded inside her brain as she took in the most awesome display of manly temptation.

Mr. Temptation lounged on one of those custom motorcycles that she'd caught on a recent TV show—a chopper. Scuffed black boots encased his feet. The faded jeans looked as if they'd been painted on, as did the gleaming white T-shirt he wore, both showing every dent and bulge of his muscled physique. Dark stubble shadowed his cheeks and chin, balancing out the honey blond hair that hung carelessly about his face.

She couldn't see his eyes behind the sunglasses, but it didn't matter. What she could see was more than enough. Everything about him screamed, "Bad Boy! Stay Away!"

Exactly what she was looking for.

Smiling, she tilted down her sunglasses to admire the view. "I bet that's a nice ride."

The biker returned her smile, dimples appearing like slashes in his cheeks. "So I've been told."

Whoa, papi. "Hhm, I guess I'll have to try that out sometime."

"There's no time like right now," he said, gesturing either at the bike or his crotch, she wasn't sure which.

Gina laughed. "Unfortunately, I'm here for business."

"Well, maybe you should think about mixing some pleasure in with the business," he told her. "I'd be happy to give you a ride you won't forget."

Go for it, girl.

"You know what? I think I'll take you up on that." Let's see how serious you are. "Give me a half an hour. I need to check in. If you're here when I come back, I'd enjoy a tour of Daytona from the back of your bike."

"And I'd enjoy giving it to you." Mr. Bad Boy Biker grinned. "The tour that is. I'll be parked over there."

He revved his engine, and then eased away from the curb as smooth as you please. Gina watched him pull into one of the front parking spaces then turned for the door, hoping her tongue wasn't dragging the ground after her. That man was trouble. And she planned to get into a whole lot of trouble before the day was done.

Matt couldn't believe his luck. Regina hadn't recognized him. Not that he'd expected her to. He'd changed a lot in the years since ninth-grade. Besides, she'd been so busy drooling she hadn't asked his name.

He grinned as he pulled into one of the spaces close to the main entrance. He'd felt her interest even before she'd pulled those shades down. A part of him was a little irked that she'd hook up with a stranger so easily even while the horn-dog in him appreciated it. Course; there was a chance that all she wanted was a ride. Just like there was a chance of a porn star being president.

As he waited, he debated telling Regina the truth—at least part of it. Sometime during the night he'd have to tell her that he owned Oceanside Customs, and see if that would put a damper on things. Telling her that she was his high-school crush probably could be saved for another day.

Matt almost lost his cool as he spotted Regina at the hotel's entrance fifteen minutes later. Painted on low-rise black jeans hugged her hips. A black t-shirt showed just a bit of belly and pulled tight against her breasts, making it hard for him to decide where to look. He thought he saw a couple of chains in there somewhere, but didn't give a damn about those or the dark shades that covered her eyes. Regina Maria Lourdes Lieberman sure had filled out since high schoool.

God damn, this wasn't going to be easy. Good thing she wasn't expecting a good guy because watching her strut his way, all Matt wanted to be was very, very bad.

Gina paused just outside the hotel's entrance. Her heart jumped, hard, in her chest. True to his word, Big Bad Biker Man was still in front of the hotel, still lounging on his bike, still looking like he didn't have a care in the world.

And still fine as hell.

She tossed her hair over her shoulders and put a little extra oomph into her walk, thankful she'd passed up the cheese Danish at the airport. He straightened up and a primal play of muscles that almost made her forget how to roll her hips. A smile curve her lips. She believed in looking good for every situation, whether she was being elbows-deep in flour or strolling South Beach. Seeing Biker Man's reaction made her confident she'd nailed biker-babe look. She'd have him give her a ride around Daytona, then she'd return the favor.

"Hey, Trouble," she said, sauntering up to him and pushing her shades up over her forehead.

"I could say the same thing to you, darlin'." He pulled his own sunglasses off. "Why call me Trouble?"

"Because you're the type of guy who makes a girl get into all kinds of predicaments she normally wouldn't."

"Well now." He smiled at her, sea-blue eyes stunning, and her blood heated. "Looks like we can both earn that nickname then, because I bet you can make a man break a couple of laws."

Just like he could make a woman break a couple of commandments, she thought. "What's your name, Trouble?"

"Matt," he said easily. "What's yours?"

"Gina."

He leaned back, eyeing her. "Well now, Gina, do I need to provide references and a blood sample, or does being on a first-name basis take care of things?"

"Fair warning." She settled her hands on her hips. "This body is courtesy of aikido. I have a cell phone and a nice set of lungs, and I'm an expert at using them."

"I promise not to do anything to make you use any of that." There was a twinkle in his eyes. "Unless you want me to."

Oh, this was gonna be good.

"You ready for your ride?" He handed her a half-helmet. Strange, she'd thought he'd be a hair-blowing-in-the-wind kind of guy.

"This is so going to turn my 'do into a don't."

"You ever been on the back of a bike, Trouble?"

"No."

"First timers have a tendency to hold too tight and freak out. I haven't had to lay down a bike in years, and I don't plan to do it tonight. It's also gonna take a while for us to get used to each other. Would you prefer the alternative?"

"Not even." She pulled the snug black helmet on, wondering if Diana Ross ever had to deal with helmet hair. She'd pull it back into an Afro-puff if she had to.

"Looks good," he said as she tucked her wild locks in. "I'll even help you fluff it back out later."

"You're just a man of many talents, aren't you?"

"Now if I told you everything, you wouldn't have the fun of finding out for yourself."

She laughed, feeling giddy and reckless and horny.

He just stared at her. "What?" she asked, a little more belligerent than she'd intended.

That slow smile again. "I'm about to piss off a whole city full of guys."

She grinned. "Then let's get this show on the road."

He straightened. She rested her left hand on his shoulder then slung her right leg over the seat. There wasn't much room, but it was a bike, not a Beemer.

"How snug should I hold you?" she asked, pressing her breasts against his back so she could speak in his ear.

"Tight enough to stay on, loose enough not to choke me," he answered. "You want the scenic route or the tourist trip?"

"How long is the scenic route?"

"Twenty-two miles, but the speed limit drops down to thirty in places. Beautiful views, though."

"Is there a third option? I'm not sure my ass could sit on the back of your bike for that long."

"I'd say something about that, but I don't want to get choked. How about a trip to the Ponce Inlet lighthouse?"

"That would be nice. Drive on, Trouble."

He turned south, easing into a speed fast enough for the thrill but slow enough not to lose her lunch. She held him as they cruised through Daytona. The afternoon sky spread topaz-blue above them while commercial properties gave way to extravagant homes. She forgot her nerves as she took in the sight of trees sweeping their limbs over the two-lane road, peeks at the ocean beyond on her left.

But it was rolling through a lush tree-clogged lane to arrive at the lighthouse that took her breath away.

"Wow, this is beautiful," she said, peeling herself off the bike. "I bet it's amazing at sunset."

"So I've been told," he said, following her. "It's a national landmark and more than a hundred years old. If you want, we can climb to the top."

Settling her hands on her hips, she bent her back to stretch the kinks out. He really was a good driver—was it called driving a bike if someone else was a passenger? She'd tensed her muscles too much on the short drive south. "No thanks. As much as I'd appreciate the view, these jeans ain't made for climbing."

"Maybe not, but I sure would appreciate the view following you up the stairs."

"I bet." She regarded him for a moment. He was either a natural-born flirter or he wanted in her jeans. Or both. Since she wanted in his jeans, it didn't matter. She hadn't had a one-night stand since college, and nothing more than solo sex since before her divorce.

Two freakin' years. It was time to fix that. And Matt looked like the perfect handyman.

The teasing light left his eyes, replaced by something that teased in a completely different way.

"Here. Let me help you with that." Standing close, so close she could see his nipples pressed against his shirt, Matt helped her off with the helmet. He smelled of sweat and salt air and something cool and wintry.

His eyes were brilliant blue even as the setting sun turned him bronze. He put the helmet on the seat behind him, then thrust his hands into her hair, fluffing it back out. It was all she could do not to close her eyes as his fingers slid along her scalp, but the look of complete concentration he wore had her fascinated.

"There." His hands slid from the nape of her neck to her shoulders. "Good as new."

"Thank you."

His left hand slid forward, his thumb brushing along the edge of her mouth. "I think I'm going to kiss you."

"I think I'm going to let you."

She expected him to immediately lug her closer and claim her lips. Instead, his thumb continued to trace her mouth as he stared down at her. What was that look about?

Then his eyes went dark, and his lips covered hers.

She didn't know what she'd expected—something a little more rough around the edges. Not this sensual press of mouths that literally sent a tingle sweeping through her body, pebbling her nipples and curling her toes. She curled her arms around his lean waist, leaning against him as her knees went wobbly.

All too soon he pulled away. She opened her eyes to find him looking down at her, a soft smile so different from the sexy teasing one curving his lips. She smiled back up at him, feeling almost giddy. "Wow."

"Yep." He took a breath like he needed it badly, then slowly put more space between them. "What do you do when you're not practicing aikido and picking up strange men?"

"I'm a caterer in Atlanta," she told him, needing the change of direction. "How about you?"

114

"Mechanic."

She grabbed his hand, turned it over. "Clean hands."

"I don't take my work home with me," he said, making no move to take his hand back. "Since I met you at the Hilton, I guess that means you're not local?"

"Actually, I'm the process of moving back to Miami. I'm here for a business meeting and then I'm headed home for vacation with my family."

"Family?" He frowned at her. "You married, Trouble?"

She cocked her head at him. "Does it matter?"

He shrugged. "I'd hate to have to drop a pissed-off husband just 'cause I took his pretty wife for a ride."

He thought she was pretty. Grinning, she held up her left hand. "Divorced." She waggled her fingers. "The ex is in the Hamptons. No worries about dropping anyone."

A cluster of tourists exited the lighthouse chattering about food. Gina's stomach growled. "Guess that's the cue to hunt for food. Can I treat you to dinner?"

"A beautiful lady wants to have me for dinner, how can I refuse? You have any particular place in mind?"

Well, now that he mentioned it... "How about one of your favorite hangouts?" Maybe she could get a good feel for what bikers considered comfort food.

"I think I know just the place."

Chapter Three

Matt took the first bridge over the Halifax River then ran the grid back north to Main. He stopped in front of Froggy's Saloon, a biker bar that catered to any and everyone who loved bikes, babes, and beer. Let's see what you're made of, Trouble, he thought to himself as he eased his bike in among the others parked on the sidewalk.

Gina strutted inside before pausing. "You want a table or the bar?" she asked him, her voice loud to be heard over the classic rock blaring overhead.

He nodded at a couple of familiar faces at the bar. Froggy's ran twenty hours a day; it was still a little early for most of its regulars. "Table's fine."

He watched her ass roll in her jeans as she made her way to a table halfway in. Damn, she made him want a beer, bad. He had plenty of practice at holding his liquor, but no way in hell would he drink and drive, especially not with her at his back.

A waitress came up to them, smiling wide. "You want menus or are you just gonna drink?"

"I'd love a bacon cheeseburger, a load of cheese fries and a Diet Coke."

Matt blinked at her a moment, then glanced up at the waitress. "Make mine the same—except make my Coke leaded."

"Sure thing. Anything else?"

Gina ordered a shot of tequila.

"Living on the edge?" he asked as the waitress left.

Gina fluffed her fingers through her hair. "I grew up on Barcardi and Manischewitz. This won't make me tipsy, but I need a little something to numb my ass pain."

"Yeah, the chopper's not exactly a touring bike for multiple riders," he said. "But I'd be more than happy to massage that pain away if you like."

She grinned at him. "You give a girl ideas."

"I sure as hell hope so. Besides, it's the least I can do, being the friendly sort that I am."

"Ooh, I like you."

116

Matt knew he was grinning like a fool, but damned if he could help it. God, he'd missed her!

The waitress bought their Cokes and Gina's tequila, then left. Gina picked up the slice of lime. "Would you mind helping me?"

"Far be it from me to refuse to help a lady in need."

"Good. Hold this." Grinning, she leaned over the table, and then pushed the lime wedge between his lips. She whisked the saltshaker off the table then climbed to her feet. "Move back."

He hurriedly pushed his chair back from the table, hoping she'd sit in his lap. Hail Mary, full of grace, Gina straddled his lap as several whoops of encouragement filled the air. "Tilt your head," she ordered softly. "I need somewhere to put the salt."

He obliged her, like he could do anything else. Tilting his head to the left, he exposed his throat. His hands moved to frame her waist, fingers lightly brushing over her back pockets. He boned right up as she slowly licked his throat, and then sprinkled salt on his skin.

She picked up the shot of tequila, and then faced him again. "Ready?"

"Hell, yeah."

She leaned forward, the cloud of her hair tickling his nose as her tongue leisurely snaked up his throat. Blood rushed straight to his groin as she tilted her head back, downing the tequila. Then her lips were on his, limejuice, tequila and salt mixing on their tongues as she Frenched the damn lime wedge right out of his mouth.

"Good boy," she cooed, tossing the lime wedge onto the table. "You deserve a reward."

She kissed him again, and it was even better without the lime. He cupped her ass. She didn't seem to mind in the least, just pressed her breasts into him even more. Whistles and catcalls rained down on them.

Their waitress brought another shot of tequila. "This one's on the house, but a couple of the guys and their ladies want to know if you're willing to share."

Matt tightened his hold as Gina giggled. "Hell, no."

Gina downed the second shot without all the fanfare, to his everlasting disappointment. But she did kiss him again, her tongue trailing a tequila burn across his lips. She pulled back with little lingering kisses, her eyes hazy. "That was fun."

"We can have a helluva lot more fun if you want."

"Oh, I definitely want." She grinned. "My cheeseburger. It's been forever since I've had one."

She slid off his lap, leaving him hard, horny, and hungry. "That was brutal."

"That was an appetizer." She settled into her chair. "It's important to enjoy every portion of your meal."

"Trust me; I definitely like to take my time when I'm enjoying a good meal."

She picked up her soda, smiling around her straw. "I'll hold you to that." She looked around the bar, taking in the rustic décor, the huge bar, the souvenir section with t-shirts caps, and stuffed gators for sale, a statue of Froggy himself. "You come here often?"

"Not enough to be on a first name basis with everybody, but often enough to eat around the menu."

"What are your favorites?"

He leaned one elbow on the table. "You thinking about catering for bikers, Trouble?"

"You never know. I like to keep my options open. So what do you like to eat? Food-wise."

"Nothing beats a burger. And ribs, if you can find someone who knows how to do them. I did a bike tour where I just mapped out a bunch of rib shacks between Georgia and Texas. Good eating, there. Wings and steaks work too. Nothing too fancy, though I suppose I can get suited up if I have to. Most of the time, I don't care what it is as long as it's meat and tastes good."

Their food came out a little later, half-pound burgers loaded with bacon, onions, and cheese, mounds of fries with even more cheese, dill pickle spears.

Matt watched as Gina pulled apart several cheese-fries, blew on them, and then shoved them between her lips.

"Oh. My. God." She thumped the table. "That is serious cheesy goodness." She chewed another mouthful. "There are no words to describe how good this is."

"Amen to that," he breathed.

"What?"

"Try your burger. I wanna see how that hits you."

With another mouthful of fries going, Gina set about dismantling and rebuilding her burger. That was pretty much when he remembered that her father was Jewish but she wasn't and from the looks of things, hadn't ever converted.

She dove into her food with a complete lack of self-consciousness that pleased him. Most women he knew would have picked at a salad even as their stomachs growled for something more. Gina moaned over every single bite in a way that had him shifting in his chair. Damned tight jeans. If she ate like that, what was she like in bed?

Why in the hell had he taken so long to find her?

"Man, I haven't had a burger like this in… I don't know if I've ever had a burger like this," she told him, plucking a dill pickle spear off her plate. "Is this the kind of place most bikers like to hang out?"

"Well now, there's bikers, then there's bikers." He leaned back in his chair. "You got some folks who only straddle the pipes on weekends. Then you've got…"

She deep-throated the pickle.

His burger hung somewhere halfway between his mouth and his plate. "I am in deep shit," he whispered.

"God, I've got to stop eating," she announced after she'd devoured the pickle. It was taking all he had not to throw her over his shoulder and run out of the bar. "Thanks for bringing me here."

"The way you sat my bike, shot tequila, and ate that burger—not to mention the way you look in those jeans—I'm definitely the one who's thankful."

She wiped her hands with her napkin, dark eyes boring into him. For a moment he wondered if he'd poured it on a little too thick. Had she finally recognized him? Maybe she was ready to put them out of their collective misery.

"What are you thinking about behind those pretty dark eyes, Trouble?" he asked.

"I was thinking that I need to find a restroom, and then get you back to my hotel room with me."

That brought his chair back to the floor. "You realize we're going to end up naked and sweaty?"

"I certainly hope so, since I bought a box of condoms from the hotel store after I checked in," she told him. "I need to work off some calories. Besides, I find myself really wanting to see what you look like naked."

Matt stood. "I like the way you think, Trouble." He threw a few bills on the table. "Course, I'm sure I'm gonna like a whole lot more than that in a little while."

By the time they'd completed the ride back to her hotel, Gina's body had hit full throttle. Two years since the divorce had obliterated her sex drive, and now it was awake and very, very hungry.

As soon as Matt made it over the threshold, she grabbed two fistfuls of t-shirt and brought him in for a full-on kiss. He responded by palming her ass and lifting her high against his chest. Her girly parts swooned.

She scissored her legs around his waist as he walked them into the room, plastering him with kisses. At the foot of the bed, he placed her back on her feet. "Be right back."

Gina pulled the bedcovers back. Horniness and nerves battled as she toed off one shoe. She was going to do it, have a one-night stand with Mr. Sexy.

He came around the corner as she hopped around trying to remove the other shoe. "Gina, there's something I need to tell you."

"What?" She straightened. "You got a communicable disease or something?"

"God, no. I'm clean."

"She moved towards him again. "You married?"

"I'm very single."

"Then what…? Oh." Her voice dropped to a whisper. "You're not a grower or a shower?"

"What?"

"Tiny penis?"

"Hell no!"

She frowned. "A vagina?"

"Gina!" He looked like he'd been the one knocking back tequila shots. "Just listen to me for a moment—"

"No." She grabbed handfuls of his shirt again, dragging it up over his pecs. And what lovely pecs they were. "This is my fantasy. If you're clean, single, and well-hung, that's all I need to know." She leaned forward and lightly bit down on his left nipple.

It was game on. T-shirts, boots, and jeans went flying in a tangle of laughter and limbs. She ended up on her back on the bed, staring up at him, breathless from the giggling removal of clothing and the piercing, hungry look in his eyes.

"You're just as hot as I imagined you'd be," he said, his tone ragged. "So freaking hot."

"So are you, Matt." A red and gold fire tribal tattoo ringed his right bicep, and something in black script encircled his left. Her eyes fell to his erection, standing proud at the center of his body. So freaking hot.

"I think you're right." She crawled up on the bed, pulled open the nightstand drawer.

"About what?"

She handed him the condom, then wrapped her hand around him.

"We're both about to end up sweaty."

"Hell, yeah." She heard him suck in a breath. "But first I need you to let go."

She did, but only to grip his shoulders, pressing kisses along his jaw and collarbone as he ripped open the condom, rolled it on. His fingers brushed against her belly and her insides trembled. Good Lord, she wanted him, wanted him so bad she could taste it.

Finally sheathed, he cupped the back of her head, slanted his mouth over hers. He pressed her back to mattress but instead of covering her, his hand slid down to cup her breast. Feeling the roughness of his fingertips on her nipples, she sucked in a hard breath. He seized the opportunity and thrust his tongue into her mouth.

She thrust her fingers into his hair, feeding on his mouth, craving more of his hand. Without her speaking he obliged her, his mouth grazing down the column of her neck, his hand sliding down her belly.

"Open for me, babe," he whispered against her breast. "Let me feel you."

Her thighs fell open, her body restless with wanting, needing. His fingers, thick, rough-tipped, skimmed their way past her belly button to the thin strip of crisp hair below. Everything—muscles, breath, blood—clenched as she waited for his fingers to find her.

The first touch, so sure, so there, had her lifting her hips off the bed. Fingers thrusting, thumb pressing, tongue teasing threw her higher and higher. He nuzzled her chin. "Come on, Trouble. Come for me."

His thumb pressed against her and she took off, crying out as her orgasm hit her. He covered her mouth with his own, drinking down her passionate cries. But she still needed more.

They rolled until she straddled him. Need made her clumsy as she balanced above him, both of them trying to maneuver her into place. Finally, she sank onto him.

"God, that feels good."

His hands gripped her waist. "Then do it again."

Drunk with desire, she rode him hard. Her hands slid up her ribcage to cup her breasts as his hips powered off the mattress, crashing their bodies together. Passion revved higher as she watched pleasure arc across his face.

"Babe, I'm sorry, I need to—" He flipped her onto her back, hooked her left leg over his arm, then began to drive into her with a speed and intensity that shook the bed and had her clawing at his back in oh-my-god goodness.

Then he shifted and he hit that spot, that sweet spot, a spot she forgot she had. She couldn't hold back, calling out as she came harder than she had the first time. Each driving thrust sent the orgasm rolling up her spine until she thought she was going to actually pass out.

"Babe, I'm coming, I'm—" He drove into her once more, his entire body stiffening, muscles cording his neck as he came with a loud, guttural groan.

After a long moment he released her, giving her a very thorough toe-curling kiss before lifting off her.

"God, Trouble. You're the kind of woman who could kill a man. But he'd sure die happy."

Chapter Four

Gina woke up smiling and energized. And very satisfied. Lord, she'd go without for another two years if it meant that she'd get sexin' like that at the end of it.

She rolled out of bed, laughing out loud at the way her muscles protested as she headed for the bathroom. Man, would she have a story to tell Kat when she got back from her honeymoon! Kat would be thrilled, even if Gina's sexcapade didn't end in marriage like Kat's had. Hell, it hadn't even ended with exchanging phone numbers.

Not that she'd wanted it to, she thought as she started the shower. Three rounds of sex—two back to back, then one after a surprisingly soothing catnap—then Matt had got dressed, got a final kiss, then got the hell out. No muss, no fuss. The perfect one night stand, full of blissful memories she could use as inspiration for solo satisfaction for weeks.

"Ugh." She thrust her fingers into her bed hair, releasing the aroma of stale cigarettes and eau de bar. She wrenched on the shower, thinking of the effort it was going to take to wash, dry, and style her hair in time to make the meeting.

Which immediately brought her mind back to her sexy biker as she grabbed her shampoo then stepped into the shower. The water felt decadent on skin still sensitized by Matt's scruffy facial hair. She hadn't had sex like that in... damn, she didn't think she'd ever had sex like that. Certainly not with Paul. Now that she knew what fla-damn sex was like, she wanted more of it. Lots more.

She scrubbed her hair, and then smoothed shower gel over her limbs. Getting some meant getting out and dating, and she didn't think she was ready for that. She had David to consider. Her son came first, always.

After moisturizing her hair and pulling it back into a bun, she called Paul's.

"Richardson residence."

Of course he wasn't home. "Hello, Martha. It's Regina. Is David up yet?"

"I'm sorry, Ms. Lieberman. Mr. And Mrs. Richardson spent last night in the city."

"The city?" "The city" meant Manhatten. Paul had said nothing about an overnight trip to the city.

"Yes, and then they're going to the water park. Shall I leave a message for Mr. Richardson?"

"No, thank you, I'll just call his cell later." She disconnected. Paul and Janice taking David into the city could only mean one thing: Janice wanted to play mommy, and Paul felt guilty for not taking an interest in his son's life. That meant a shopping spree for things David didn't need and Gina would have to play bad cop.

She tossed her phone on the bed then went to get dressed. No use borrowing trouble yet. She knew when she'd been awarded primary custody of David that she'd automatically given Paul the role of the "fun" parent, the one who would let David stay up late, have another cookie, and go on cool vacations, while Gina would make her son brush his teeth, do his homework, and eat his broccoli.

Doing the best for David was the biggest reason for returning to Miami. Both her grandmothers lived there, her parents spent half the year there. Miami had been home until she'd gone to college, and she believed that being near family would be good for both of them.

Dressed and made up, Gina grabbed her briefcase and headed downstairs. To live in Miami, she needed to work. She had personal and professional connections she could use, but landing the biker event would still be a coup highlighting her versatility as a caterer.

In the lobby she searched for an appropriate area to wait. Legends Sports Bar already had some early lunchers heading in, though most people were probably out on the beach or the Ocean Walk Shoppes next door. Doc Bales looked to be closed, as did the Clocktower Lounge.

"Gina?"

She turned. Slicked back blond hair caught her attention, as did the wide shoulders caught in a topaz blue dress shirt. Black trousers and dark shoes completed the business casual look, but there was no mistaking that body or those eyes hidden behind gold-rimmed glasses.

"Matt, what are you doing here?" *Why are you dressed like that?*

"I'm here to see you."

No, no, no. This couldn't be happening. "I can't talk to you right now. I have to meet a client."

"I know. I'm the client."

She felt her jaw drop open. "You're the what?"

"I'm Matthew Ryan, owner of Oceanside Customs." He held out a business card.

She automatically reached out and took the card, imprinted with

124

an image of a pair of menacing yet beautiful bikes parked before a storefront. The words Matthew Ryan, Owner jumped out at her.

Heat crawled up her cheeks, singed her ears as she took a step backward. "What is this?"

"It's a business meeting, isn't it?"

The urge to do bodily harm swept over her. She had to grip her briefcase to keep from swinging it at him. Only the thought of causing a scene and damaging her mini laptop kept her from swinging. "Do you meet all your potential business partners like that?"

"No." He focused on her. "You're special."

"Special?" Her voice climbed, and she forced it back down with an effort. She glanced around the partially empty lobby. She didn't want to cause a scene. She had her reputation to think of.

Right. If she'd thought about her reputation, she wouldn't have straddled his lap and sucked salt off his neck. She certainly wouldn't have gotten horizontal with him. Paul would have a field day with this.

"Oh God." She grew ill at the thought of what her ex could do with the information. She had to clench her jaw against the bile that threatened. "You did this deliberately. My ex-husband put you up to this."

"I don't know your ex, and nobody can put me up to anything, especially this."

Her knees went weak. Thank God. She'd outlive her own stupidity. Taking a deep breath, she pushed away from him, gathered what dignity she had left. "Then if you'll excuse me, I think this whatever this is is over."

"Gina wait." He made a grab for her arm. "Can we talk?"

"No. We can't talk. It's taking everything I've got not to go off up in here."

"I can explain—"

"Explaining should have happened yesterday. Before we did the nasty. I have nothing to say to you." She headed for the guest elevators.

He followed. "The catering deal is legit. So's the money we offered. That's completely separate from this."

"It is not separate! I don't sleep with my clients"

"That's good to know. I don't either."

"And I have no intention of starting now."

He grinned. "Even better."

She just stared at him. "Are you listening to me?"

"I don't want you sleeping with clients either."

"You think this is funny? I'm serious!"

"So am I."

"You know, you've got a lot of nerve." She leveled a finger at him. "One, you're assuming I'd ever go there again. Two, you're assuming pleasure means more to me than business. Do you really want to go for the idiot trifecta and assume that I'm going to ever forgive you for this?"

"We didn't do anything wrong."

"Didn't do anything wrong?" She gaped at him. "I have a reputation to maintain!"

"And you think I'm going to ruin it somehow?" That had him moving away. "What, you think I'm gonna go into the nearest hole in the wall and brag about this hot catering chick I bagged like you're some sort of notch in my fucking handlebars?"

"You're putting words into my mouth."

"Am I?" His eyes grew stormy. "Oh, I get it. It's not the fact that a client would spread a rumor, it would be the fact that it's coming from me, a biker with a G.E.D. who spends his days up to his elbows in bike parts and torch fumes. Do those words fit your mouth better?"

Oh no he didn't. "Projecting much?"

She stepped closer until only the thickness of her briefcase separated them. "You know nothing about me, all right. If I was worried about your education or had a problem with you being a biker, you wouldn't have had a chance in hell with me. What matters to me is what you do, not what you are. And what you did is unforgiveable."

To her amazement he smiled, and it lit his entire face. "You haven't changed, have you Gigi?"

She froze. "What did you call me?"

"Gigi."

Her throat tightened as memories came back to her like waves rushing ashore. "Only one person called me that."

Blue-gray eyes stared up at her. "I know."

"He was my lab partner in biology and draft class."

"I know."

"But he fell in with the wrong kind of people, and dropped out of school."

"I know."

She thumped him in the chest. "Damn it, can't you say something else besides I-fucking-know?"

"I'll think of something while I catch my breath."

"I need a drink." She spun on her stilettos and marched toward the sports bar. "And you're buying."

Matt sat at the bar, wishing he'd asked for some rum to go with his Coke. Gina sat beside him, swirling a straw in a strawberry smoothie. She hadn't said anything since ordering, which he supposed was a good thing. He wasn't wearing her smoothie, which was an even better thing.

She pinned him with an accusatory glare. "You're Matty Ryan, former friend, lab partner, and fellow geek."

"Yeah." He tried not to wince over the word "former."

"You thought it would be fun to prank on me because?"

"It wasn't a prank. If I'd introduced myself as your client, you would have been all business. If I'd introduced myself as your high school buddy, you would have made it just about friends. I wanted more than that."

"You sure got it, didn't you?"

He leaned closer. "I didn't force you to hop on the back of my bike, babe. If you didn't want it, you wouldn't have invited me to your hotel room."

Her fingers unclenched on the bar rail. "This was supposed to be a hit-it-and-forget-it thing," she said. "It would have been much better if I didn't have to see you again. But it's you, and now it's complicated."

He wasn't sure what to make of that, so he kept quiet.

She blew out a breath. "Let's just start at the beginning. What happened? Why did you drop out?"

"I didn't have a choice. I don't know if you remember, but I was in foster care since I was five. My first foster parents were cool. I would have done anything for them. After they died I got shuttled around. The last set, all they care about was the money. The old man was a real pain in the ass, made sure I knew how lucky I was to be staying with them. Crap happened, and they kicked me out. I fell in with street racers. I helped them fix their bikes and they didn't beat me up and gave me a place to sleep. The rest is history."

She thumped him on the forearm. "Why didn't you come to me? I worried about you. I thought you might have gotten arrested or worse."

He couldn't control his shock. She'd cared. Pleasure drove out the ache to his gut. "I didn't know—I had the hope of every teenaged boy, but I didn't think I stood a chance. When I got up the courage to talk to you about stuff like that, the stuff at home started."

"I went by your house," she confessed. "They said they didn't know

127

where you went and they didn't care, and that you weren't welcomed back. I made my dad go to the police and report you missing."

She'd done all that for him? No one had cared for him back then. He stared at her, his throat uncomfortably tight. "Thank you."

She sniffed. "For what? Thumping sense into you?"

"No." He caressed her cheek. "For caring about me."

"Yeah, well, don't think it's going to win you any points," she said grumpily. "I'm still ticked at you. I mean, why do all this? Why go to all this trouble?"

"I thought about you. A lot. I wanted to know how you're doing."

"There are easier ways. Google. High school reunions. I've got a contact form on my catering website."

"I guess I just wasn't sure how you'd react. You always thought of Matty Ryan as your nerdy friend, a sidekick to your fabulousness. I didn't mind," he added quickly when she began to protest. "It's exactly what I was. I've changed a lot since then."

"Understatement of the decade."

"Maybe." He grinned. "I wanted to be able to relate to you on your level."

"What level is that?"

He snorted. "You're kidding, right? I was one of the freaks. I didn't have a chance back then. I'd like to have a chance now."

Gina sighed. "I don't know what to think."

"As long as you don't think it's creepy or crazy, I'll say that's a great start."

She gave a small smile. "It's not creepy. Much. The jury's still out on crazy. I would have been thrilled to see you at the reunion."

"It's this coming weekend, you know. Were you planning to go?"

The smile faltered. "I'm still thinking about it. The move back is taking a lot of my time, and too many people would gloat to hear about the end of my marriage."

"Then let's go and show them up by having a good time."

He wrapped a hand around hers. "I can't apologize enough for not being straight with you, but I don't regret last night. Do you?"

"No." She fanned herself. "God no."

"Then I should remind you that there's more where that came from." He dropped his hand to her knee.

This time she laughed. "You're evil. But I like it."

"Good. Spend the next couple of days here, and go to the reunion with me. Cater my Biketoberfest party. If you think it's a conflict of interest, recommend someone else for the job, but I'd really like you to do it."

She turned to him. "You screwed me out of my common sense. I can't believe I'm not kneeing you in the nuts and I'm going to go to the reunion with you."

"I swear you won't regret it. Now how about we talk about food, fun, and fast bikes? Then I can give you a tour of my humble enterprise."

She looked at him, clearly hesitant. "You're serious about all of this?"

"I've never been more serious in my life."

"All right then." She opened her briefcase. "Let's talk appetizers."

Chapter Five

"Regina Maria! We were expecting you yesterday!"

"I know, Nonny." Gina threw her arms around the diminutive woman's neck, returning the bear hug. "You know how stuff happens. Where's Nana O?"

"Is that my baby girl?" A voice called from the back of the condo.

"Hi Nana."

Nana Marie strutted into the living room with her crisp white capris and screaming red top. Nonny Lieberman and Nana Ortiz shared a smart three-bedroom condo in a high-rise overlooking Biscayne Bay. Both women barely came up to Gina's shoulders, but what they lacked in stature, they more than made up in shock value. There were moments when Gina thought they could make Dr. Ruth blush.

Right to the point. "How are you doing? Are you dating?"

Nana O flanked her on the couch, effectively caging her in. No one had thought the two would get along much less live together after their respective husbands died, but the women hit it off fabulously well, traveling, shopping, cooking together. The only problem Gina could see was that their favorite hobby was pestering her about marrying again, or actually for real, since neither had considered Paul that much of a catch.

"Not really." Not a real lie she thought to herself.

"Well how are you going to find a nice young man if you don't look?" Nonny wondered. "David needs a real father, not that sorry, jet-setting sperm donor."

"Nonny!"

"Don't mind Hannah," Nana O said, patting Gina's hand. "But she's telling the truth. We've talked to some of our friends and think we've come up with a list of good men who are much better than Paul. Once you get settled in, we can call—"

"Okay I met someone!"

Did she really say that? Looking from one hopeful face to the other, Gina realized that she actually had. She put her head in her hands. "Oh God."

"Don't take the Lord's name in vain," her grandmothers admonished in unison. "Tell us about him."

Well, she'd stuck her foot in it. Might as well get into the hoo-hah up to her neck. Better to let them think Matt has potential than to suffer through their attempts at matchmaking. "His name is Matt Ryan. I knew him in high school."

Nonny L sniffed. "Doesn't sound Jewish."

"Or Latino."

"He's not," Gina said, then told them something she'd knew would make them happy. "He owns his own business up in Daytona. He wants me to cater an event for him."

"Is he a doctor?"

"Is he a lawyer?"

Gina lifted her chin. "He designs custom motorcycles."

Nonny frowned. "Like Pimp My Ride or American Chopper?"

"Pimp My... what do you know about those shows?"

"Sweetie, I'm retired, not dead."

Nana leaned closer. "Is he hot?"

Gina shot to her feet. She'd forgotten how dizzying it was to be double-teamed by her grannies. "Do you both say stuff just to shock me?"

"It's a valid question," Nana said. "He owns a business, that's good. And designing motorcycles, that means he rides them too. But for you to be interested, he's got to be hot."

"You do like them pretty, dear," Nonny added. "Paul's nice looking. His only talent is his ability to attract women with money."

"Which explains why he's with Janice." She'd been amicable about the divorce until she'd found out Paul had been seeing Janice while still married.

Nana coughed. "So, this Matthew, he's not going to crack any mirrors, is he?"

"No, he won't." Gina pulled out her phone and showed them Matt's picture, then told them just about everything she'd discovered about her old friend over the last several days. "He's a good guy that had some bad stuff happen to him, but it's all behind him now. He's different from high school. I mean, he's still funny, still a little geeky, but my God, did he grow up fine."

Nonny leaned over to Nana O. "She's got that look in her eye."

"I know. I'm so glad."

Gina folded her arms. "Do I even want to know what look you're talking about?"

Nonny shrugged. "Probably not."

"Tell me."

"That's the look of someone who's had really good sex," Nana explained. "I know that look."

"So do I." They both sighed.

Gina's mouth opened. "That's what I get for asking. I don't want to think of either of you with my granddads."

"Who's talking about them? I'm talking about Silas down in 12-A. He's a bit younger, but he keeps up okay."

Nonny nudged Nana O. "I don't think the girl wants to hear about our dating lives."

"Especially not when you're getting more action than I am," Gina added. "I think I'm jealous."

"Then you should invite your Matthew down for the weekend. Show him around Miami. Let us meet him."

"Don't even try it, Nana," Gina warned, wagging her finger at them. "Matt's coming down so we can go to the reunion together, but I don't think I want to let him anywhere near the two of you."

The grandmothers exchanged looks. Nonny spoke. "He's taking you to the reunion? It's that serious then?"

"It's not serious. It's not anything."

"Have you told him about David?"

"I didn't see a reason to."

"Why not?" Nana asked, after exchanging another look with Nonny.

Gina marched over to the balcony doors needing air. "This will be over after this weekend anyway."

"Are you sure about that?"

"I have to be." She turned back to her grannies. "Matt's fun. I'm glad we had a chance to get reacquainted. I enjoy his company, his sense of humor, the way his mind works, and damn, he's hot. But he lives in Daytona and I'm closing on a house here. Then there's David to think of."

"What? You think Matt won't like David, or David won't like Matt?"

"I don't know. I don't think there's any reason to put them together to find out."

"Where's my real granddaughter?"

Gina turned to Nonny. "What do you mean, Nonny?"

Nonny threw a hand up. "I don't recognize this coward who looks like Regina. Where's the Regina who defied her parents by becoming a caterer? The Regina who went on a culinary tour of Europe by herself? The Regina who makes sure her son is exposed to arts as well as sports so he won't grow up to be a cretin like his father?"

"She got chewed up when her husband traded her for a richer model." She hated when Nonny read her the Riot Act by breaking out the Book of Hannah, as the family affectionately called her sermons. Having someone who came up to your navel giving her a dressing-down was so not fun.

"Regina Maria." Nana Ortiz placed a hand on her forearm. "David accepted Janice, mostly because of what you did. Why would it be any different with Matt?"

"He's not the same Matty Ryan I knew back then."

"Well what does your heart tell you?"

"It's too early to bring my heart into this. I've only known this Matt for three days."

"So? Maury knew he wanted to marry me in four days," Nanny told her. "I knew the first day that he was the one, but I didn't tell him for a week."

"I knew Rodrigo was the one by the end of our first date," Nana O said. "We were engaged in a month. Your parents dated two months before your father popped the question."

The two older women shared a smile. "Knowing sooner instead of later runs in the family, sweetie."

Gina felt her mouth drop open. "You haven't even met him and you're on his side? How does that work?"

"We're on your side, bubelah, and if you could see your expression, you'd know why." Nonny joined them. "Your eyes lit up when you described him. I don't remember you being gaga over Paul. Paul was the safe choice. Matt sounds like the right choice. Raising money for charity? Next, I suppose you'll tell me he rescues animals too."

Gina ducked her head. "His dogs are both shelter dogs."

Nana grinned. "When do we meet our future grandson-in-law?"

Chapter Six

"I'm in love with your grandmas," Matt told Gina the following night as they left her grandmothers' condo for the reunion.

"Good, because they were sizing you up," Gina said airily, still grinning over his reaction to seeing her in her gold sheath dress. "The separate bouquets were a nice touch. They want to have you for dinner."

"Really?" He smiled. "I'd love to have dinner with them, especially if it earns brownie points."

"They want to have you for dinner," Gina said, "while that might earn you points, I'd have to kick your ass to the curb. I can't date someone who did my grandmas."

He stumbled. "I think I just threw up a little. Not that I think doing your grandmas is gross—I mean, I don't. I mean, if I was sixty-five I'd think they're hot. Oh hell, will you just kiss me so I can shut the hell up?"

She kissed him. "You're cute when you're flustered."

"Yeah well, apparently the women in your family have a talent for flustering me. Especially when it's a grandma pinching my ass. So when do I get reintroduced to your mother so we can make it a clean sweep?"

"Slow down there, biker boy," she chided him. "We've still got a reunion to get through. Don't you think you've done enough charming of the women in my family?"

"Not even a little." He held open the door of a compact black SUV. "Don't think I didn't notice you saying that you're dating me."

"I did not."

"Did too. It's all in the interpretation. By the way, did I tell you how smoking hot you look?"

"Yeah, but I don't mind hearing it again."

He captured her gaze. His voice was low, warm, and sincere. "Regina Lieberman, you're more than smoking hot. You are the most incredible woman I've ever known."

She blinked. With her grandmothers' words still ringing in her ears a day later, Gina knew she was close to falling for this man. Words caught in her chest, desperate to break free. Instead, she cupped the nape of his neck, leaned closer, and then kissed him.

A horn sounded behind them. They broke apart. Matt gripped the wheel. "Will I lose brownie points if I throw it into reverse and ram this guy?"

"I'll help. You're so getting more than laid tonight."

"There's more than getting laid?" He pulled the SUV over. "You know, my hotel's not all that far away."

"Oh no you don't," she chastised him. "Going to the reunion was your idea. I greased myself into this dress and we're not leaving until I show it off."

"I'll be more than happy to help you show it off."

And that's exactly what they did. In fact, Matt was definitely the center of attention. As the night wore on, Gina felt more like an accessory than a date.

A couple of hours later, she was beyond ready to leave, and not with Matt. "Did you enjoy yourself?"

"Better than I thought I would," he admitted as he pulled out of the parking lot. "I guess high school didn't suck as bad as I remember."

"Well especially not now, when you're doing so much better than many of the people who teased you." She folded her arms across her chest. "Designing bikes for movies, hanging out with A-listers and rockers. I gotta wonder, if that actress you dated was too busy to come to the reunion, and that's why you hunted me down?"

He slowed to a stop. "I screwed up, didn't I?"

"Yeah."

"And you're pretty pissed right about now."

"Pretty much."

He sighed. "I'm an idiot."

"Give the man a prize."

"I'm sorry. And stupid. Stupidly sorry."

"If I'd known all of this was just an elaborate trick to get back at everyone at school—"

"No." He threw the car into park. "Finding you was never about showing up the idiots in school. I shouldn't have treated you like a prize I'd won, but Gina, that's how this feels to me. Like I'm finally being rewarded for doing the right thing all these years."

"You think you can sweet-talk your way out of this?"

"It's not sweet talk. It's the truth. We wouldn't have worked back then. Right now, being here with you after straightening my life out and doing right…it makes me believe that good stuff can happen to good people."

Tears blurred her vision. "Dammit, Matty, how am I supposed to stay mad at you when you say stuff like that?"

"I'm betting that you can't."

"You're making this up to me, you know."

He eased the vehicle forward. "Absolutely. How about multiple orgasms? Or Cuban food? Or both?"

"You sure know the way to a girl's heart."

"I don't care about other girls. I care about you."

He was laying it on pretty thick, but damned if she cared. She reached over, wrapped her fingers around his on the gearshift.

"You're forgiven. Let's get back to the hotel."

She gave herself a private talk for the remainder of the drive. It wouldn't do to think of how this was probably the last night she and Matt would get to spend together. Even if they both wanted more, it wouldn't be easy. She was in the process of moving back to the state, but there was some serious distance between Daytona Beach and Miami Beach. They both had businesses that required a lot of attention, and Gina had to think about David. She couldn't abandon her son for weekend trysts, and she was certain that either she or Matt would find the occasional sex not worth the trouble, no matter how amazing it was.

Still, she put all of that out of her mind as Matt unlocked the door to their suite, held it open for her. As she stepped inside, her mouth dropped open. The seating area had been set with a bouquet of roses, a bottle chilling in an ice bucket, and two place settings.

She spun to him. "How did you do this?"

He grinned as he jettisoned his jacket and stripped off his tie. "I called the hotel as soon as we decided to leave. I thought it would be a good way to end the evening, and I like chocolate."

Wrapping her arms around his neck, she kissed him thoroughly, pouring more than she should have into it. "Thank you, Matt."

He huffed. "I'm pretty sure I'm the one who's supposed to be thanking you."

She shook her head. "No, I mean thank you for this weekend. Thank you for finding me. I guess I can even thank you now for tricking me."

He offered a teasing and tentative, "You're welcome?"

"I'm being serious." She sighed as she crossed the room. "I can't tell you how much I appreciate this. You've made me feel like a woman again."

"When did you not feel like a woman?"

Damn. "Don't worry about it," she said, lifting a serving lid to reveal a slice of chocolate mousse pie with swirls of chocolate and raspberry sauces decorating the plate. "If I recall, you're supposed to be apologizing to me right about now."

He didn't take the hint. "Your ex?"

"Yes and no," she answered. "Mom, wife, and businesswoman. I've been all of those for the last decade. I forgot what being a woman and feeling sexy to a man was about. Thank you for reminding me."

"You're sexy, Gina. Everything about you is sexy." He moved closer, his nearness causing her skin to tingle. His lips skimmed her left temple. "Like your hair."

He traced his way down her cheek. "Your mouth." His lips brushed hers before sliding down her neck.

Her eyes slid shut on a sigh.

"Your throat. That sexy collarbone. The dip between your breasts." He pushed the dress straps off her shoulders. "Especially your breasts."

Her dress fell to the floor. She heard him take a deep breath, and she knew her red lace strapless bra and matching bikini panties had done their job. She reveled in the roughness of his fingertips as he reached behind her to unclasp the bra. Her nipples pebbled when he freed her breasts. She rested her hands on his shoulders, anticipation clenching low inside her while she waited for the warmth of his mouth. "Please, Matt."

"No, I think you need just a little…there."

The touch of coldness popped her eyes open. Her breath came fast as she watched his finger, running with chocolate and raspberry, slowly paint her nipple. She whimpered when he lowered his head, swirling his tongue over the sauce-covered peak while thumbing the other.

Another trip to the dessert plate, then he drew circles on her stomach. "The softness of your skin is sexy, too."

His mouth skimmed below her belly button as he knelt in front of her, hooking his fingers into the waistband of her panties. "These are very sexy," he said, sliding them down her legs and helping her step out of them.

"What about my shoes?"

"Leave them," he rasped. "They're part of the sexiness too." His fingers brushed her thighs.

"What about the rest of me?" she asked, breathless with full-blown lust.

"Sorry. I got distracted by your sexiness. The rest of you—the back of your knees, your ankles, your toes—everything about you is sexy. The bend of your right elbow is my favorite place. And this, this is a close second." He dipped his tongue inside her.

She groaned digging her fingertips into his shoulders as her knees threatened to unhinge. His fingertips dug into her buttocks, guiding her back and into the chair he thrown his jacket on to.

She clamped her knees. "I'm going to soak your jacket."

"Don't give a damn," he muttered, expression tight with desire. "Open for me, Trouble."

She did, balancing her heels as he positioned her where he wanted her. The sweep of his tongue had her arching off the chair, pressing her against his mouth, needing his touch, needing him, needing everything he gave.

He pressed even closer, plundering, demanding, coaxing, and teasing. She wanted to hold back, wanting it to last. Just like every other defense she'd tried against this man, her attempt crumbled in the face of Matt's relentless sensual onslaught.

Her body stiffened as ecstasy swept through her like an electrical charge, tearing a long, singing moan from her. He continued his stroke gentle and soothing as she managed to separate her consciousness from her clit.

He pressed a kiss to her belly then looked up at her, his expression entirely too self-congratulatory. "Ready for dessert?"

She fought to catch her breath. "What about you?"

"Can you stand up right now?"

"Uh…no."

"Enjoy dessert." He smiled. "There's time for me."

Tears clogged her throat. She lowered her chin, turning to focus on the confection and not the emotion that threatened her. Her mind roiled as she took several bites without tasting them. Dessert was so not what she wanted. She wanted—she wanted—what in the hell did she want?

"Gina."

She glanced up to see Matt standing in front of her, very naked and very aroused. He held a hand out to her. She automatically took it, and he pulled her to her feet. "Let's go out onto the balcony."

She held back, acutely aware that she wore nothing but blood red stilettos and her grandmother's rubies. Don't think about your grandmothers. "But that's outside."

"I know." He grinned at her, switched off the lamp, leaving the room in darkness. "It's late, we're a few floors up and a storm's coming in. I think we'll be okay."

"You know, I could resist you if you weren't so good at this," she said, allowing him to lead her through the sliding glass door to the surprisingly large balcony edge with fat pale stone balusters.

"Then it's a good thing I was motivated to succeed." He licked the back of her neck, causing her to shiver. "Grab the railing, babe."

She did, wrapping her fingers around the stone resisting the urge to look down. Sea and sky spread purple-black around them, the air thick with the promise of a storm. No one was about and the balustrade, hitting just below chest height, had wide enough panels for a view and privacy. But if any of the other guests came out on their balconies, they'd see them. Out here. Naked. Having sex.

Her insides liquefied.

His hands slid down her back slowly, leaving goose bumps in their wake. She shivered from the sensation. He stepped closer, his chest against her back, and she shivered for an entirely different reason.

"You've given me the best week of my life, Gina," he said into her right ear, his hands settling on her hips. "But I think my best memory will be being out here with you with the storm rolling in, listening to you come."

"Matt." She broke off as his right hand cupped her heat, his middle finger slipping inside.

"Yeah?" The roughness in his voice contrasted with the expert gentleness of his left hand on her breast, the calloused tips of his fingers teasing her nipple to a perfect, painful peak.

She forgot about words, her awareness reduced to the magic of his hands pulling pleasure from her body, the hardness of his erection pressed against her butt cheeks.

He held her close against him, moving her like a dance, his fingers setting a pace for her body to follow. Pleasure rolled through her like the waves to shore. She reached up and back to encircle his neck, turning her head to seek out his mouth for a kiss. He kissed her hungrily, pressing against her, his fingers circling her pleasure button again and again. "Come for me, Trouble," he whispered in her ear. "Show me how much you like it."

As if she needed his voice to push her over, she came, a short, hard release that left her craving more. She pressed back against him, silently demanding.

"Gina?"

"Do it," she ordered. "Do it now!"

He shoved his thigh between hers, forcing her stance wider, one hand splayed across her back. Then she felt his cock as he guided it between her thighs. She tilted her hips, angling her body to receive his. A groan of pure pleasure slipped from her as he pushed inside her waiting sheath, hard and hot and thick, filling her completely.

Sensation washed over her, heady and incredible. Lowering her head and gripping the railing for all she was worth, she shoved back against him, driving his cock deeper into her waiting sex. Matt took that as permission, hands clamping to her waist as he began pounding into her.

She heard the slap of their bodies, the sensual ripples rolling through her, driving her higher. The ocean boiled in front of her, thunder flashed in the distance, the wind caught at her hair. Nature's ferocity called and she answered, demanding Matt to follow. Waves buffeting, bodies crashing, wind tossing, all combined to throw her over the edge.

Matt slammed against her, lightning-quick thrusts as powerful as the approaching storm. His callused fingers dug into her hipbones as he caught her against him, a loud groan seeping from his lips as he came.

Her legs trembled as he withdrew from her. His hands were gentle as he turned her around, pulled her into his arms. Unable to help herself, she rained kisses onto his forehead, his cheeks, and oh-so-sexy mouth.

Matt held her close, unable to stop touching her, kissing her. Wanting her. The rain finally caught up to them, the pelting drops cold. Laughing, he pulled her inside. "Be right back, babe."

He slipped into the bathroom to dispose of the condom. Just seeing Gina's silhouette against the stone balcony, that perfect ass and legs, all he'd wanted was to ride her like there was no tomorrow. But there was tomorrow and he wanted it, and the day after. And the day after that.

He caught sight of himself in the mirror, the dopey grin that reminded him of a Sesame Street character. Who knew that having sex in a thunderstorm could be so damn good? Course, Gina was a force of nature all by herself.

He stepped out of the bathroom to find both rooms still in total darkness. He could just make her out, standing at the open door, silently watching the rain sheeting down. "Hey, are you okay?"

"Just watching the light show." She turned away from the balcony. "I'll be right back."

He moved to the bedroom, flipping on the light and pulling back the bedcovers as she took her turn in the bathroom. They'd had three full days together. Three days, but it felt longer. It felt right.

His hand fisted the bedcovers. He had the feeling that Gina thought all they had were these handful of days. He couldn't believe that. Gina could have still been married, he could have still been on the wrong side of everything. But they weren't. He'd found her again, the one person who'd kept him from self-destructing even if she didn't know it. He'd convince her to try for more.

"The bed looks comfortable."

Matt's heart tightened in his chest. It did every time he saw her. It'd be damned annoying if he wasn't so gone for her. Hopefully she'd be around long enough for him to get used to it.

He slid in, made room for her. "Come and find out."

Gina crossed the room to him. He held the covers up for her and she tucked right up next to him, her hand lightly stroking his chest. This, this was what he'd been wanting for so long it had become a dull ache in his chest. Being with Gina was everything he knew it would be.

Her voice came as a soft breath across his heart. "What are you thinking?"

"That I'm the luckiest bastard in the world who's glad you're such a forgiving person."

Soft laughter vibrated through her as she pressed a kiss to his heart. "How can I not be, considering how good you are at apologizing? You're so good at it, that I think I need to do a little apologizing of my own."

She licked her way down his chest to his navel, and he sucked in a hard breath in response. Goosebumps broke out along his skin, his cock stirring in anticipation. At that moment, he would have sold his soul to have her mouth surrounding him. Luckily he didn't have to.

After coming like a freight train out on the balcony, he didn't think he had another go in him. But whatever Gina wanted, he'd give her. He tried to be all cool and macho, but she was so roll-your-eyes-to-the-back-of-your-head good. His hands dug into the mattress as his orgasm tightened his balls moments before breaking free. He groaned long and deep as Gina's mouth launched him high, sent him flying, brought him back down.

"Gina." Breath sawed in and out of him as he felt the need for her like an ache in every damn pore of his body. "God, Gina."

She rested her head on his belly, her fingers just a light touch on his balls, as if soothing him. "I won't forget this, Matt. This has been the best weekend ever."

There was a distinction, but damn if his sex-addled brain could figure it out. Instead he just pulled her up until her head rested on his shoulder. Draping an arm about her, he fell into a satiated sleep.

Chapter Seven

When Matt awoke the next morning, Gina was gone.

Throwing back the covers, Matt rolled to his feet—and caught sight of Gina sitting in a robe on the balcony, watching the sun rise.

Relief filled him. He quickly found a second robe, pulling it on before joining her. "I thought you'd left."

"I was going to," she admitted. "But I didn't think that would be fair. Or brave."

Uh-oh. "What do you have to be brave about?"

"Saying goodbye to you, to this."

Dread filled him. "Why does it have to be goodbye?"

"I'm not saying that we'll never see each other again," she said, pushing her hair away from her face. "I've agreed to cater Biketoberfest, after all. I'm just saying that we won't be able to see each other like this."

"Give me one good reason why."

"I have a son."

"You do?"

She nodded. "David is eight. He's spent the last month with my ex and his current wife. My parents are picking him up and we're going to meet up with them in Orlando for our family vacation next week."

She brushed her hair back from her face. "I wasn't trying to hide my son from you. I just didn't think there would be more than this, or that I would want more than this. But there is, and I do, and so you need to know."

The tightness in his chest eased. "I want to meet him."

"You want to meet Davey?"

"Of course I do."

She stared at him. "You want to meet my son?"

"You being a mother doesn't changes things. Why would it?"

"I don't think you realize how important something like that is. Kids are impressionable and they can get attached to people pretty quick. David doesn't get to see his father often, which is part of the reason we're moving back here, so he can be closer to his grandfather. I wouldn't want to introduce David to someone I wasn't sure was going to be around for a while."

He folded his arms across his chest, trying not to get angry with her. "You think I'm not a long-term guy?"

She laid a hand on his arm. "Try to understand where I'm coming from. I have to protect me, but most importantly I have to protect David. You and I knew each other for a few years when we were teens and a few days as adults. We know that we're good in bed together, but that's all that we know. How do we know this could work?"

"That's why we need to try this. We have to take a chance, Gina. Why don't you want to try?"

"This is overwhelming. You're overwhelming, and I'm gun-shy. It's bright and shiny and new, and I can't think around you. I wanted you so bad last night that I didn't even think about a condom. I'm not on anything, Matt."

"I remembered," he assured her, mind reeling at the thought of having kids with Gina.

"But I didn't. It didn't even cross my mind. All I could think about are those arms, that mouth—"

"And my sense of humor?"

She cut her eyes at him. "Every single part of you, especially that part. You're making me stupid with orgasms, making me greedy and selfish and wanting to toss everything to be with you, and I can't think like that. I'm moving David back here to be closer to our family. There wasn't supposed to be room for anything other than David and my catering and I'd resigned myself to that."

She shook her fists at him. "Then you come roaring into my life, and you're hot and you're charming, and then you have these geeky moments that make you so sweet and you blow through every defense I ever had. But you're in Daytona. How can we think about trying this?"

The look in her eyes tore at him, but it also gave him hope. He knelt beside her. "If we want this, we can make it work. We just take one step at a time, one day at a time. And the next step is meeting David. What do you say? Will you introduce me to your son, Gina?"

She wrapped her hands around his, kissed his knuckles. "Okay. I'm taking Nonny and Nana O up to Orlando to meet up with David and my parents next week. Maybe, maybe you could come to Orlando for the weekend?"

"I'd like that."

Matt had asked to meet her family for a picnic at a park and as soon as he pulled up, Gina knew why.

David's eyes bugged as he caught sight of the pair of motorcycles in the trailer. "Awesome!"

"Smart man," her mother murmured as Matt got out. "Not bad on the eyes either. I see why Nonny and Nana keep talking about him."

She watched as Matt opened the back driver's door, and two dogs bounded out. One looked to be a lab mix, and the other was a dark bundle half its size but twice as loud. Matt hooked leashes on both, and then headed their way.

Her mother harrumphed. "Oh, that boy really doesn't play fair, does he?"

"Boy's playing to win," Nonny declared. She moved forward to catch up with Nana, who was in the process of greeting Matt with a hug and a pat to the butt.

"God help me." Gina joined them. "You brought bribes, I see."

"I couldn't leave my guys at home, and I figured I could use all the help I could get," Matt answered with an unapologetic grin. He looked too good for her peace of mind in faded jeans and a Tampa Bay Bucs t-shirt. "The dark one's Pepper, AKA Mr. Psycho, and the Lab mix is Sandy. Sit, boys."

Both dogs dropped. David pressed against her. "Mom?" He'd been asking for a puppy for a year. This was going to be trouble.

She turned to her parents. "Mom, Dad, this is Matt Ryan, my friend from high school. Matt, you remember my dad, Stephen, and my mother, Carmen."

Matt shook her parents' hands. "It's a pleasure to see you again after all this time, sir, ma'am. Mrs. Lieberman, I have missed those dinners you let me crash."

Carmen Lieberman beamed. "Well, we'll have to fix that real soon, won't we?"

Great. Just like that, he'd charmed her mother. Gina cleared her throat, dropped a hand to her son's shoulder. "This is my son, David."

She held her breath as Matt and David eyed each other. Matt stuck out his hand. "Nice to meet you, David."

David minded his manners, shaking hands quickly. "Do they bite?"

"Only empty shoes and Frisbees," Matt answered. "Maybe later we can play catch with them."

"'Kay." He stepped away from Gina, craning his neck to see the bikes. "Your motorcycles are cool!"

"Thanks. I'm delivering the red one to a client, but I own the blue.

Would you like to see it?"

Her son's face lit up like a Christmas tree topped by a menorah. "Can I ride it?"

"I think that would worry your mom a lot, and I'd kinda like to stay on her good side," Matt answered to her ever-loving relief. "But I tell you what. If she says its okay, we'll take some pictures of you sitting on it so you can show your friends. How's that?"

"Awesome. Do you really make motorcycles?"

"I sure do."

David immediately began pestering Matt with questions about motorcycles. Nonny and Nana seemed keen to know more too, which made Gina fear for the next road trip her grandmothers planned.

"Is that really the same gangly, pimply boy who used to hang at our kitchen table eating all our food?" Steven wondered. "He's so different."

"I know," Gina said softly. "But that's really Matty Ryan. I think he's infatuated with me."

Her mother clucked her tongue. "Mami, this show he's putting on is not about infatuation. Not even close. How do you feel about him?"

"Tingly," she answered truthfully. "It's good and it feels right, which is freaking me out. But I can't even think about that until I see how he and David get along."

"Why don't we watch how it plays out while setting up lunch? Steven can spy for us, can't you?"

"Sure thing." Her father moved off. "I've got some questions for him anyway."

"Baby?"

He paused. "Yes, dear?"

"Don't even think about hopping on that thing. I can't ride you if you're broken."

Her dad winked. "Yes, dear."

Gina coughed. "I think I just threw up a little."

The day got better from there. Matt played catch with David and the dogs, fixed lunch for her grandmothers, talked home repair with her dad. She had to keep pinching herself to be sure she wasn't dreaming. Then he announced he was leaving.

"I've got to deliver this bike," he told her. "Besides, it's better to leave 'em wanting more?"

"You really don't play fair."

"I'm not playing." His smile faded. "Do you think David liked me?"

"I'm trying to remember the last time I've seen David laugh so much and just play like that, but I can't." She blinked rapidly. "So thank you for that."

"No, Gina. Thank you. You have an amazing family, and once again, you're letting me share them with you. I can't tell you what that means to me."

She wrapped her arms around him. "You're part of the family now. My grannies wouldn't have it any other way. Both of them want to convert you, though."

He laughed. "Then I better leave before they make me choose. I'll call you to see about the next visit."

"Next visit?"

"Did you think I was kidding about making this work? I'm going to wear you down eventually."

"Wear me out is more like it," she muttered.

"That, too, Trouble. That too."

***

"So, what did you think of Matt?" Gina asked David later as she tucked him in for the night.

"He's cool." Her son stared up at her with sleepy dark eyes. "Is he gonna be my second daddy?"

"Wow, you sure are moving fast," she said, managing a light laugh even as her heart stumbled a beat. "We haven't talked about anything like that yet."

"But you like him, right?"

"I sure do. But I want to know if you like him too."

David nodded. "He likes to play and doesn't mind getting dirty and stuff. Daddy and Mama Janice don't like it when I play outside, and they don't have a real dog like Sandy and Pepper and Mama Janice's dog doesn't do anything but sit on her lap and whine all the time."

He stared up at her with an expression way too serious for an eight year-old. "Do you think he likes me?"

"He totally likes you," Gina reassured her son. "I'm not the one he challenged to an Xbox duel."

David laughed. "Mom, you don't even play Xbox. When can we see him again?"

"We have to work that out, but Matt will be glad to know that you like him."

"Promise?"

"I promise."

That seemed to satisfy David, because he immediately sank into his

pillow and drifted off. Gina's thoughts, however, wouldn't let her sleep.

Matt had rolled into her life like a bulldozer, demolishing the barriers she'd put in place after discovering how Paul had cheated on her. Like Paul, Matt had good looks and charm, but there the similarities ended. Matt wanted her and made no effort to hide it. He gave as good as he got with her grannies. He was thoughtful and easy-going with her family as if they were his own.

A memory came to her, a memory of sitting on the patio with Matt at her parents' place more than fifteen years ago, talking about their dreams. Even then she'd wanted to be a caterer. "What do you want to be, Matt?"

"I already told you. I want my own family."

"My family is your family until you get your own."

"Is it?"

"Of course. Mom and Dad like you, and you're already over here all the time. I don't think we'd get along so well if we were brother and sister, though."

He'd hung his head. "You're probably right."

It had been the last conversation she'd had with him.

Obviously being her brother had never been Matt's goal. She didn't want that either. She wanted to give Matt what he wanted, what he deserved more than anything: a family to love and welcome him. But with his business firmly established in Daytona and her roots running deep in Miami, how could she make it work?

She didn't have the answer, but she'd find one. Somehow they'd make it work. With her entire family pulling for them, how could it not work?

Chapter Eight

"Regina, it's Paul. Do you have a moment?"

She looked affectionately across the backyard at her two men as they attempted to teach Pepper how to play dead in the late August heat. The little dog was too hyper to do more than play dazed, but they had a good time trying. She headed inside, pulling the patio door closed behind her. "Paul? What's wrong?"

"David's told me about that gentleman friend of yours, and I use the term 'gentleman' loosely."

She cocked her hip against the kitchen counter. "I assume you're talking about my gentleman friend Matthew Ryan, and I'm not using the term loosely at all."

"So it's true? You're sleeping with a biker?"

"What business it is of yours, especially since you didn't consider sleeping with Janice to be my business. We don't share a bed when David's with us."

"You let him stay with you? While David's there?"

Gina blinked in disbelief. "Have you suddenly found the morals you were missing while married to me?"

"I'm David's father—"

Gina snorted. "Please. Don't make me pull out the good parent card."

"Look who's talking about good parenting. Allowing David to be exposed to criminal elements and a dangerous environment isn't good parenting. I won't stand for it."

"Criminal elements?" Her grip on the phone tightened. "You mean the misdemeanor arrest when Matt was nineteen? The case was dismissed. Is that what you mean?"

"If you know, then you can see why Janice and I have some concerns."

"Really. Is that D.W.I. charge from last year still hanging over your head?"

"Now, Regina, my past is not the issue here. You know my only concern is for David."

That was it. "Now you're concerned for David? Where were you for

his Little League games?"

"That's not fair. We work hard"

"Work hard? You married your money. That biker I'm dating built a multi-million dollar company from scratch using his brains, his muscles, and his sweat. You don't even sweat during sex. That biker is out in the back yard on his hands and knees teaching my son to train a dog. You've never been on your hands and knees for anything. That biker treats my son like a person, not a fucking accessory. He respects my parents and my grandmothers."

"I really don't think—"

"Shut the hell up. This has been two years coming and I'm going to say my piece. Matt comes down from Daytona every other weekend and helps David with his homework, his art projects, and his pitching. You have two nannies who know more about my son than you do. Matt is a kind and decent person and we all love him. So I don't give a good goddamn what you're concerned about. And-"

"Regina—"

"Still talking. If you cared so much about my son, you would have honored our family and our vows. But you know what? You did me a favor when you left. Now, I have done nothing but wish you and Janice every happiness. I don't care if you can't extend me the same courtesy, but I'll be damned if I'll let you threaten me. So I am warning you just this one time: don't you start with me, because if you start it, I will finish it."

She had to use both hands to disconnect and put down the phone. Gripping the edge of the counter, she lowered her head, fighting to calm her nerves, her rapid breathing. Anger sent little shocks vibrating through her entire body. How dare he? How dare he?

Don't cry. You didn't cry when he left. You didn't cry when you found out he cheated. Don't you dare cry now.

Blowing out a breath, she wiped at her eyes then turned, running right into Matt and David. She held it together for a nanosecond, and then they were both there, shielding her in their arms.

She clutched them tightly, realizing in that moment that she would do whatever it took to keep them both. Paul had no idea what a mistake he'd made.

"Mom?" David's voice broke as he pressed his face against her. "I'm sorry I told Daddy about Matt. I e-mailed him the picture with me on the bike and he asked about Matt and I told him. I didn't mean to do nothing wrong."

"You didn't do anything wrong. You had every right to tell your

father about Matt." She ruffled his dark curls and tried to give him a reassuring smile. "He's a part of our family, after all."

Matt's grip on her shoulders tightened, but he remained silent. She gave them both a final squeeze then stepped away. "Why don't you go get cleaned up, and we'll go out to dinner? I'll let you pick the place, okay?"

"'Kay." David headed off to his room, head down and feet dragging.

Her shoulders slumped as soon as her son slunk around the corner. "How much did you guys hear?"

"More than you'd want." He turned her around, lightly brushing his thumb across her cheek to chase a stray tear. His brilliant blue gaze intensified. "Did you mean it?"

"Mean what?"

"That you love me. All of you love me."

She rewound the conversation with Paul. Yep, she'd said it. "I guess it would have been better to tell you before I told my ex, huh?"

"I wouldn't mind hearing it again for the first time."

Her hand shook as she brushed a lock of hair from his eyes. His beautiful eyes, shining with something she'd resigned herself to never seeing again. It was a simple thing lift up, guide her mouth to his. He responded automatically, parting his lips to take her breath, give her his. A shudder wracked him, his lips forming her name.

Heart tripping a beat, she closed the distance between their bodies, sealing his mouth with hers. Her arms curved around his shoulders, her hands thrusting into his thick hair. Falling...fell...fallen. She was gone for him as she'd never been gone for Paul. So it was easy to say the words and mean them. "I love you, Matt."

Everything about him relaxed. "Good." He breathed deep, his forehead resting against hers. "God."

He seemed shaken, and it shook her. "Did you doubt it would happen, considering how hard you've worked at it?"

"Yes. I've been in love with you for a long, long time. Boyish infatuation when I was acne-covered and hormonal, maybe. But it's only grown stronger, and deeper, and truer. You know my life went to hell when I turned sixteen. Home was hell before that. The only bright spots I had were you and your family."

He gathered her hands. "I made it through. I survived getting beaten by my foster dad. I survived getting beat up by bikers. I survived a weekend in county lockup. I survived because one day, I wanted to be able to find you and your parents and at least say thanks. Thanks for

being nice to me, for caring about me, for giving me good memories to go with those of my first foster parents. Maybe I'm looking back through rose-colored glasses, but having those memories kept me from going the wrong way."

He stopped, swallowed. "So when I think of family, I've always thought of you. I just want to love you, Gina. You and your son. And your parents and your nannas."

"Good thing, cause we're a package deal." Her heart lightened. "But first, I have to deal with Paul. He's forgotten I've got Jews who survived Germany and Cubans that escaped Castro in my family and that Mom's a lawyer."

"I think I actually feel a little sorry for the bastard." Matt shook his head. "And now the moment's gone. So why don't you go freshen up yourself, while I get David. I think he can use a little reassuring."

That alone would have been enough to love him. She kissed him again, and the last of her fear and anger melted. "Be right back."

Matt went to David's room, knocking on the door before pushing it open. David sat on his bed, clutching one of his model bikes. Sneakered feet thumped against the side of the bed. "Hey, Big D, you ready?"

The boy sniffled. "Is Mom mad?"

"Not with you." He sat beside David.

"I don't like it when she's crying."

"Me either." So Paul had made her cry before. Matt liked the man less and less. He'd pay for making Gina cry.

"I don't think my dad likes you."

"He's just worried about you and your mother." In a twisted sort of way.

David stopped kicking the bed. "You gonna go away?"

"Not without coming back. If you want me to."

"I like it when you come here. So does Mom. And Pop-pop and Mami and the nana-nanas." He glanced up quickly, then back down. "If you wanted to be my second daddy, you could be here all the time."

A second sucker-punch to the heart in less than thirty minutes. "I'd be proud to be your second dad. You're an awesome kid. I'd like nothing more than to spend more time with you and your mom. But there's some grown-up stuff we have to work out."

"She don't like it when you leave," David told him. "She says Sunday is Sad Day and Friday is Fun Day."

"What's Saturday?"

David looked up at him. "That's Family Day."

Matt thought his heart would burst right out of his chest. Everything

he'd ever wanted was under this roof. All he had to do was claim it.

"I'll make you a deal. You help me keep your mom happy and I'll find a way to make every day Family Day."

"You mean it?" Hope sparkled in David's eyes.

"Absolutely. And you know, you can call me and talk to me whenever you need to. I'm not gonna try to take your Dad's place, but I will try to be here if you need me." He stuck out his hand. "Deal?"

"Deal!"

Chapter Nine

Where was Matt?

Gina resisted the urge to pick up the phone again, but the silence was beginning to get to her. She'd spoken to Matt a few hours before, when he'd said he was already on the way. He should have arrived already.

September had flown by. Carmen Lieberman had gleefully called her ex son-in-law, who'd then called Gina all contrite with promises to "trust her judgment" from now on. She'd bought into an existing catering business after meeting the owner at a dinner party she'd catered at her grandmothers' condo. Life was good, so good she felt like she'd never left Disney World. Except that it seemed as if she and Matt had less time to spend together than ever.

To be fair, planning and executing their Biketoberfest festivities had consumed a lot of their professional time. She'd had a lot of groundwork to do in Daytona before she could cook the first dish. But the gig last week had been a success on multiple levels. Her food had been a hit, and so had the donated bike featuring graphics David had helped with. Matt had told her that the investors had been impressed and things were looking good. Just what things, she had no idea, but she really hoped he hadn't been speaking of any of the leather-clad women strutting around.

That had been last week. She hadn't expected Matt to come down this weekend, but he'd promised that he would. She wanted to see him.

She wanted to propose to him.

They'd proven they could do this. It was just like having a traveling salesperson as a spouse. They'd split the office in two, the dogs had beds in David's room, and the garage was Matt's. He and David were like two peas in a pod. They were just like a family--except she was seriously tired of him sleeping in the guest bedroom.

It was time to do this. And at three months and counting, her family thought she was behind schedule.

The phone rang. She snatched it up, saw Matt's number on the caller ID. "Where the hell are you?"

Rich laughter came through the line. "Someone's ready for the weekend to start. I'm almost there, I just got delayed with a few

logistics."

"What sort of logistics?"

"Don't you want to hear the real news?"

News? "What sort of news? Did the deal go well?"

"It went better than well. With the new investors buying in, the expansion is a go."

"Expansion?"

"Babe, we're opening another shop. Oceanside is going to remain the place for classic choppers, but Miami Metal's going to cater to flashier street bikes and gear, and supply bikes to movie and video shoots. The Japanese group already want an order."

Gina's heart stopped. "Did you say Miami Metal?"

He laughed. "Wondered when you were going to catch that. Angel's taking over running the Daytona shop and I'm gonna establish the Miami location. You're talking to the soon-to-be CEO and chief designer of R & M Customs."

"Soon to be?" R & M Customs?

"Yeah. I told everyone that I couldn't start anything until after my honeymoon."

"Honeymoon? Are you asking me to marry you? Cause I gotta tell ya, being proposed to over the phone sucks."

"Then look out the window."

Oh no, he didn't.

Gina snatched back the curtain covering her picture window and stared into the encroaching dusk. Sure enough, she could see a lanky figure leaning against an SUV, holding a bouquet of flowers in one hand and a phone to his ear with the other.

It was hard to breathe. "Is that really you?"

He laughed. "Come outside and find out."

Coordination left her as she dropped the phone onto the couch and tripped to the door. It took a couple of tries to spin the locks open, throw open the door and run right into his arms. "Hi."

He kissed her, long and deep. "Hi yourself."

"I was going to propose to you," she confessed.

"Really? I had this speech prepared and everything."

"Heaven forbid I should deny you your moment." She disentangled herself. "All right. I'm ready."

"I want to be with you, Gina. I want to be part of your family, be the dad I never had to David. I want to tell our grandkids how we were high school sweethearts who took fifteen years to realize it. I want it all, babe, and I want it with you."

She couldn't seem to force enough air into her lungs to say anything other than, "Oh, Matt."

He pulled out a ring box, then knelt. "I love you, Regina Maria Lourdes Lieberman. I've loved you since the ninth grade. Either marry me and put me out of my misery or tell me hell no, and let me go on a tequila bender for the next few months until I drink you out of my system."

The grip on her heart eased. "That doesn't sound like a healthy choice to me."

"There's only one choice for me. Marry me. We'll work everything else out."

"That's a mighty big plunge you're asking me to take."

"You've already dipped your toe in the pool. I'm just asking you to jump in completely."

"If I jump, you damn well better catch me."

He opened his arms. "Jump."

She did, leaping into his arms. He caught her high against his chest, laughter throttling out as he swung her around.

"I'm going to spend the rest of my life making you happy," she declared. "And our family is going to spend the rest of your life making you crazy."

"I hope so. I certainly hope so."

"I gotta call Nanna and Nonny, and my parents. And I need to go get David from my parents' place. He'll be thrilled."

"They're all waiting for us at Bella Noche."

"They are?"

"Yeah. I told them I'd either be coming with you after you said yes, or I'd be coming by myself and need one of every dessert on the menu."

She smiled up at him, her heart close to overflowing. "Do you think it's all right if we're a little late?"

"I don't think they'll mind, Trouble. I don't think they'll mind at all."

She grabbed his hand. "Then come on. You're about to get into a whole lotta trouble."

Enjoying the Ride

By
Kelley Nyrae

Dedication:

Mom, even though romance books aren't your thing and I blush at just the thought of you reading my books you've always been one of my biggest supporters. My dreams are your dreams and that means so much to me. I love you and thanks for everything you do for me.

Acknowledgement:

Big thanks to Angela and Alexis for your help with snowboarding information. Any mistakes are my own. Also, to Amy for again being my second set of eyes. You rock!

Books by Kelley Nyrae:

Getting Lucky with Luciano
The Emperor anthology—Trenton's Terms

Chapter One

Evangeline Sinclair stared out the car window at the snow. A whole crap load of snow to be exact. "Damn, girl, it looks really cold up here. I thought you said this was supposed to be a vacation." Evie didn't do cold. She grew up in Southern California and though Big Bear was only a couple hours away it was a different world. Hell, she didn't even know how to drive on these icy and snowy roads.

"It is a vacation, Evie. The whole idea is to get a change of scenery, you know? Mountains, taking advantage of the early snow, and hot, athletic men who need to be warmed up," Mia answered.

Yeah, that sounded good. Or even better Evie wanted someone to warm her up. To set her on fire. They spent the last several years attending college, where they met, then law school and both ended up passing their bar exams on the first try. They deserved a vacation.

She earned a vacation. After the past few sexless years she needed to cut loose and make up for lost time. She had one long weekend to do it. After days of begging and pleading Mia finally talked her into making a pact to have a sex-filled fling on their vacation. The idea freaked her out at first. Now she couldn't wait. After blowing off a little steam she'd return to her life, where everything was in order and where a job awaited her in Sacramento. The job would require a move but she'd do anything for her career.

Being a lawyer had been her dream since she was a small child. She didn't grow up having much. Her father had been sent to prison for a crime he didn't commit. Her mom worked her ass off to support her and her younger brothers. Years later her dad was exonerated but that wasn't enough. She vowed never to let that happen to someone she defended.

But this weekend wasn't about that. It had nothing to do with work, her parents, or any of her other responsibilities. This weekend was about freedom. About fun. About sex. "You don't have to remind me what this vacation is about. I'm ready to cut loose. To be one with nature even if I do freeze my ass off in the process. I don't know how you handled growing up here."

Mia laughed as she pulled her black Range Rover into the resort

parking lot. "You are such a wuss. We haven't even stepped out of the car yet."

"I don't need to step out of the car to know its cold out there. All that powdery white stuff on the ground says it loud and clear." Coming to Big Bear hadn't been her first choice. She didn't even know how to ski or snowboard but Mia could be damn persistent when she wanted something and for reasons she didn't know, Mia really wanted to come home.

"I think you'll love it here if you give it a chance, Evie." Mia ran her hand through her curly hair.

Really, she didn't doubt that. She gave her a hard time but she was much more excited about the weekend then she let on. Not just the whole find someone to have hot, sweaty sex with part either. She looked forward to getting out of the city and trying something new.

They pulled into a parking spot and Mia killed the engine. Evie couldn't speak. She sat tight-lipped, staring in awe at their beautiful surroundings. The resort wasn't as large as she expected but still wasn't small by any means. It looked like a large, A-framed cabin. Connected to the back was a larger squared building, still made with large logs. It must house the resort suites. To the left of the building sat a couple private cabins. All nestled in white capped trees, and mountains to the right.

"Damn, girl. I've never seen anything like it," she didn't try to hide the amazement in her voice.

Opening her door, Mia said, "I told you. Wait until you see the inside. It's to die for."

Evie put a beanie over her shoulder length, light brown braids then pulled on gloves before wrapping her red scarf around her neck. She already wore her fluffy jacket. Mia skipped the beanie and gloves but donned the same kind of over-stuffed jacket except hers was black where Evie's was white. "Let's get our stuff and head inside. I want to check this place out."

They quickly grabbed their bags from the back and made their way inside the resort. When they walked in, Evie dropped her bag in awe. The interior was all a dark, red wood. The whole building had an old fashion, elegant feel, reds and gold's gracing the walls and the accessories. While they stood in the doorway looking around a man approached and offered to carry their bags to the check-in counter. "Damn, I could get used to this, girl."

"I knew you'd love it if I got your butt up here."

They both giggled while walking to the counter to get their room keys. They'd reserved connecting rooms. Normally they would share but

if they did find boys to play with they wanted to have their own rooms but also be close enough incase either one needed each other.

When they entered Evangeline's room she noticed it was just as gorgeous as the rest of the resort. The room had a rustic feel. The king sized bed had a large wood headboard and a dark brown and black comforter. There were matching bedside tables, a dresser, and enclosed TV case. "I likey." Evie walked over and sat on the bed with a smile.

Mia looked at her, a suspicious glint in her eye. "You know, this is going to be the best weekend of your life. Get dressed and we'll go to the restaurant for dinner."

Evie's heart beat nervously as she dressed to go down to dinner. She was excited for their pact, but nervous too. The scariest part, Mia got to pick her party boy and she got to pick Evie's. Oh boy. This would be an adventure. But one she couldn't wait to embark on. Throwing on her lingerie, a pair of tight black pants and a white, v-neck sweater that showed her cleavage, she looked in the mirror making sure she looked okay before knocking on the door that connected to Mia's room. Mia opened the door seconds later.

"Let's get this show on the road. You told me there would be a gang of hot guys for us to choose from. I'm ready to start shopping," Evie sauntered through the door.

"Who are you and what did you do with my best friend?" Mia had her curly hair hanging loose down her back, wearing a red fleece top and a pair of white pants. "I had to practically blackmail you into this idea earlier."

Mia was right but she didn't want to think about that right now. Then she might start to question the decision again. She didn't want that. She wanted a man, she wanted to let loose. "Well, I'm game now. Grab your purse and let's get the hell outta here."

They walked to the resort restaurant and were quickly seated by the host. Only a few empty tables littered the establishment. The majority of the people in the room all looked around their age, mid twenties to mid thirties. Evie scanned the room searching for single men. She had to pick someone delicious for Mia. From the looks of things they'd have a lot to choose from.

A few minutes later their waiter came to deliver water and menus. Quickly she picked her meal and a drink. The food didn't really matter tonight. For the first time since she could remember she felt free. None

of her responsibilities lingered over her head here. She had four days before she had to get her act together. No matter what, she wanted to enjoy this time.

The waiter approached their table a little while later carrying their drinks and food. "See anything you like?" She asked Mia.

"Not yet. I'm looking for something very specific for you."

"Hot with a nice body will do fine," she kidded.

Evie scanned the room while she ate. About twenty minutes into her meal she set eyes on the perfect guy for Mia. He sat at a table with a couple other guys drinking beers.

"There," she said pointing across the room. "That's your guy."

Mia licked her lips. "Hell ya, he's Latin and looks good enough to eat. I'm on it."

"You're so crazy, girl. Now if you would just hurry up and find my guy."

"I'm looking, I'm looking," Mia replied. "I want you to enjoy this weekend. I have to find the perfect man."

The longer they sat there Evie's nerves started to set in. Her emotions warred between excitement and fear. Could she do this? Could she sleep with a guy she didn't know?

"Quit it. I know what you're thinking and you can stop right there. You need this more than I do." Mia patted her hand. Even though they'd only known each other since college Mia knew her better than anyone. Obviously a little too well.

"What if the guys we pick aren't interested?"

Mia laughed in her face. "They're men. We're women. End of story. A guy will never turn down the chance for hot sex."

She couldn't help but laugh too as she picked up her glass from the oak table and took a drink. She'd never seen so much wood in one place in her life. The rustic feel was offset by crystal chandeliers throughout the room. Off to the left was a bar with one bartender serving drinks to a couple patrons.

"Hey Ryan. About time you showed up," the female bartender said waving towards the door. Mia whipped her head around, Evie following her line of sight. Standing in the middle of the doorway stood a God in faded, loose-fitting blue jeans, a black t-shirt and a long-sleeved white shirt underneath it. She would have never thought she'd find a guy like him attractive but she couldn't turn away. The guy was fine.

His hair was blond, disheveled and spiky on top like he hadn't brushed it all day. His body was tall, lean, but solid. A slight stubble coated his square jaw, a cocky grin on his lips. This man didn't lack confidence in

the least. She could see it in his eyes, in the way he leaned against the doorway, winking at the bartender.

"Hey, Wendy. How's it been tonight?" he replied to her.

Evie watched as he sauntered to the bar, took a seat, and a swig of the Corona she handed him. Damn, too bad she couldn't have him. It looked like he might be involved with the busty woman behind the bar.

"That's him," Mia said eyeing him as well. "He's your fling."

"You must have had a little too much to drink tonight. Looks to me like he's already spoken for." Unfortunately.

"Looks can be deceiving. My guy might have a woman too. The only way for us to know is to ask. If they aren't available we start over."

Sounds like a plan. If she had any doubts before they died when she set eyes on the blond. He looked so relaxed, so hot, so like he knew what to do with a woman. Exactly what she needed. Her body started to come alive, tingling and aching at the thought.

Taking a deep breath, she built up all the courage she could and stood up. "I'm going for it. Don't forget to get your man too," she said as she started to walk away.

Mia laughed. "Guess this means I'm getting the bill." Evie kept walking. She was going to get her man.

Chapter Two

Her knees quivered but she kept her stride. When would she ever have a chance like this again? She was in a town where no one knew her, she had no responsibilities. After this weekend life would go back to normal. She'd be responsible later. Not tonight. Not on this vacation.

Evie held her head high taking the barstool next to the man she hoped to become very personal with, very soon. She sensed his strength, his masculinity the second she sat down. He smelled ruggedly delicious. Veins popped out of his obviously strong hands as he grasped his bottle of beer. Without a word, she sat next to him listening to his deep, gravely voice as he continued his conversation with the bartender. Please don't let her be his woman.

"Can I get you a drink?" the bartender stopped her conversation to talk with Evie. Her skin pricked with awareness as Mr. Sexy turned her way while the bartender spoke. He smiled. Her nipples hardened at the relaxed, grin on his face. This guy was too hot for his own good. But not for hers. He was perfect for what she had planned for him. Now if she could just get the balls to talk to him.

First things first, she needed to find out if they were attached and if not get rid of the bartender. "I'll have a Pina Colada." She walked away to get her drink leaving them alone. But probably not for long. Once she made her drink who knew how long the bartender would sit there bending over the counter so her cleavage popped in his face. Hm, maybe that wasn't such a bad idea. Evie giggled to herself at the thought.

"Cute laugh. Want to share your joke with me?"

She was surprised to hear him speak to her. She stayed silent while he picked up this bottle and downed the rest of his beer. Damn the man had sexy hands. Long, strong fingers. She'd always been a hand kind of girl. Nothing did it for her like a sexy pair of hands and arms.

"I can't tell ya. If I did, I'd have to kill you." She winked at him.

"And why's that?" he asked.

"First of all my mama taught me to never talk to strangers. Second, a girls got to have some secrets don't you think?" Amazingly the flirtation came easy. With so many years since she'd done it last it was a miracle she remembered how.

"I'm Ryan," he reached one of the hands she'd just admired toward her to shake. "Ryan Barnes." His grip was tight but not overbearingly so. She liked the feel of his hand on hers, it increased the beat of her heart making her feel faint.

"Evangeline Sinclair," she replied. "But my friends call me Evie."

He still held her hand. "Well Evie if I get to use the nickname does this mean I'm not a stranger anymore?"

She hoped not. She wanted to know this man very well, intimately. "Well I don't know. I have to know a little more about a person before I consider them a friend. All I know about you is your name." And the fact that you're sexy as hell and I want you to hold more than just my hand in the very near future.

Ryan let go of her hand just as the bartender came back with her drink. "Put it on my tab," he told her. The bartender winked at him before walking away. Guess that answered that question. They weren't involved. "What else do you want to know?" He had the sexiest voice she'd ever heard. It was rough, masculine but also relaxed, like he didn't have a care in the world.

"The usual." She let him take it from there. You learned a lot about a person by what they found important in their lives. Depending on how he answered it would tell her what really mattered to him. Not that it really made a difference. It's not as if they were forming a life long relationship but she also didn't want to spend her time with a complete jerk or someone who she couldn't relate to either. She hoped to find someone who she could not only enjoy sexually this but also someone she could have a good time with in other ways.

"You sizing me up, Evie?" his tone was playful, fun. Wet panty inspiring.

"Maybe."

"Well maybe I don't want to play that game, Honey. If you want to know something, you're just going to have to ask." He signaled to the bartender to bring him another beer.

So he played hardball. She could respect that. Hell it made her want him even more. "What brings you to Big Bear?"

"The snow, what else? There's nothing like the freedom of racing down the mountain on my board."

His voice was full of passion. Even though she didn't understand the allure of freezing cold air, falling down or getting hurt, she admired his obvious love of the sport. "How long will you be here?"

He smiled. "As long as I want. As long as there's snow on the slopes or I find other ways to keep myself busy I'll be here." That sounded nice.

Real nice. She hoped to keep him very busy while she was in town.

"What do you do for a living?" she had to ask. This weekend wasn't about work but she couldn't help but wonder how he could spend all his time here if he had a job to go to.

"Don't worry, I'm not just some snow bum. I run my own business."

Evie immediately felt guilty for her thoughts. She didn't want to disrespect the first man in years to make her nipples hard before they had the chance to even engage in foreplay. "I didn't mean-"

"No worries. It takes a lot more than that to hurt my feelings."

She didn't doubt it. He seemed like he let everything roll off his back, like he didn't take anything too seriously. But he must. If he owned his own business that wasn't a small feat. There had to be something he took seriously. Evie sipped her Pina Colada, her body already felt intoxicated but it had nothing to do with her beverage. She was drunk on lust. "Are you here alone? No friends or anyone with you?"

"Why Honey, you want to keep me all to yourself?" his raspy tone turned sultry, flirtatious. Mia picked the perfect guy! This was going to be a piece of cake. A delicious piece that she couldn't wait to sink her teeth in.

"Maybe." Before she made her move on him she wanted to get to know him a little bit better first. "So you're a big snowboarder, huh? I have to admit I don't see the draw."

Ryan turned toward her, leaning on the back of the stool. His movements said relaxation better than a pamphlet for an all inclusive vacation to the Bahamas. "You don't like to snowboard? That's a crime around here."

"I don't really know. I've never done it but to tell you the truth I'm not real fond of the whole cold thing." Boy did she feel stupid sitting in a ski resort talking about how much she didn't like snow. Didn't make a whole lot of sense but then this trip wasn't really about the snow.

"I think you picked the wrong place to vacation, Honey. In case you didn't realize this is a ski resort." Then he winked at her all sexy and inviting. She held in a groan. Ryan Barnes was a walking orgasm. Everything he did turned her on even when he was pretty much calling her foolish.

"No shit? I must have missed my exit. This whole time I thought I would be spending my time at a beach house." He laughed and she couldn't help but join him. He had a good sense of humor. Big plus. Just by their easy conversation she could tell he was someone she'd like to spend her time with. Even if he wasn't drop dead gorgeous.

"I guess you can say I'm big into snowboarding. I spent a few years in the pros but it wasn't really for me."

She couldn't have been more shocked. He didn't seem like the type to be a professional snowboarder, not that she knew what a professional snowboarder looked like. Ryan seemed like he didn't mix business with pleasure and from the glint in his eyes snowboarding was definitely his pleasure. "Wow, why'd you stop?" He looked her in the eyes making her heart do a flip-flop in her chest. His dark grey eyes entranced her, captured her and she couldn't turn away from their stormy depths. "I can't tell ya or I'd have to kill you," he returned her line from earlier. It was much more fun on the giving end rather than the receiving.

He took another swig of beer. "Why are you in Big Bear in the winter if not for the snow?"

Ah oh. The subject came about a lot sooner than she wanted it to but hey, might as well put it all out on the table. She just had to build up the nerve. "Funny you should ask. I have a specific plan for this week and I'd like you to be a part of it." Uncertainty flooded his face but quickly evaporated. Thank God. She needed him to be excited, to wonder what she had up her sleeve otherwise she'd never get through this. Her nerves were already shot.

Ryan leaned toward her. "I'm listening."

"My best friend and I passed our bar exams a few weeks ago. The past few years have been about school and school alone. No time for, play, men, or," she stalled a second before continuing, "sex." Ryan perked up really quick at her last word. He sat up in his barstool.

"Are you making a move on me?" Interest flashed like a bolt of lightening in his eyes. Yes!

Evie sat there a minute trying to decide how to put this. She didn't want to sound like a slut. This wasn't something she'd ever done before or anything she planned to do in the future. Glancing behind her she noticed Mia was gone as was her guy. Were they together? Had she already propositioned him? Her nerves were starting to get the best of her.

"I don't want you to think this is something I've done before. It's not like I go around sleeping with men I don't know but my friend and I decided to let loose a little. To reward ourselves for the past few years of hard work. I really want to feel free this weekend, to have some fun." She rubbed her hands together nervously. "Damn this is a lot harder than simple flirting."

Ryan grabbed her hands. His fingers were calloused like he spent a lot of time working outdoors. Her body temperature started to rise. "Let

me make this real simple for you. I'd like nothing more than to spend the weekend with you if that's what you're asking." A mischievous glint sparked in his eyes, "But, you're going to have to do something for me too."

Ryan couldn't fucking believe his luck. How often did a beautiful, funny woman approach you and ask you to have a fling with her? He must have done something right because God was rewarding him today. When the sexy, mocha-skinned beauty sat down with him tonight he hoped for some good company before he headed to his cabin for the night. Never did he expect this.

Especially from one of the most beautiful women he'd ever seen. Her eyes were a smooth, honey brown with long, dark lashes that couldn't help but hold his attention. That wasn't the only thing about her that grabbed him. She had sexy full lips that begged to be kissed, long legs, curvaceous, womanly hips, and a rack to die for.

And she was funny, obviously smart, and had a sarcastic mouth on her that kept him on his toes. Oh, and did he mention she was hot? Oh yeah, this was definitely his night. The only downer was her dislike for the snow. It really shouldn't matter since he'd only know her for the next few days. He liked her. If she wanted a good time, he'd show her one. In the bedroom and out.

"You know, most men would be happy with the offer of hot sex. I pick the only guy who wants a favor too," she said with a smile.

"Hot sex, huh?" Damn that sounded good. "My favorite kind." She looked embarrassed and turned on at the same time. Damned if his cock didn't begin to stir. "And it's not really a favor. More of a request."

He planned to have her no matter what. She offered and he'd accept. No fucking way would he turn her down but he wanted her to get out with him too, to experience what he felt when he glided down the slopes. The feeling was almost as good as sex. Almost. "You said you wanted to have fun this weekend. I'm just offering you more than just the sexual kind. We'll do that too," he added with a wink. "And it will be more than just fun."

"I need to find out what this request is before we go any further. We also need to set ground rules: we don't sleep with anyone else while we're together, we both understand it ends when its time for me to leave, and most importantly, protection must be used at all times."

"You put a lot of thought into this." She amused him.

"Of course."

"Sex shouldn't be about thought, Honey. Well, except for the protection part. That's always a must for me as well. It's about attraction, connection, pleasure." And he couldn't wait to pleasure her. All sorts of thoughts flowed through his mind. What kinds of noises would she make when she came? Did she like top or bottom? How would she feel clamped around him?

Evie stuttered. "That's exactly what I'm looking for. Emphasis on the pleasure part."

He laughed heartily. "Believe me I'll put a lot of emphasis on satisfying you." She shuddered, a smile gracing her plump lips.

"So what's your request?" she asked. "We still haven't gotten to that part yet."

"I want you to spend a day in the snow with me. I'm going to show you what snowboarding is all about."

Half hour later Ryan sat in his cabin hoping like hell Evie didn't change her mind. After she agreed to meet him the next day for their snowboarding lesson he bid her goodnight and headed for home. He probably could have taken her with him. After all, that's what she wanted this weekend but he hadn't. What she planned shouldn't be taken lightly. He wanted to give her a night to sleep on it and make sure she really wanted to have a weekend of sex with a stranger.

She was a nice woman and the last thing he wanted is to give her something to regret. He could only pray he wasn't making a big mistake because he wanted Evangeline Sinclair with a burning intensity that could rival a wildfire.

Chapter Three

Evangeline woke up the next morning to Mia knocking on their connected door. Last night she'd quickly said hello to her sleeping friend to make sure she got in alright. Neither talked about their night deciding to wait until morning. Getting out of bed she walked over and opened the door.

"How'd it go?" Mia quickly asked after they both sat on the bed. "I know you liked what you saw when you looked at him but was he feelin' you too?"

"Do you doubt my sexual allure?" Evie raised an eyebrow. "Like you said, he's a man, right? Of course he was interested."

Mia hugged her excitedly. "Damn girl this is going to be a great vacation."

"So I take it you scored with my choice for you too?"

Mia looked down at the bed. "Hell ya. I met him and we had a good talk as well."

Perfect! She couldn't be happier. She and Mia both deserved a good time so badly. Coming to the resort was the best decision they could have made to release their inhibitions and to gain sexual freedom.

"So give me details?" Mia asked.

"Girl you couldn't have picked a sexier man. Ryan is all that and then some. He also seems like a really good guy. He's funny and carefree. I think he's just what I need to relax." Mia looked so happy she would have thought she planned to hook up with Ryan rather than Evie. Not that her friend would do that. "There's only one thing about him that so isn't my thing?"

"What's that?"

"Can you say obsessed? The man loves snowboarding, used to be a pro and for some reason thinks I'll love it too. He's going to teach me how."

A loud howl of a laugh escaped Mia's lips.

"It's not that funny." She threw a pillow at Mia.

"You on a snowboard? I wish I could be there to see it."

Because of that comment Evie became a little more excited about the whole snowboarding thing. She didn't back down to a dare easily and

without actually speaking the words Mia just dared her to learn how to snowboard, to do it well, and to enjoy it. "Just wait until this weekend is over. I'll not only be a pro at riding a snowboard but Ryan too." They laughed together before separating into their own rooms to get ready for the day.

They met in the resort lobby. Evie sat on one of the couches while he approached her. "First things first you need different clothes if you're planning to board." He held out his hand to help her stand.

"Ooh. Shopping? This day is getting better by the minute." *Especially since I get to look at your fine ass all day.*

"Don't get too excited." He led her to the door. "Today our goal is one stop shopping so we have time to get a little bit of practice in." Evie followed him to a black F250 truck.

"Nice ride." She jumped into the truck, Ryan getting in on the driver side.

"Thanks. She's one of my girls."

"One of your girls?"

"Yep." They pulled out of the parking lot before he continued. "I have three, my truck and my two favorite boards."

"And how often do you ride your…girls?"

He turned toward her cocking his brow. "Now there's a loaded question. I ride them every chance I get. And practice makes perfect, Honey. I'm damn good at what I do."

She bet he was. Soon she would know first hand. Her body came alive with the thought. She tingled in places she almost forgot existed. "Well I'm glad I'll get to practice with the best."

Ryan shifted in his seat. "We better stop now or we won't make it to the board shop."

"And that's a bad thing because?" He gave her a look of warning. "Okay, okay. I'm done with the sexual innuendo for now. I'm actually a little excited for my snowboarding lessons."

"Only a little bit? I'm telling ya, you'll love it. There's nothing like it in the world."

"We'll see."

"Yeah we will."

They arrived at the snowboard shop a few minutes later. The ride felt even short today with Evie in the truck with him. She was great company, refreshing, funny, confident and gorgeous. He fought to keep his eyes on the rode while he drove. Her luscious body called to him. Her honey eyes held a sweet sparkle to them but he had a feeling Evangeline Sinclair was anything but sweet. Well, except for sweet tasting, that he didn't doubt. He couldn't wait to find out first hand.

"So what do we need?" She asked when they walked in the store.

"Pants, boots, and a hoody. That should get you started. You can get the rest back at the resort."

He watched her scan the racks her curvy little body swaying and coming close to giving him a woody in the middle for the store. He still couldn't believe his luck. Out of all the people in the resort he was the one she chose to have a fling with. He didn't want to disappoint her. He'd show her a good time this weekend if it killed him. Not that he was worried about the bedroom part. Chemistry pulsed between them. He just hoped he was right about her enjoying the slopes.

"Since you're the expert why don't you go ahead and pick what I wear." She pointed to one of the racks.

What he really wanted to be picking for her was some sexy lingerie, snowboarding gear came in a close second. Those two circumstances were the only times he liked shopping. "Sounds good to me." They walked the store, Ryan grabbing a pair of white Roxy snowboarding pants, boots and a pink hoody. She gave him sizes as he picked clothes from the racks. The fact that she didn't shy away from letting him know what size she wore turned him on more. He loved confident women. And her sizes were just what he liked, real, not Hollywood standards.

When they walked up to the counter he reached into his pocket to pull out his wallet. Since this was his show he didn't want her to pay for something she hadn't planned on doing in the first place.

"What are you doing?"

"Paying."

"You must be crazy. No way will I let you buy my clothes, Ryan."

"This whole thing is my idea anyway. I don't want you to put out your vacation money on something I'm pushing you into doing in the first place."

She laughed. The beautiful sound headed straight for his cock making him stand to attention. If he was honest he'd admit it also had a strange affect in his chest too. He wouldn't think about that though. They didn't know each other well enough for her to affect him that way. He admired her independence but still part of him didn't feel right about her forking

out her own hard earned money for his pleasure. And that's exactly what it was. He couldn't wait to show her his world.

"I'm willing to compromise. How about we split the bill?"

Her eyes gave a clear window to the wheels turning in her head. He could tell she was a thinker, everything planned and plotted. Thank God she made the choice to let loose this weekend. He was even happier she decided to do it with him. All night he'd been primed and ready for her. Sleeping was a bitch but he finally caught a few z's. She would be worth his lack of sleep. As long as she was here he didn't plan to get much sleep over the next few days.

They'd be too busy.

"Sounds like a deal to me." They each took out their wallets and paid their respective amounts.

"Want to grab a quick bite to eat before we head back? There's a café next door. The food's good."

"I'm starved. I didn't have breakfast this morning."

Ryan shook his head at her. "That's your first mistake, Honey. You need food. I plan to keep you very active."

She again laughed while they walked into the café. He liked that about her. Though she was responsible, a thinker, she also knew how to laugh. They had a sexy banter going between them that he couldn't get enough of.

"I'm going to hold you too that, you know?"

"I'm counting on it."

Evie ordered a big bowl of potato soup, a ham sandwich and hot chocolate. She wanted something to get her body warmed up before they went back out into the cold. Not that Ryan wasn't already making her body temperature rise a couple degrees every time he looked at her. It's a wonder she didn't catch fire. He had her that hot. If he was athletic as she thought he was she couldn't wait to see what he had in store for her. In the bedroom. The slopes, she was a little nervous about.

She studied the little café while Ryan continued to eat his steak and eggs. It was cute, homey. The walls were red brick, with an actual fire place on the far wall. It wasn't lit, probably for safety sake but it added character to the room. The tables were all small, two person tables. Though the place was packed it was still quite, relaxing. She decided she'd have to come here again before her trip was up.

"You about ready to go?" he asked after finishing up his food. She

had a few bites left in her bowl but was stuffed.

"Yeah, let's get going." Ryan threw a twenty on the table and walked toward the door. She followed stopping only to grab her jacket off the coat rack next to the door.

Half an hour later they were back at the resort getting equipment for Evie to use on the slopes. Ryan did all the picking, choosing what he thought would be the perfect board for her. They tested to make sure his choice reached just below her chin and then to see if she was goofy-footed or standard. Luckily she was standard. The other didn't sound like a good start even though Ryan assured her it wasn't a big deal.

"We need to get you a helmet," he told her.

"I have to wear a helmet?" She touched her braids "Well that just ruined my sex appeal," she kidded.

Ryan leaned toward her. "Nothing could ruin your sex appeal, Honey." She almost melted. Just the sound of his sexy voice did that to her.

She dressed in the gear they bought at the store and a few minutes later they were in the snow at the teaching section.

"Isn't the point to go down a hill?" she asked knowing the question was foolish.

"Honey, you aren't going down the mountain the first time you put the board on your feet. There are a few things I want to go over with you first. It will be a good couple hours at least before we attempt the slope. Depending on how you do, it might even be tomorrow."

"Tomorrow?"

"Maybe not." He shrugged "I have a feeling you'll be a natural. If not then I just guaranteed myself more time with you."

She'd give him all the time he wanted. Snow boarding or not.

Before they began Ryan started to explain the parts of the board to her, the tip, tail, stomp pad, and other snowboarder terminology. Evie paid close attention. Studying she knew. After years of college it was one thing she could say she was really good at.

As he talked to her, explaining the different steps they'd be taking today, she could see how much knowledge he had of his craft. Her respect for him grew. The man was smart.

"Okay, let's get you on the board." Evie stepped into the binding while Ryan bent to her feet and latched some kind of leash.

"What's that for?"

"Keeps you from losing your board when you crash."

She couldn't help but smile. "When I crash, huh? I don't even get an if?"

"No offense but I'd be damned surprised if you didn't end up on your sexy, little ass a few times today. It comes with the territory."

This was starting to sound less and less like a good time but she gave her word she'd do it' so she would.

"We picked a good day to start," he told her. "We got a few fresh inches of snow last night. That will make it easier for you."

Please, she didn't need easy. She could learn no matter how hard it might be. "I guess someone's looking out for me."

"Yeah, that's what I said after meeting you last night," he said with a wink and a smile. Shivers assaulted her body and it had nothing to do with the cold, crisp air. It was all because of Ryan. Damn this man is fine.

Before she had the chance to reply, he stood and their lesson began. It was probably better that way. Otherwise she might have begged him to take her to her room right now.

Chapter Four

The lesson started out not at all like she imagined. Ryan made her learn to walk with her board first. He taught her to "skate" with the board, how to pivot and steer. He explained the stomp pad, how to rest her foot on it, told her how important it was while riding and exiting the lift.

"Next you get a lesson in riding the lift itself."

She wondered how hard it could be to get on and off a damn lift. Didn't you just sit down then stand up? She could handle that. As if he could read her thoughts he said, "Believe me. It's not as easy as you think."

He was right. They practiced exiting the lift multiple times, each one either ended with her on her read end, or wobbling before she caught herself. On the hill he started teaching heel and toe edging which was another obstacle she had to overcome. This whole snowboarding thing was a lot harder than she thought. He was right. She'd already landed on her ass a few times today. Every time she fell, he tried to teach her the correct way to fall.

"I didn't know there was a correct way to fall. I'd rather just stay on my feet the whole time." That sounded like the best plan to her.

"I'm sure everyone would like that. It doesn't work that way though."

Evie watched Ryan demonstrate and listened carefully. She was determined to do this and do it right. One thing she couldn't stand is not being able to do something. She had to succeed.

"You're doing great, Evie. I think you are almost ready to go at it for real. I'll show you a couple more exercises to make sure you have as much control over the board as you can then we'll give it a try." He looked down at his watch. "And we've only been practicing about a few hours. That isn't bad."

"Control is one thing I can do." Yeah, she liked control.

"Me too, Honey. I can't wait to have you give a little bit of it up to me."

She started to get wet and not from the snow. Part of her wanted to call off the lesson right now but she was starting to really want to know

how to do this. She liked a challenge. Thrived on it was more like it.

They worked about another half an hour before he asked, "You ready to give this a try for real?"

This week is about letting go, being free. "Let's do it."

They took one more trip up the lift. This time, on the way down, she'd really get to experience snowboarding. She'd get to see if she shared Ryan's love of the sport.

Her nerves prickled as she exited the lift. She was a ball of fear and excitement rolled into one. As if he sensed her emotions, Ryan grabbed her hand squeezing it before he let go and they walked to the beginning of the slope. He went over a few last minute instructions, reminding her how to ride, turn and eventually stop. Then they were on their way.

The wind flowed around her, cold, strong but also freeing. She felt like she never felt before, the snow beneath her board, like she was flying. All the stresses in her life, worrying about her new job, paying back her student loans, everything flowed out of her body and into the wind as she soared down the mountain. Her body felt shaky but she managed to keep her balance as she went.

All too soon she approached the end of the slope, struggling she tried to remember how Ryan told her to stop her board, how to try and keep herself from falling. It didn't work. She crashed into the soft, white snow. Her ankle twisted and pain erupted as she went.

Ryan couldn't be more proud as he watched her work on all the exercises he'd taught her. She joked, but took it seriously which was important. And like he thought, she was a natural. He could tell she was a little discouraged it was taking so long but that's the name of the game. She didn't realize how good she was actually doing.

Then he saw her go down.

Unfortunately, the way she grabbed her ankle told him it wasn't an injury free fall. Damn. He got to her as quickly as possible. "Are you okay?"

"Oh, just broke my ankle, that's all."

Guilt hit him with the force of a knock-out punch. His feelings must have shown on his face because she said, "Not really. I'm sure it would hurt a lot more if it was broken. Not that it doesn't hurt." He could see the grimace of pain on her face. "I think I just sprained it."

Like that wasn't enough. He might have just ruined her whole trip by insisting she snowboard with him. Who knew how long she'd be

laid up? "Let me look." He helped her take off her boots. Sure enough her ankle was swelled and discolored. "Shit, Honey. I'm so sorry." He signaled to one of the workers to come over and instructed him to grab their equipment. He would take Evie. He hoisted her in his arms, she was warm, her feminine curves molding in his arms. She even smelled of sweet honey. How did he not notice that before?

She winced.

"Did I hurt you?"

"It's okay. Just the movement." Ryan tried to walk as gently as he could as he carried her away. The last thing he wanted to do was hurt her anymore.

"You must really spend a lot of time here if employees do what you say." She said tilting her head toward the man carrying their equipment. Then changing the subject she said, "You know, I could probably limp to wherever we're going but it's not often a muscular, gorgeous guy carries me. I decided I want to take advantage."

He loved the fact that she still joked at a time like this. Maybe she wasn't as straight laced she thought? "I thought I was the one taking advantage? It feels damn good holding you, Evie."

For the first time since he met her he saw her cheeks blush. The smile on her face made him want to bend and kiss her sweet lips. He didn't. Not yet. He wasn't sure if things were still a go. "So you think I'm gorgeous, huh?" He asked trying to darken the red tint to her cheeks. It worked.

"You know I do. I wouldn't have made the proposition I did if I didn't think you were hot."

He almost tripped.

"Ouch. Let's try not to hurt my ankle anymore, shall we?" she asked grimacing because of pain but slightly smiling because of her joke. "Where are we going anyway?"

"I'm taking you home with me." Now he was the one with a smile.

Ryan's comment almost made her forget her pain. She wanted him and wouldn't let a small ankle injury come between herself and the chance to have him. She was a fighter. "Why aren't we going into the resort?"

"I'm always here. I have one of the cabins." An ornery look on his face.

"Are you taking me to your house to take advantage of me?" She

hoped so.

"Nope. I'm taking you there to examine your ankle. Depending on how it looks we'll decide if I need to take you to the hospital or not." Damn. That isn't what she expected to hear.

"I'm fine." And she was. Sure it hurt but all the hospital would do is x-rays that she didn't need before they told her to wrap it and try and stay off it. She could do all that herself, well, except for the x-ray part of course.

"I'll be the judge of that." He turned up the path toward a lone, log cab in the trees. She couldn't help but think about being stranded there with him. Just the two of them. His hard body against hers made her nipples start to pucker. He generated enough body heat for the both of them, hot and masculine.

"Looks like I'm not the only one who likes being in control."

"Nope," he answered simply before opening the door to his cabin. She couldn't believe he didn't lock it. But then maybe that's what small town life was like. He must be here enough that he trusted the people who worked here to watch his belongings.

The first thing she noticed when he carried her over the threshold was the smell. His cabin held the same distinct, manly, rustic smell that Ryan carried. She felt him here. She hadn't known him long but this place fit him. There was a small, open kitchen off to the right of the front door. The living room was small with one couch, TV, coffee table and a fire place. There were two closed doors on the other side of the room which she assumed to be the bathroom and bedroom.

Ryan walked straight over to the forest green couch and set her down. "All right. Let me have a better look." He propped her injured ankle on the table and removed her sock.

"Oooh. Ouch. That hurts, Ryan. Be careful." She knew she sounded like a baby but couldn't help it. Her pain escalated when he touched her.

"I'm sorry, Honey. I've almost got it." His gravely voice was soft, caring, comforting. She didn't notice he'd completely freed her foot.

"Maybe I'm more goofy-footed than I thought," she laughed poking fun at herself. "I can't believe I hurt myself my first time out." Warmth shot from her foot up her body. Ryan lightly skated his fingers across her ankle. Her body shuddered in delight from the simple touch.

"Don't be hard on yourself. It's natural to fall." He turned his steel gray eyes toward her. "You're right. It's an ugly sprain but I don't think it's broken. You don't look in too much pain but I'm thinking we should bring you to the hospital just in case. I'd hate to be wrong or risk the pain

getting worse for you."

Pain was the last thing she felt right now. Not with his calloused hand on her ankle, his dreamy eyes locking with hers. Horny fit her mood so much better. Then Ryan moved his hand and she felt the slight throb of pain. She could handle it. She wasn't one to rush to the hospital for something like a sprained ankle. "We don't need to go to the hospital. I'm good."

He didn't look sure. "I feel bad, Honey. What if you're hurt more than we think?"

"We'll wrap it up and if it doesn't start to feel better, I'll go in. I'd hate to spend part of my much needed vacation in the hospital," she continued to plead her case.

He shot her a mischievous smile. "If you don't go to the hospital you have to stay here with me. I'm going to take care of you and make sure you have the vacation you deserve."

Oh yeah. She could handle that.

Chapter Five

"I'm going outside to grab some firewood." Ryan handed her a phone. "Why don't you call your friend? I'll write my phone number down. I want you to give her my number and tell her you'll be staying with me. I want her to know you're safe and where to find you if she needs you for anything."

Evie saluted him. "Aye-Aye Captain."

Ryan bent over her on the couch and touched his lips to hers.

For the first time in her life she felt "the zing". Her body came alive with the sensation. He coaxed her lips open with his tongue and dipped inside. If masculinity had a taste it would be Ryan. Their tongues mates sensually, giving and taking. He brought his strong hand behind her and grasped her head deepening their kiss.

Another zing. It formed deep in her belly and shot throughout her body making her want to explode from the pleasure. When he moved, rough whiskers rubbed against her face reminding her how ruggedly handsome he was. She couldn't take anymore. It was too much, too soon. As if he read her thoughts, he pulled away.

"If I don't stop now I won't be able to at all. You taste too damn good." She watched as he backed away from her writing his number down on a piece of paper. "Make that call, Evie. I'll be back in a few minutes." He handed her the sheet and walked out the door.

Outside, Ryan leaned against the side of the cabin. The air around him blew brisk and cold but his body felt aflame. If he hadn't walked out the door when he did he would have taken her right there on the couch. Injured ankle and all. Her kiss was amazing. Like nothing he ever felt before. He'd almost come from a damn kiss. A kiss! What the fuck was that? This wasn't his first trip around the block but he felt like it. When his lips touched hers he was fifteen again, scoring his first slip of tongue.

And he wanted more.

Now.

He knew he couldn't have what he wanted. Not yet. He felt too guilty for her injured ankle. He shouldn't have even walked out on her when he did but he'd barely had hold of his control. Shit he hadn't even wrapped it yet. What an ass.

He started to stack wood in his arms. A few minutes later, after he had better control, Ryan had a plan. Somehow he still had to make sure she had a good vacation. She deserved it. He could tell she worked hard all these years and he wanted to give her the reward she sought. He'd pamper her, take care of her and then, ravage her.

Evie couldn't slow down the erratic beat of her heart. It pounded in her chest. She could feel it in her throat. Kissing Ryan was everything she imagined and then some. The throb in her ankle spread to the apex of her thighs in remembrance. Quickly, before he came back in the house she dialed Mia's cell. Her friend answered on the second ring.

"Hello."

"Hey, it's Evie." Her voice quivered.

"Girl, I've been wondering about you. You get some yet?"

She let out laugh. "Not yet. I hurt my damn ankle trying to snowboard."

"Are you okay?" Concerned etched her voice.

"Yeah, I'm good. My ankle hurts and it's swollen but it isn't that big a deal. I'm in Ryan's cabin." She couldn't hold back her excitement. "He wants me to stay here. I don't know if he means just for tonight or what. I know he's feeling guilty that I hurt myself so I'm sure he just wants to make sure I'm okay."

"I'm sure he wants a lot more than that, girl."

"I hope so." If his kiss was any indication Mia was right. "Anyway, he wants me to give you his number in case you need anything." She read the number to her friend. "I'll call you in the morning, k?"

"Love you."

"Love you too, girl."

Evie went to hang up the phone when Mia added, "And have fun."

She planned on it.

A couple minutes later Ryan walked in the door his strong arms filled with wood. He set it down next to the fireplace and came back over to her examining her ankle. "We need to get some ice on it. I should have done that before I went out but if I didn't leave when I did it would have been a lot longer until I got around to getting you ice."

She doubted that. He acted too concerned about her to get sidetracked too long. "And why is that?"

"Because the wrong head was in charge." He caressed her ankle. "I'll be right back."

He went to the freezer and pulled a tray out before grabbing a large baggie and towel from the drawer. He filled the bag with ice, wrapped it and brought it over, holding it to her ankle.

"Damn that's cold."

"Here, hold it for a minute while I get a fire going." She grabbed the icepack letting him get to warming her up. The fire would be a good start. She counted on the man himself to really turn up the heat. If his kiss turned her into such an incinerator what would his be able to do with his hands, his mouth, his cock. A moan slipped past her lips.

"Honey, you do that again and damn the fire."

She almost told him okay but it really was cold in his cabin. She needed the fire to take the edge off. "Sorry."

"Don't be. It was sexy as hell. Just save the moans and groans for when we're in bed together."

That she could handle.

Ryan made quick work of the fire. "It's a small cabin so it should warm up pretty fast. How do you feel?"

"It hurts but not enough that I can't handle it. I'm afraid I got your couch a little wet though. My pants are damp from falling in the snow."

He ran a hand though his hair. "Sorry. I didn't think to get you something to wear earlier. I'll grab some clothes then help you in the bathroom to get changed."

A minute later he was back, taking the ice off her ankle before he bent to lift her in his arms. While he was in the room he changed as well, putting on a white T-shirt that hugged his muscles in all the right places and black, cotton pants.

"You don't have to carry me." She spoke the words but really her body pulsed at the idea of being in his arms. All he had to do was touch her and she came alive, he was like a drug, if she wasn't careful she knew she'd become addicted to him.

"I know I don't have to but I'll use any excuse I can to get you in my arms."

Sweet talk didn't usually do it for her but with Ryan everything he said, did, turned her on. Once in his small bathroom he set her down on the closed toilet. "Here's a pair of sweat pants and a sweat shirt for you. There's Aspirin or Tylenol in the cabinet if you want to take a couple to help with the pain. I'll be right outside the door when you're done."

She was going to smell like him. The scent she couldn't get enough of, trees, crisp fresh air, and powerful, masculine man was going to follow her around the rest of the night. As if Ryan wasn't temptation enough his own, his distinct aroma which she labeled, sex appeal would fill her nostrils with each breath. She would die if he didn't take her to bed soon.

Evie slipped out of her clothes and into his. She felt warm, comfortable in his baggy gray sweat suit. Opening his medicine cabinet she grabbed a couple Tylenol before opening the door to catch her ride. "A woman could get used to this, you know?" She asked while he carried her into the kitchen.

"You don't strike me as the type who would take advantage." He knew her better than she thought. The thought warmed her insides. He walked her to the kitchen setting her down in one of the wood chairs at his small table. Pulling over a chair with a pillow on it he propped her ankle up and returned the icepack.

"You set this up for me while I was in the bathroom?"

"Yep. I'm going to cook some dinner. Part of the couch is still wet so I figured you could sit in here and keep my company."

"You need any help?" She could hop around the kitchen if need be.

"Nope. I want you to relax."

"I'm not helpless."

"I know." He pulled a couple cans of tomato soup and a loaf of bread from the cabinet. "But I am a simple man. Not much of a cook so we're having soup and grilled cheese tonight. I hope that's okay."

"I can always grub on some grilled cheese sandwiches. They're my favorite."

"What a coincidence, Honey. They're my favorite too."

Ryan opened a bottle of wine and poured them each a glass. Evie sipped hers while he grilled the sandwiches and warmed the soup. Thank God she wasn't the kind of woman who turned her nose up at a simple meal. He hadn't lied when he told her he was a simple man. That's part of the reason he'd quit the pros. He snowboarded for the love of the sport not for recognition. He thought he'd enjoy the cameras but he hadn't. In the end, he walked away back to the life he loved here and hadn't looked back since.

They made small talk while they ate, laughing and drinking wine. She

was smart and fun to be around. Besides being sexy as all hell she was kick-back, down-to-earth just like himself. When they finished eating he asked, "Want to move this back into the living room?"

"Sure," she answered simply. He grabbed an ace bandage, a couple blankets and a pillow laying them on the floor in front of the fire. The couch was still wet so it gave him the perfect excuse to lie down next to her. He brought the wine and glasses in setting them on the coffee table before going back in for Evie.

"Is this alright with you?" he asked. When she nodded yes he laid her down in the middle of the pallet. He sat down and put her feet in his lap. He stayed away from her injured ankle, massaging her other foot. "So how was your first full day in Big Bear?" he asked meaning the words as a joke but she looked serious when she replied.

"Great. It's been exactly what I need."

"Really? You needed to fall on your ass and hurt your ankle?"

"You know what I mean." She gave him a smile that almost stopped his heart. He realized he wasn't moving his hands. He was just staring at her, unable to move or turn away. There was something special about her, something different. Her eyes diverted down. Did she feel it? Was she just as surprised as him by the connection between them. She downed the last of the wine in her glass. Trying to sidetrack himself he refilled both their glasses.

He started gently brushing his fingertips across her injured ankle. "Is this okay? Am I hurting your ankle?"

She shivered. "It tickles a little but feels good."

"So, tell me why you decided to become a lawyer." He wanted to learn as much about her as possible.

She stayed quite a moment before answering. "My dad. He convicted of a crime he didn't commit. My mom had to work two jobs to take care of me and my little brothers. We went through a lot not having my daddy around."

"Like what?" He hoped he wasn't overstepping any boundaries by asking. Sure this weekend was supposed to be about sex but she fascinated him. He wanted to get to know her on every level, not just sexually.

"The typical. I became a mom at twelve, helping anyway I could to care for my younger brothers. I cooked dinner, did laundry, and went to school. Not that my mom didn't try but there are only so many hours in a day."

"Jesus. I'm sorry. That had to be hard."

"It was but we survived okay. That which doesn't kill you will only

184

make you stronger." As if he didn't respect her enough before, it grew by leaps and bounds now. Her strength amazed him, touched him like no other woman he'd ever known.

"You should be proud of yourself." He continued to rub the pads of his finger on her swollen ankle. He wanted to touch her any way he could.

"I don't want to sound conceited but I am pretty damn proud of myself. It wasn't easy. I worked my ass off. That's why I wanted this weekend so much. I need to do, to have something just for myself."

He smiled inside not wanting to look life a goofy, school boy who was about to lose his virginity but the idea of her wanting him all to herself appealed to him. "I'm honored you chose me, Honey." When he looked at her he noticed her eyes were becoming heavy.

"Me too, Ryan. I think this is one of the best decisions I've ever made." He didn't know if it was the wine or exhaustion but she drifted off to sleep.

Chapter Six

Evie stirred in the most comfortable bed she'd ever slept in. The blanket covering her was soft, felt like it might be a down comforter draping over her. The pillows were fluffy, her head sinking in. Opening her eyes, she looked around. This must be Ryan's bedroom and it was gorgeously masculine. The bed was large with a dark oak frame. The bedding a deep midnight blue. Across from the bed was a matching dresser with a small space heater next to it, turned on and facing the bed.

He had two shelves on his wall, one with snowboarding trophies, the other with beautifully detailed wood carvings of animals. Why would he bring this many personal items to a resort cabin, she wondered. She snuggled deeper in the bed drenched in Ryan scent. He was such a sweet man. He'd taken care of her yesterday, carried her, cooked for her, massaged her, talked to her. She couldn't remember the last time anyone had taken care of her. It had been a damn long time.

The scary part was she feared he was starting to mean more to her than just a bed buddy. Hell, they hadn't even made it to bed together yet. She'd ruined that by falling asleep last night. Leave it to her to fall asleep the night she was supposed to make love to a gorgeous, sexy man. Have sex. Not make love. She'd be smart to remember that. She had to leave tomorrow afternoon. Her heart sank at the idea. Maybe they could stay in touch when she left. They could still be friend's even if it were long distant ones.

Evie left the comfort of Ryan's bed and limped into the bathroom. She looked down and realized he'd wrapped her foot in an ace bandage after she'd fallen asleep. Her heart beat so fast she became dizzy. The man was one of the nicest she'd ever known. After relieving herself she threw a handful of warm water on her face and opened the door.

"Jeez, you scared the shit out of me," she said to a very dishevled, tired looking Ryan.

"You should have yelled for me so I could carry you in here." He said his deep voice almost angry. "I don't want you to hurt yourself."

She patted his bare chest, Good God how could she have just noticed he didn't wear a shirt? His arms and chest were broad, muscular.

Oh yeah, his arms were just as sexy as she knew they would be. His chest had a light dusting of dark blond hair. She followed the trail downwards. It disappeared below his the elastic in his pants. Continuing down she eyed a large bulge.

"Morning wood," he said. She didn't have to look him in the eyes. She felt his intense stare on her. "If you don't stop staring like that I just might have to do something about it."

"I--" she tried to reply but couldn't. In the flash of an eye Ryan had her in his arms and back on the couch. The blankets from the floor last night were now there.

"Let me look at your ankle."

"It's fine."

He ignored her words and looked himself. It was still discolored but some of the swelling from yesterday had gone down. "It looks a lot better." He wrapped it again.

"I'm glad you think so, Dr. Barnes," she kidded.

"I'm hungry. Would you like some breakfast?"

She looked at him, sexy as hell, and so damn caring she could almost cry. "No." Then she leaned forward and kissed him. She wanted him, not food. He took over leaning her back against the couch. He kneeled on the floor, between her legs, his bare torso touching her shirt clad chest. He kissed her senseless.

His tongued mated with hers, deeply swooping in and out of her mouth making her dizzy with lust. She felt his urgency, his hunger for her as his mouth devoured hers. Spirals of delight flowed through her body. Pulling away slightly he traced her upper lip, then her bottom with his tongue. All she could do was moan in approval. A soft laugh escaped him before he sucked her bottom lip into his mouth gently, released it, then nipped it with his teeth.

She'd never, ever been kissed this thoroughly in her life.

It felt as if his mouth were on her whole body, the pleasure was that great, that overpowering. His lips again captured hers in one more mind-blowing, soul-reaching kiss before he seared a path down to her neck with his tongue. Evie pushed herself into the couch, tilting her head back to give him better access.

"I knew Honey was the perfect name for you," he said against her mouth. "Your skin tastes so sweet. I want to eat you up." Then he licked a trail from her neck to the pulse at the hollow of her throat, kissed her there then traced his tongue back up toward her ear, stopping to kiss her every few seconds. He nibbled, than sucked her earlobe into his mouth while he buried his hand in her hair. She'd never been this wet, this

turned on especially from just a kiss. But then, what he was doing to her was more than a kiss. It was every happy, pleasureful, joyous event in her life all balled into one moment.

"I wanted to do this to you so badly last night, Honey." His mouth was again by her lip, whispering against her.

"You should have woken me up," she said breathlessly. "I would have been accommodating."

He laughed deeply. "Lean up." Ryan pulled away from her so she could sit up. Before she could blink he had her shirt off and pushed her back into the couch. Then he stood up, lifted her hips and pulled his pants down her legs careful not to hurt her ankle. "Oh, fuck," he fell back to his knees. She fought the urge to cover herself up. All she wore were white panties and a bra. "I knew you were going to be beautiful all over, Evie." He placed a soft, fleeting kiss to her knee, than softly kissed a path up her thigh.

His stubble scratched her leg as he went. It felt good, he felt good. She buried her hands in his silky, blond hair. His kisses were soft, slow, sensual. When he made it to her panties, he surprised her by biting the top. They pulled away from her skin, then he let go and they snapped back against her. He kissed her stomach, dipped his tongue in her navel then dragged it up to the front clasp of her bra.

Her body burned with desire. He was the most sensual man to ever touch her. She quivered from the inside out, her body eager for the release that she knew would come shortly. Her heart thudded, wanting to burst free. Then he stopped and looked her in the eyes. "I don't want you to have any regrets about this weekend, Honey."

"I won't Ryan. I want you more than I've ever wanted anyone in my life."

Her words played again in his head. "I want you more than I've wanted anyone in my life." God he hoped so. She had him hard as steel but it was more than that, she was more than that. He didn't know how he was going to let her go. Pushing the thoughts from his mind he looked at her coco colored mounds. Her breasts were large with purplish colored nipples.

Leaning forward he sucked one peak into his mouth. He could die a very happy man right now. Well, maybe not quite yet. He still didn't know what it felt like to be buried deeply inside her. All the way to the hilt. He couldn't fucking wait. He continued to suckle her nipples first

one then the other. Evie writhed beneath him, moaned, and whispered his name. He wanted to give her so much pleasure she'd never be able to forget him.

Running his hand down her supple body, he dipped below her panty line, parting her lips. She was drenched. Fuck yeah. Pushing his finger inside her, he felt her silky, heat for the first time. They moaned in unison. "I don't know how much I can take," she said to him, her voice coming out between shallow breaths.

"You can take whatever I give you, Honey. That's what this weekend is about. Pleasure, fun, everything you've been missing." Then he added another finger and started to move them inside her. Her tight channel clamped around his fingers as he pumped them in and out. She felt so right beneath him, like everything that he hadn't even known he'd been missing. Her sharp panting breaths fueled him. Not that he needed anything extra to keep him going. She was enough. Gasping she moved along with him and then came on a scream.

***

Evie's heart thudded like a herd of elephant threatening to burst free from her chest. She lay there beneath Ryan fighting to catch her breath. So many mixed emotions swirled throughout her body she didn't know what to think. She felt more for Ryan than she should. This was about more than sex. But it couldn't be. She couldn't let it be. She had a career to start, her life to get back to.

Neither person spoke as they laid there both breathing heavily. Ryan stirred on top of her. When he did her stomach let out a fierce growl.

"I thought you said you weren't hungry."

She hadn't been. Not before he gave her such a workout. God, if he was this intense with foreplay how would it be when they finally made love? She couldn't fathom. "You helped me build an appetite," she said with a smile. "But we aren't done yet. I'm the only one who has received any pleasure today."

He looked at her, seriousness in his steel gray eyes. "Believe me, Honey. You've given me pleasure. Everything about you gives me pleasure." Evie could feel the heat in her cheeks. "I'll make something for us to eat." He stood up pulled her with him. He handed her the sweatshirt but nothing else. I was big on her so it covered her mid-thigh.

"Sit down. Do you like omelets?"

Her stomach growled again. "Obviously my tummy wants to speak for herself."

"Great."

"I can help. I'm not crippled you know."

"Who said you weren't helping?" He grinned. "I'll bring some veggies over and we can both chop them." He washed his hands then grabbed a couple produce bags from the fridge, went to the sink to wash the vegetables and then brought them to the table. He grabbed two knifes, a bowl, cutting board and a small plate. "I only have one cutting board," he said joining her at the table.

"You really must spend a lot of time here, Ryan. You seem so at home, it fits you so well here."

"That's because I am at home here," he popped a piece of raw bell pepper into his mouth. "This is where I live."

What? He lived at the resort? "Why? How?"

"It's mine," he shrugged his shoulders.

"You own the resort?" She was in shock. She didn't know why but she was.

"Yeah."

"Why didn't you tell me? Not that it matters."

"I don't know. The locals of course know but it's not something I usually announce to women I meet on vacation."

Her heart sank even though it shouldn't. What they had wasn't anything more than a weekend of sex no matter how it felt. And from the way he made it sound, it wasn't out of the ordinary for him either. He probably did this kind of thing on a regular basis. "Don't want to flash the bling to your weekend playmates?" she hated that her voice sounded so angry, so hurt.

"Hey," he said grabbing her hand. "That's not what I meant and you know it. I just like my privacy, that's all."

Yeah. Whatever. It didn't matter anyway. She was his playmate just as he was hers. "I know the score, Ryan." She started chopping again. "Let's get this breakfast going. I'm starved."

***

They ate their breakfast in near silence. She tried to push the hurt aside but she couldn't. She was falling for him as stupid as it was. But she wouldn't, couldn't do anything about it. She'd try and enjoy what they had left of the weekend, then go home and try to forget Ryan Barnes.

"Do you think we could get out of here for a little while?" she asked after breakfast. She didn't want to leave him but also needed a little space before they ended up in bed. She needed to clear her head.

"What do you want to do?"

"I'd like to explore the town a little bit. Walk around, look at some of the shops or something." Her ankle was still sore, but she could make

it. They'd just wrap it and she'd take it easy, try not to put much weight on it.

"What about your ankle? I don't want you to hurt yourself anymore." She gave him a look that told him what was up. "I know, I know, you can handle it." He grabbed her around the waist and pulled her close. "Why don't you take a shower with me and then we can head out?"

Then they'd never leave. "Can't. I don't have any clothes to change into. I'll head back to my room and meet you in the lobby in an hour."

Chapter Seven

Ryan insisted on helping her get back to her room before he showered. She let him get her as far as the main resort entrance before she finally shooed him away. He was sweet but she could take care of herself. Always had and would continue to do so after the weekend was over. She enjoyed his pampering too much. She couldn't let herself get too used to it.

She showered and got ready before making a quick call to Mia. She answered telling her she was having a great time with her friend and said they'd talk later. Thank God. Evie was so happy Mia found someone to have a good time with this weekend as well. She would have felt so guilty if they guys she picked for her didn't work out.

Evie wrapped her ankle in the ace bandage again before slipping her boots on. She tucked her pants into the fake fur top of her boots, ran her hand through her braids then limped down to meet Ryan. Ryan who lived in Big Bear, Mia's hometown. Who knew, maybe she'd but lucky enough to run into him again? The town was small and if Mia visited again she could go with her. Don't even think like that, girl. You agreed to have a weekend with him. That's it.

He was in the lobby talking with one of the resort employees. She hung back not wanting to interrupt him while he was working. Working! She still couldn't believe he owned the damn resort and she didn't know. Not that it mattered. She just didn't like not being in the know. That came along with being a lawyer. She was nosey like that.

He noticed her standing in the background, winked and continued his conversation. A minute later he was by her side. "You know I'm going to insist you lean on me while we're walking today."

"Oh yeah? What if I refuse?"

"Then I'll be carrying you around town. You pick." He put his arm around her waist. Evie leaned against him as the walked toward the truck. Her ankle didn't hurt much at all. She'd taken a couple Tylenol while in her room and it had taken most of the pain away. But she decided not to tell him. Why pass up the opportunity to be close to such a sexy, strong man? Mama didn't raise no dummy.

They were in town a couple minutes later. It wasn't much of a town

but endearing all the same. They walked the streets going into to each shop they passed so Evie could look around. Ryan had to have seen all this stuff a hundred times before. It touched her heart that he was willing to do it again with her. And she wasn't a quick shopper. She meandered around looking at antiques, souvenirs and learning tidbits of town history.

People smiled, waved and some even stopped to talk to them everywhere they went. No one looked twice at her even though she was obviously an out-of-towner and attached to Ryan's arms. Was that a good thing or a bad thing? Either they just didn't care, welcomed everyone to their little town or they were used to seeing Ryan with snow bunnies on vacation.

Not that she was a snow bunny.

A couple hours later they were heading back to the resort. "You remember that guy you saw me talking with earlier?" he asked.

"Yeah."

"He's worked for me a long time now. Real good guy. His nephew is here on vacation. He's been hounding Josh to ask me to board for him. I guess he wants to go pro one day. I've been putting it off the past couple days but I don't want to let the kid down. When we get back I'm going to take a couple trips for him. You can stay in my cabin. I don't want you on your feet any longer than need be today."

She really, really wanted to see him snowboard. "Can't I watch?"

"If you want. I wasn't sure if you'd want to. I know it isn't really your thing."

"Hey. I was having a good time once I got out there to learn. If the damn mountain wouldn't have gotten in my way I would have been just fine."

He laughed. "You did good too. Like I said, it's normal to fall, Honey. Its just unfortunate you hurt yourself."

"Story of my life. Anyway, I was starting to have a good time."

"Well, we'll have to do it again some time." Then as if realizing his mistake he added, "If you ever come back for vacation that is."

They were quiet the rest of the ride. Once they made it back, Ryan paged Josh and let him know he was ready for his nephew. The little boy was a cutie and looked at Ryan like a rock star. He bent to eye level, talking with the kid, telling him about snowboarding, what it meant to him and about the pros. The little boy hung on his every word as did Evie. She wanted that. Wanted to love and enjoy something as much as Ryan obviously did.

Her heart raced in her chest. He was so sweet, so patient with the boy, answering questions and treating the kid as his equal. Ryan stepped into his board and skated with it over to her, he kissed her quickly on the lips and then left for the lift. She watched him go, her hand somehow found it's way to her mouth trying to savor the feel of Ryan's lips on hers.

He was absolutely amazing. Beautiful, graceful, and powerful. Evie watched him soar down the mountain, turning, jumping, cutting corners sharply. She didn't know what to do when he came racing toward her. He was going so fast she had no idea how he could stop. Right before she thought he was going to mow her down he skidded to a stop a couple inches in front of her.

"Damn, you can ride."

He took off his goggles, winked and said, "You ain't seen nothing yet."

Ryan and Evie had dinner in the resort restaurant before going back to his cabin. Her nerves were on edge. Tonight she would get exactly what she wanted, what she'd come here for. Tomorrow she had to leave. The thought didn't feel right. She wasn't ready to leave yet. It's just because this is your first vacation in like…forever actually. That's why you're feeling nostalgic. She knew that wasn't the truth. It was Ryan. He'd gotten under her skin and she didn't know what to do about it. She had to leave, had to get to work and he lived here.

He sent her into the cabin while he brought in more firewood. She took off her boots and socks propping her ankle while she nervously waited for him. Her hands shook, her heart pounded in anticipation for Ryan. He came in a few seconds later making a fire. They didn't speak. He disappeared into his room coming out changed into sweat pants and a t-shirt and carrying the same blankets they laid on the night before.

"You want to lay by the fire for a little while?" he inclined his head toward the fireplace.

She did. Warmth started to flow from the fire place, the rustic smell of burning wood tickled her nose as she watched the flickering red and yellow glow. "I'd love to."

Ryan laid the blankets down. She got down to her hands and knees and crawled over to join him after he sat down. "Now that's a position I could get used to seeing you in." He said the words playfully but she could see desire brewing in his eyes. The time had finally come and she was going to take advantage of it. She couldn't wait any longer to have him.

Without replying she continued to crawl toward him like a lioness stalking its prey. His sultry smile shot straight to her heart. "I want you, Ryan."

He rose to his knees, lifting her up to hers as well. "Thank God because there is no fucking way I could stop myself now." He brushed his fingers across her cheek. "I'm going to take you in so many ways, Honey. All night long." Then his lips came down crushing hers.

He didn't have it in him to go slow. His hunger for her built up in his body too powerfully to control. He starved for her. Ryan's tongue pushed past her lips possessing her mouth. His tongue swept every corner, every inch of her mouth as her body molded his. Her small hands roamed his body, wrapping around him, rubbing his bare back under his shirt.

He was so hot for her. Her touched fueled the fire that already burned for her. Grasping her head with his hands he deepened the kiss and started to lean her back. Following his lead she laid down. He covered her body with his. His erection nuzzling in the warmth between her thighs. Needing to get her naked he opened the button on her jeans with one hand. The zipper followed.

Evie laughed against his mouth. "You are way too good at that. I don't even want to know how much practice that took."

He smiled kissing her softly. He left her mouth kissing her collar bone before pulling her shirt over her head. With one hand he unhooked her bra letting her breasts pop free. "I'm good. What can I say?"

"You're cocky."

"That too," he said with a wink.

Game time was over. Back to unwrapping his piece of sweet chocolate. He kissed down her body, going between her breasts. He wanted to suck her pert mounds into his mouth but knew if he did he'd never finish getting her undressed. His lips reached her open pants. He hooked his fingers into her jeans and panties pulling them down her legs. Ripping off his shirt, he bent and kissed her ankle before spreading her legs wide.

He stared at her glistening center. At that moment he knew he could never get tired of looking at her. She was perfect. Perfect for him. Ryan bent toward her, his tongue came out licking her wet heat from top to bottom. Her body ground against his mouth as a pleasure-filled moaned echoed through the room. He opened her with one hand, his tongue dipping between her feminine folds. He lapped up her sweetness, becoming drunk on her taste.

Ryan swirled his tongue around her. Evie bucked. He smiled against her and did it again and again until she came against his mouth, whispering his name. I love you. He didn't even try to deny the words as they drifted into his head.

Chapter Eight

Evie was exhausted because of the powerful orgasm that just shot through her body. Ryan definitely knew what to do with his tongue. She wanted to do it again. But first she'd return the favor. He lay between her legs, his blond head resting on her belly. He felt so good, so right laying on her that she almost didn't have the heart to move him. But she wanted to do this. Wanted to pleasure him as he'd done to her.

She pushed him off her and onto his back. He looked at her, desire and confusion in his eyes. "My turn to play," she told him. Evie grabbed his sweat pants and started to pull them down his legs. He'd gone commando. His long, thick erection sprang free from his pants as she lowered them. She sat there, enamored a minute, unable to think of anything else but Ryan's beautifully, masculine body.

He stirred bringing her back into the moment. She finished pulling his pants down before wrapping her hand around his shaft. He growled, grabbing her stopping her from moving it.

"Damn woman. I want to explode just from your touch." His voice was deeper, rougher even than usual.

"I like driving you wild, Ryan. Let me." He dropped his hand to his side and Evie took advantage rubbing her hand up and down his cock. It wasn't enough. She bent down, lowering her mouth over the tip then back up again.

"Oh God, Honey. You drive me wild." She pulled back briefly only to twirl her tongue around the head of his penis. Then she lowered her mouth again taking as much of him as she could. He was a big man but Evie wanted to make this special, to give him as much as she could. He dug his hand in her hair as she went, up and down, licking, sucking and teasing his cock.

His musky, manly scent filled her nostrils, fueling her on. This man was so hot, so sexy. She wanted go give him the ultimate pleasure. "Evie, Honey, you have to stop."

She ignored him and continued to work him with her mouth. He was close, she could tell. "Honey," he pulled back, lifting her head away from him. "I want to be inside you when I come. We have time to play later. Right now, I need to be inside you."

Oh God, she would do anything for his man. In a matter of a couple days he'd become so much to her. He respected her, took care of her. How was she going to leave him behind? It's a fling, Evie. That's all. But she knew that wasn't true. He was so much more.

Somehow Ryan got out from under her and lifted her in his arms. She had been so sidetracked she had no idea how he'd done it. "I want to take you in my bed, Honey. I want to smell you on my sheets when you're gone."

When you're gone. Why did she have to leave? At this second, here in his arms she couldn't remember. He laid her down on his over-sized bed. The heater was again turned on in the corner. She had a feeling the two of them could generate enough heat without it. Her body was already over-heated. This man had her on fire.

Lying on top of her Ryan sucked one of her nipples into his mouth. Her body burst, coming even more alive. She didn't think that were possible but with him it seemed anything was. He teased her nipples with his tongue, first one then the other. It was the sweetest sensation she'd ever felt. She held him close, running her hands all over his neck, shoulders and back while he suckled her breasts.

"I can't wait any more." He leaned over and reached into the bedside table. He pulled out a condom and quickly sheathed himself. "No regrets, right?" he asked lingering over her.

"No regrets." As soon as the words left her mouth he pushed inside her in one gentle stroke. He filled her up, reached her soul. Her body tingled, burned with delight as he started to move inside her.

"You feel even better than I thought you would." He pulled almost all the way out of her before pushing himself inside again.

"You're not so bad yourself, Ryan." She was breathless, struggled to speak. He was better than not so bad and both of them knew it. He bent down kissing her senseless as he thrust in and out of her body. Ryan touched her soul-deep on every level, mind, body, and heart. Every part of her body felt a heightened awareness. She felt him from the tips of her toes to the top of her head.

Unable to hold back any longer, Evie came in an earth-shattering climax, Ryan's name on her tongue. He followed right behind her.

Minutes later, after they both recuperated, Evie finally spoke. "That was…fantastic Ryan."

"I told you snowboards aren't the only thing I know how to ride," he said with a grin.

She smacked his arm and then curled up against him. He held her naked body and wished to God he never had to let her go.

"Well I thoroughly enjoyed that ride."

So did he. More than anything in his life. He loved her, wanted her to stay. She was strong, funny, smart…beautiful. Great in bed. Ryan pulled her on top of him. "Time to test your riding skills, Honey."

Without hesitation she grabbed another condom and rolled it on.

They made love through the night. Ryan hadn't wanted to. The night would end faster that way. Finally the sun started to peak through the blinds in his room. Her vacation was over. Evie would be leaving today. Unless he could talk her into staying. Hell, he'd even go with her if she'd have him. He trusted his management to run the resort while he was gone. He could come back every other month and check on things. Stop getting ahead of yourself. "Honey, wake up." He shook her lightly.

"Again?" she purred in his ear.

He loved that about her. She'd fallen asleep multiple times last night. Each time he'd awakened her for another round she had been ready, willing, eager. "No, Honey. You asked me to wake you up early. It's morning."

"Oh." Was that disappointment in her voice? He sure as hell hoped so.

He kissed her before getting out of bed tossing one of his over-sized sweat shirts to her before dressing himself. "I'll make us a quick bite to eat while you shower." He left her in his room. He needed a little bit of space. She was a special woman and he loved her but he didn't want to interfere with her life. She had plans and they didn't include him. This was supposed to be a fling for her, it was his own damn fault he'd gone and fallen in love with her.

About thirty minutes later she came out of the bathroom dressed in her own clothes. They drank coffee and ate pancakes making small talk. Every now and again he'd catch her staring at him. What was she thinking? For the first time in his life he wanted to be someone else. Mel Gibson in the chick flick where he could read women's minds to be exact.

"I better get going," she told him standing up at that table. "I'm sure my friend is wondering where I've disappeared to."

He stood up and walked her to the door. She looked a little lost, confused. Did she feel what he did? "Bye," she opened the door and tried to walk out.

He grabbed her and pulled her into his arms kissing like crazy. Trying to show her how he felt.

"Wow."

He couldn't ask her to stay, ask her if she wanted him but he had to let her know how he felt. "I love you, Honey."

She looked at him, smiled, a tear streaming down her face and walked away.

She was a mess. Ryan had said he loved her and she walked out on him! How could she do that? She loved him too, there wasn't a question about that she just didn't know what to do about it. She had plans and they didn't involve staying here. Hell, she didn't even know if she'd like living in the snow. Sure she'd enjoyed her weekend here, she even wanted to give snowboarding another try but could she live here?

A soft rasping sounded on the connecting door to Mia's room. "Come in," she called.

"What's wrong?" her friend asked rushing to her.

"Ryan told me he loved me and I walked out." She covered her face with her hands.

"Do you love him?"

"Yes, I do. I know it's stupid and we were supposed to come here for a fling but I do. I love him and I don't know what to do about it."

Mia looked happy, a smile graced her face and before she hugged her. "You're in love, girl. What do you mean you don't know what to do?"

"I have a job waiting for me. A job kind of job that isn't a high demand in Big Bear. Plus I don't know if I can just move here on a whim for a man. What if it doesn't work out?"

Mia shook her head, stood up and started to pace the room. "You need to ask yourself if he's worth it. Some people look for love their whole lives. You found it in one weekend. I can't believe your thinking of giving it up for something as small as geography."

"That isn't little, Mia." When she said the words she knew it was. If she really loved him, they'd make it work. There had to be bigger towns close by that she could go to to look for work. She'd have to travel, but everyone in California traveled to go to work. Ryan was worth it. Whatever she had to do it was worth it.

"Finally seeing the light?" Mia asked. Evie jumped up and hugged her friend. "I'm glad. Since I'm going to be staying around here too it will make things a lot easier having my best friend around."

"What? Your guy? Did you fall in love too?" She couldn't believe this.

"Naw. I didn't even get any this weekend," she threw her arms in the air. "You picked a man with a girlfriend for me to try and fling with."

"Why didn't you tell me?"

"I didn't want to ruin your weekend. Plus, I had this planned the whole time, you know? I'm getting a job in Yucaipa. It's about an hour down the mountain."

Evie wondered if she looked as confused as she was.

"Think about it, girl. I insisted we come to my hometown for vacation? I decided we'd have a fling. I decided we'd choose each other's man. Did Ryan tell you he grew up around here?"

The truth donned on her. Evie sat on the bed unable to believe the lengths her friend had gone through.

"I knew you'd be perfect for each other. He was one of my best friends in high school."

She was shocked, awed, and a little bit annoyed. But then, it had all worked out. She couldn't be mad at her best friend for introducing her to the love of her life. Even if she did do it in an underhanded way. Everything was perfect.

"You said you were with your friend when I spoke to you."

"I was. A friend from high school. I didn't say which friend."

"You told me you spent time with your man that first night!"

"I said we had a good talk. Which we did. When he told me he had a woman I bid him goodnight."

She had to give it to her. Mia was sneaky. "Mia, you're a trip, girl. You know I love you but I'm out of here. I'm going to get my man."

Evie ran out through the resort like a mad woman. Her ankle throbbed but she didn't care. She had to get to Ryan and tell him how she felt. She burst through the doors and out in the snow with no jacket on. When she reached Ryan's she pounded out the door. "Ryan. Open up. I need to talk to you."

He came to the door looking frantically gorgeous. His blond hair wet a towel wrapped around his waist. "For God's sake, Honey. What's the matter?" He pulled her inside. "Where's your jacket?"

"I love you too," she blurted out. "I had to tell you."

"You just realized that?" he asked with a smile.

"No I knew I was just...I don't know, being stupid. But I'm saying

201

it now. I love you." He pulled her close. Hugging away her fear and the cold that set into her bones.

"What are we going to do? I'll go with you. Where ever you go. You can't get rid of me now."

His words made her love him even more. "I don't want you to go anywhere."

"So you just wanted me to know you loved me but you don't plan on doing anything about it? I won't let that happen, Evie. Not after knowing how you feel."

"I don't want you to go anywhere because I'm not going anywhere. I'm staying here. With you. If you'll have me."

He picked her up. When he did she wrapped her legs around his waist. "What about work?"

"We'll make it work. I'll find a job in one of the bigger cities close by."

"I thought you didn't like the snow."

"You're worth it. Plus, it wasn't as bad as I made it sound. As long as I have you the rest will fall into place."

He kissed her. She felt him bone deep. "Now let's get you out of this towel. I'm ready for another ride."

The End

Flow

By
Simone Harlow

Dedication

To Rhonda Thanks for letting me borrow your kid
To Nikki, Thanks for making my surf stuff right and not laughing at
me cause I'm a shoebie
To the wonderful Ladies of the IMRR loop Bama is just for you.
To Kelley, Natalie, Karen, thanks for joining me on this ride.
To Seressia and Kym. You two always make me want to naughty.
To Miriam Thanks for letting me be naughty.

Bio

Simone Harlow is a former Catholic school girl who worships at
the altar of Prada, loves tequila and will always strives to be her naughty
best.

Books By Author

The Lotus Blossom Chronicles #1
What White Boyz Want
The Happy Birthday Book of Erotica
The Merry XXXmas Book of Erotica
Down and Dirty Vol 2
Heatwave: Sizzling Sex Stories
Red Hot Erotica
Erotic Anthology: Bedtime Stories

Chapter One

Robey Wade counted to ten and stared her boss Dan Nolan right in the eye. "I completely understand that you gave the promotion to your frat buddies' son."

Dan's nut brown face relaxed. "You do?"

"Why wouldn't I?" Robey forced her lips into a smile, forbidding herself from losing control of her emotions. That just wasn't her style. As she was fighting the urge to stick a paper clip in her soon to be ex boss's eye, she neatly placed her bonzi tree in a card board box.

Dan took a big breath and smiled. "I thought you might be upset."

Robey shook her head, the smiled still on her face as she placed the photo of her and her sister Julia next to the tree. Obviously Dan didn't understand that she was an ambush predator. She liked to just sit and wait until her target got comfortable and then she'd pounce. "Well if you were concerned that I'd be upset that I didn't get a job that I so richly deserved, then maybe you should have given me the job."

Dan's smile slowly faded as her words apparently began to sink into his lying two faced head. "Now Robey--"

She held up her hand interrupting him. "Don't you worry your pretty little head, Dan I'm not mad." But she had every intention of getting even. Eventually.

"Why are you cleaning out your desk?" His eyes widened as she put her coffee cup into the box.

Did this man really graduate from Harvard? Did he really run a major investment firm? Did it really take this long for the light bulb to go on in his head? "Because it's time for me to be moving on."

"Where?"

Was that a look of sheer panic in his brown beady eyes? "That's not your problem now, is it?"

He put his large hand on her box. "Robey, I'll give you a raise."

Roby resisted the urge to tug her box away from him, but that would have looked like a loss of control on her part and she didn't want to do that. "I don't want your money. I make plenty of it on my own and over the next six months as the 35 accounts I handle find out I'm no longer working for Nolan, Arnold and Bennington and their contracts are up for renewal, then I'll be taking your money." She flashed him a big cheesy I got you by the buster browns grin.

"You can't--"

This man had hired her four years ago for not only her money making skills, but her people skills. When she left so would her clients. "Did you think there wouldn't be a problem when I didn't get the promotion?"

"But--"

She held up her hand. Silly man. "Oh I get it. I was supposed to have a little hissy fit, rant and rave and get it all out of my system, and then I was supposed to go back to work and pretend nothing ever happened. Sorry to disappoint you. That's not my style."

"You can't take my clients."

"I won't have to take to them; my clients will come all on their own." Now the old boy was beginning to see the error of his ways and he wasn't liking it.

Dan puffed up his chest. "I'll sue."

Now he was threatening her. As if he could intimidate her. Not on her worse day. "Go ahead. I'm still leaving."

"Please Robey, I'll give you a bigger office."

She loved this office, it had view of New Jersey. This was a view of how far she'd come. How her hard work and sacrifice had paid off and now she'd hit the glass ceiling, she had to give it up or she'd never respect herself. "Save it, I'm out Dan." She waved her hand toward her soon to be former office door. "Handle your business."

Dan turned and walked out of her office closing the door.

The second she heard the click, the tears almost flowed. She'd loved working at N.A.& B. She thought working for an all black firm would be great and that nothing would stand in her way. And since one of the partners was a woman, she didn't think gender would be an issue. Steve Jackson did okay, but he was no wonder kid, he just happened to be born in the right family. Robey sniffed and she bit the bottom of her lip, she wasn't going to cry. At least not here. She forced her infamous control to steel her. She'd cry alone, like she always did, in the shower where it was safe. When she got home she was going to drink a supersized Martini and have a whole bag of Cheetos, followed by a pint of Ben and Jerry's Chocolate Chip Cookie Dough ice cream. And when she woke up from the salt, sugar, and alcohol induced coma, she'd call her older sister Julia. Then she'd have a good long cry.

Then she'd decide what she was going to do with the rest of her life.

Two weeks later the warm sand eased between Robey's toes and she wasn't sure she liked the sensation. Sandals shouldn't be worn on the beach. She watched another wave crash on California's Laguna Beach shoreline and the thought of her out in the water was enough to melt all the relaxer out of her hair.

Her sister Julia pulled her black Gucci sunglasses down her nose. "Could you stop looking like you're going on the death march?"

"Black girls don't surf."

Julia belted out a big laugh. "Who told you that bullshit?"

Nobody, but since she was about to learn how to surf and she really didn't want to, it sounded good to say. "I think I read it in Essence."

Julia put her arm around her shoulder. "You're the one that wanted to change your life."

"I'm in Los Angles, living in my sister's pool house, with no job. I'm good on the change tip. I don't need to learn how to surf." Okay that wasn't all true. In the last two weeks three of her clients at N.A. & B. had jumped ship and already hired her. Another four had promised to make the leap as soon as their contracts were up. So she wasn't really out of a job. Just very part time.

"Trust me, yes you do."

"No I'm pretty sure I don't."

"I've paid for the lessons." A stiff breeze blew Julia's loose cinnamon curls across her face. She pushed the curls behind her ear revealing her perfect no makeup look across her skin. The blousy white cotton shirt whipped across her toned body.

As if that ended all arguments. Well it did since both sisters' were pretty tight with a buck. Robey couldn't let her waste her money and get a good night's sleep.

Her sister looked all hippy chic. She just looked so natural and earth goddessy. Julia used to be all designer power suits and New York City cutting edge glamour. Since she transferred to California, she changed. Had it been three years since they both had the time to see each other? Had her career been so consuming? "I'm going to take my ten free surf lessons and I'm going to be gracious that you spent the money, but I'm still not going to like it."

"That's the spirit." Julia patted her shoulder and flashed her some kind of mysterious I-know-the-secrets-of-the-universe-and-you-don't smile.

Robey snorted. "You do know that when you go in the ocean; you become part of the food chain right?"

Julia sighed. "No shark is desperate enough for food to bite your up-tight ass."

Now there was the old Julia in that remark. Robey felt herself relax. "Ah, thanks I think."

"That's your surf instructor."

Robey followed her sister's finger and saw him. Her eyes widened as the tall tanned blond god standing next to the life guard stand talking to a couple kids. He had to be at least six feet tall. Okay Robey had never really been ga-ga over white guys, but at this example of sheer male beauty she was ready to make an exception. Golden blond hair that was stylish shagging surrounded his beautiful face. This man was the epitome of California hotness. Broad shoulders with abs she could wash her panties on, he stood there like the world was his for the taking.

There were strange things going on in her stomach and further down. And to think she was dying to go to Disneyland for a wild ride. Not anymore. He was the ride she wanted to get on. And stay on for a long time.

Welcome to California, baby.

"Bama." Julia raised her hand and waved.

The man in navy blue shorts turned around and waved. He held up one finger and turned back to the kids.

He did not have a name like that. "Bama? What kind of stupid name was that?

"He's from Alabama. It's his nick name."

"Is he a redneck surfer?" She laughed at her own stupid joke.

Julia gave her the look that usually made trees wither and die and make Robey wish the San Andreas Fault line would open up and take her now.

Okay Robey felt shame for the assumption. She had been taught better. "Sorry."

He stopped talking to the kids and started walking over to them, his long muscular legs crossing the distance with ease. Then the man smiled. And it was dazzling. His full impact of sexy just didn't really hit her until those beautiful lips parted to reveal pearly white teeth. Perfect, straight, and white. God she was such a sucker for great teeth. She started tingling all over. She hadn't dated in a long time.

"Isn't he beautiful?"

After hearing the breathy sigh come out of her sister's mouth, Robey whipped her head around and stared at her. Oh hell yes. But that kind of surprised her that her sister would notice. "Isn't tall black and handsome your type? Or has Cali changed that for you?"

Julia shrugged. "I know pretty when I see it. I've been trying to get him signed with the agency for years."

Robey bit her bottom lip. "You have a great job."

"God can you see that face and body on forty foot screen?" Julia sighed.

God yes she could. She'd buy out the theater just to have him all to herself. "He's not an actor?"

"He's the only guy in the state of California that doesn't want to be an actor slash model. Which is why I like him so much." Julia elbowed Robey. "You'll love him to."

Well at least she'd like to.

Mr. Tall blond and tanned finally reached them. "Hello ladies." Bama held out his hand to her. "You must be Robey?"

She just shook her head, because the full impact of those sky blue eyes and perfect white teeth just turned her brain to mush.

"Pleased to meet you." His southern drawl was deep and sexy. "Call me Bama."

"Mmmmm." Words just didn't want to seem to come out of her mouth she reached out and took his large hand in hers. Heat just meandered up her arm slow and sexy and she just hung on for the ride.

He didn't let go of her hand. "You're shaking. Are you sure you want to learn how to surf?" He turned to Julia with a questioning glint in his eye.

There was only one thing she wanted to do with him. What every right thinking heterosexual woman wanted to do with a man like him.

And surfing wasn't it.

Chapter Two

Travis 'Bama' Anderson stared at Robey Wade thinking she was going to faint at any second. Her hands were clammy and her cinnamon brown eyes were glazed over. She was beautiful but scared out of her brain. And she still hadn't said a word. "Ms. Wade, are you okay?"

Julia patted her back a couple of times. "She's fine. Aren't you sis?"

"I want to learn."

Sure ya do. Bama hoped that skepticism was showing on his face because he was so not believing her. What was Julia up to and how was it going to smack him upside the head. He smiled at her again. "Of course you do."

"How hard can it be?"

He was debating on whether to tell her the truth or not. Surfing wasn't just a sport it was a state of mind. "Surfing is hard enough to make it interesting, but easy enough to make it fun."

"Great!"

Damn she had a pretty mouth. Her full lips were quivering and she reminded of him a rabbit watching one his daddy's dogs running straight for it. He smiled at her. This woman didn't even want to go near the ocean. "I like your enthusiasm." He turned to Julia, making a mental note to extract some kind of payment for dumping her sister on him. "I'm gonna take you sister to the shop and we'll get her gear together."

Julia leaned over and gave him an air kiss. "Just bill me. Robey when you're done just give me a jingle, I'm going to shop." She left with a wave of her hand.

"Do you and sister get along?"

"I'm starting to wonder."

They started walking toward the boardwalk lined with shops. "You know I can refund her money. Surfing is something you shouldn't be forced to do unless you want to." He noticed she walked with grim determination. And in a strange way he admired that. This woman wasn't a quitter.

"Look, I'm at this fork in a road in my life. I shouldn't be afraid to do something new."

"I'll give you that, but you could take up knitting. It would be less …"

"Dangerous?"

"Surfing isn't dangerous." He said the words hoping he sounded convincing. A smart man would have told her to go home and try another hobby, but for some strange reason he had this instant attraction to her and he wanted to hang out with her for awhile.

She held her arms up. "Oh I don't know, shark attack, concussion, and drowning take your pick. It's dangerous."

"That's not what I was going to say." Yes he did think it, but he would have never said. This woman liked control. The secret of surfing was to let nature take you where it wanted to and enjoy the ride. He could tell by the tight bun at the nape of her neck and the perfect make-up this one was the one who liked to call the shots.

She stopped. "Besides do I look like a knitter to you?"

Bama shrugged. Do knitters have a certain look? An ex girlfriend of his had more tattoos then the local Hell's Angels and she liked to go to the ballet. He never judged people on what they looked like. Well except now, he could see she didn't want to surf. "My dad knits."

"He does?"

"He's a surgeon and it keeps his fingers nimble." Bama jiggled his fingers. And he also liked to hunt and skin his own game too, but he wasn't going to tell her that part.

She laughed. "You set me up for that."

He liked the sound of her laughter and now he was determined to make her laugh some more. If he wasn't mistaken, she didn't seem to have a lot of fun lately. "I'm not that devious. I'm just making a point."

Robey stood a little taller. "I'm going to learn how to do this even if it's just prove to my sister I can." There was a whole lot of steel laced in her tone.

They reached his surf shop Bama Dawg and he held open the door for her. "Well okay, but you going at it with the wrong attitude."

For a second, she just stared at the open door. "I can master anything I set my mind to." She hurried through the entry into the noisy shop. "I don't like to fail."

"We all fail." The best lessons he ever learned were from failing at things.

She shook her head, and a strand of hair actually escaped that tight bun. "Not if you don't give up."

He resisted the urge to twirl his finger around her dark hair. "This is going to be interesting."

She gave him a tight smile. "I'll do my best."

He was sure she would. And frankly, he'd love to see what her best was. Especially if it involved them naked. "What size do you wear?"

Robey held up two fingers. "Two."

He eyed her up and down. She was slender but her curves were in all the right places. She could stand to gain a few pounds. She had this incredible bubble butt that filled out her walking shorts. He just wanted to touch it. For a short woman she had the longest legs. He'd bet anything if she loosened up a bit she be a helluva ride in bed.

"Is there a surfing uniform?"

"No. Why don't look around the shop for something that catches your fancy." His imagination was good enough to put her in a wetsuit or a pair of board shorts. Unless you slapped a Prada label on it. Julia had been the same way, when she came into his shop two and half years ago. He snuck another peek at Robey and he knew he had his work cut out for him. And he wondered if he was that good.

She rummaged through some of the bikini tops on a circular rack. "I have a question."

As if he wasn't expecting her to ask about a thousand of them by now. "Yes?"

"Is Bama your really name?"

"Nope."

Robey stopped examining the bikini tops. "Well, what is your real name?" She had an expectant look on her mahogany colored face.

Bama shot her a innocent smile. Now was the time to teach her a little life lesson. "Is it important?"

Her full red lips pursed and her brown eyes narrowed. "Not really."

He figured he was about seven seconds from pissing her off, but he couldn't resist the temptation to play dumb with her. "Then why did you ask?"

"I'm making conversation." She shoved a hanger across the metal rack so hard it screeched.

He took a slow deep breath, she wanted him to think she didn't care, but he knew better. Hell if she could have made sparks on the metal rod, she would have. "I see."

"Is it top secret?"

"No." He picked up a red string top with little hearts on the cups and handed it to her.

Her hand went to her slender hip. "Then why won't you tell me?"

"Because this conversation is like surfing."

She rolled her eyes and shook her head. "What did I just miss?"

"Grasshopper, you need to go with the flow. You attack everything like you're at war. Me and surfing are not about attacking. Just go with it and you'll get what you want out of the ride."

"My head is spinning so hard I don't even want to know it anymore." Robey put her fingertips on her forehead and closed her eyes

Bama had to stop himself from laughing. That would have been bad. "Yes you do."

Her manicured hand went up in the air. "Trust me, I'm over it."

"It's Travis."

"Don't care." Robey turned her back on him and started examining another rack of one piece bathing suits.

He leaned over and whispered in her ear. "Of course you do."

She whipped around so fast he had to take a step back. She was on fire. "Do you spend a lot of time in the sun?"

Holding his arms up his supplication he answered. "Surfer."

Robey huffed. "I could tell."

She had no idea how much fun he was having. Maybe it was bad, but he just couldn't help himself. "Robey Wade you make me laugh." She held up a plain dark blue bikini top and matching bottom. A bit conservative, but they would look good on her slender body and fit in all the right places.

"I'm thrilled beyond belief."

He pointed to a wall with some of his boards. "Pick a board."

She stared at her five choices. They weren't his best boards or that expensive, but they'd do for a newbie, who probably would never hit the water again when she was done with her lessons. "Is this all I get to chose from?"

"These are right for your size and skill level."

Another one of those disbelieving looks crossed her face. "How can you tell?"

After about ten years in the business, he could match a person with a board within five minutes of meeting them. "It's my business to know these things."

She pointed to a blue board with an orange sun in the middle. "But I like that one."

Bama was impressed, she knew her boards. "That's a prototype. It's not ready for sale."

"Then why do you have it out?"

He wasn't ready to trust his new baby to just anyone especially not to a newbie. "I'm waiting for the right person to come in to test it for me."

Her black eyebrows rose. "You really designed that surf board?"

If he wasn't so sadly mistaken, she sounded like he just graduated from dragging his knuckles on the ground. "Yes, I did."

"Wow."

Bama enjoyed that she was impressed. "Thanks I'm glad you like it."

"I just thought you were a surfer."

He pointed to the name Bama Dawg above the dressing rooms. "I also own the shop."

Robey nodded with approval. "You are just the surfing triple threat."

"Why does that impress you so much?" Bama crossed his arms over his chest and rocked back on his heels.

She tilted her head and studied him for a second. "That's an odd question."

He didn't know her well enough to know if she was stalling, but he didn't suspect that she was. But then maybe he didn't want to hear the answer. He wanted her to like him for him, not what he was. "Let me put it another way. Why did the business man impress you and the surfer boy didn't?"

It's as if a light went on in her eyes. "Ah…"

He touched his chest. "I'm still the same guy." Why he felt like he had to justify this was beyond him, normally he didn't care what most people thought of him, but he wanted her to like him.

"That makes me sound like a snob."

"I didn't say that." But he couldn't help but wonder if it was true. God knows he didn't want to be, but there was just something about her he liked. A lot.

Robey pointed a long finger at him. "But you were thinking it."

She was a cagey one. "Good comeback, but you still haven't answered the question."

Her tiny fist went to her hip. "Is this one of those going with the flow lessons you're trying to teach me?"

He really liked her spunk. She gave as good as she got. And she knew how to keep him coming back for more. "I'll answer your question if you answer mine."

She pointed to a board with a rose on it. "I want that board."

Lady, I'm not letting you off that easy. "That's not the question."

"Yes I know." Her tantalizing brown eyes narrowed. "I'm trying to control the conversation again."

He laughed. "You're good."

Her smile was wide and genuine. "Thank you."

"So now that I'm a business man do you like me better?"

Shaking her head, she continued to smile. "I didn't say that."

Now she was making him work for it. "But now if I ask you out for dinner, I have a better chance of getting a yes now that you know I'm more than just a beach bum."

Her perfectly groomed eyebrows rose. "You want to go out with me?"

Hell yeah. He took a deep breath and calmed himself down. "Very much."

"Do you go out with all of your students?"

She'd be the first he'd ever asked out. "Nope."

Robey gave him a long probing stare as if his body language would tell the truth. "How do I know that for sure?"

Besides giving her the list of his former students there was never any way that she'd know for sure, but there was one person she could ask directly. "You could ask your sister."

Her mouth dropped open for a second or two. "Julia took surf lessons?"

He almost howled with laughter at the look of disbelief on her face. Julia had come to him about four months after she moved here. He suspected the surf lesson was not the only reason, she came to him; she'd been lost in California and needed someone to help her 'get' California. One of her fellow agents who came here from Kansas gave her his name and they'd been friends ever since. "She took to it like a duck to water and I didn't ask her out."

"Yes."

Just for a fraction of a second the world stood still, then reality sunk in and he made sure. "For dinner?"

"Yes.

"Cool." Discreetly he wiped his sweaty palm on the back of his board shorts. When was the last time he sweated asking a girl out for dinner? That was just some snarky shit. Something about her just punched his ticket.

"But only if you promise to take me to Pinks."

He would call in a favor and get a table at some hip Hollywood restaurant. Now she went and really impressed him. "You like hot dogs?"

Her eyes widened and she looked so sweet and innocent. "Doesn't every girl like a good wiener?"

He smiled and a little tingle ran down his spine and his boy got all excited. Down boy, Daddy's workin' here. Now that was the best double entrendre he'd heard in a long time. He had to give Robey points for that answer. Now he had to decide on whether to follow it up or just keep going? "I like a girl who likes her wieners, but I can afford to take you to the Ivy." He just went with the flow; he was really good at that.

"I don't care about movie stars." She waved her hand with flair. "And just so you know you being a business man as opposed to just a surfer had no impact on the fact that I'd have dinner with you. I make my own money; I don't need a man for that."

He could have wiped his forehead in relief. "I was just testing you."

Robey rolled her eyes. "Sure you were."

Well if that didn't open a door to a lot of interesting possibilities. "What do you need a man for?"

She pointed a blood red finger nail at him almost poking him in the chest. "If I have to explain then maybe you've been out in the sun to many times."

Things were looking up. He'd just been handed a gift from the gods. "Tight."

She mouthed the word. "And that means what?"

"Tight is good. Tight is very very good."

Pointing to the board with the rose on it again, she said. "I really want that board, dude."

She may not know a thing about surfing but she could pick the best board for her body type, and as it so happened he designed the board a few years ago. Somehow some way this was going to be a lot more fun than he expected when he first met her. That excited him a lot.

Robey was a surprise and he was the type of man who loved surprises.

Chapter Three

Bama was nervous. He hadn't been edgy on a first date since he was about eighteen and going to the senior prom with Lana Weaver. By the time he'd picked her up he'd puked three times on the drive over. And now his stomach was feeling a little queasy.

He was feeling a little strange taking Robey to Pink's. Pink's wasn't a first date kind of place. It was established relationship territory. When you knew each other or it was some place you took you out of state relatives so they could get a taste of California life. But not the place to go to impress. He was glad she picked it and not him. Damn now he sounded like he watched Oprah or some shit.

After swallowing a big bite of chili cheese dog, Robey leaned over and trained her gaze on him. "So tell me how you started designing surf boards?"

He shrugged his shoulders. "I like to surf and it seemed a logical step."

"After what?" She dabbed each side of her mouth with a paper napkin.

He wondered why she didn't even have a crumb on her side of the table. The woman ate like a queen. His step mom would be impressed. "I have a degree in Aeronautical Engineering from Cal Tech."

The soda was halfway to her mouth and she stopped and put it back down. "You are unexpected."

Bama faked surprise. This confused everyone when he told them how he got into designing boards. "I am? In what way?"

"Well no insult intended, but you don't radiate geek to me."

Now that was fresh, no one ever called him that. He liked that she didn't hold anything back. "What do I radiate then?" But then again maybe he didn't want to know.

Jabbing the table with a long nail, she smiled. "Travis, you just had to be the coolest guy in high school. You're so laid back."

He liked that she called him Travis. Not many people did anymore. "Not always."

"We'll get to that later. So you went to school to design planes and ended up designing surfboards." She tilted her head and studied him for a second. "It seems like such a big leap. Why?"

It didn't to him. Now he was flying on the water and he was doing it under his own power. Once she learned to surf, she could see that it was the ultimate high. "A few months before I graduated, my dad had a heart attack and he thought he was going to die and he told me to stop trying to be someone I wasn't. He said I loved surfing and there had to be money in it, so follow my heart."

Her full lips curved into a smile. "You're father is a wise man."

"Not always, but he quit his job doing plastic surgery to the rich and shameless and started doing charity work and he said it saved his life and his second marriage."

Again surprise registered in her face. "Nice but is he living on PB & J sandwiches now?"

"Nope stepmom's from money. So we do okay. What do you do?"

"Julia didn't tell you?" Then she took another sip of her soda.

Now he was glad he didn't ask Julia because he got to discover her all for himself. "I didn't ask."

"Why not?"

He didn't want to know. That would affect his perception of her and he wanted things to be fresh. He liked to discover things about people by himself. "Because it's not what you do, it's who you are that's important, but to be honest I'm kinda figuring it to be something high pressure."

"I'm a … was an investment counselor."

Now it was his turn to be surprised again. Like he'd been when she showed up in the sexy purple sundress and the loose hair she was sporting tonight. Which happened to him so little. He figured her for work 24/7 just like Julia used to be. "You don't have a job?"

Her mouth fell open for a second, but she recovered quickly. "Don't look so surprised."

He grinned. "I was hoping I wasn't."

Robey shook her head and her loose hair danced around her shoulders. "I have some private clients now and I'm looking to expand, but I want to keep it small."

She just looked so sexy sitting there smiling. This is the woman he saw beyond the tight bun. He wanted her. Badly. "I hate the money side."

"What?"

He didn't know how to read that. He remembered she said she didn't need a man with money, but she certainly liked to have it. "By the about to drop dead look on your face, I'm thinking you're shocked."

Robey fanned her face. "Making the money is the most exciting part."

"I said it wrong. Money is great. I like helping people, having fun and getting paid for it. What I don't like is worrying about the bottom line all the time. It's stressful and it sucks all the fun out of my business."

She said nothing.

Stopping himself from reaching over and shaking her, he said. "Robey are you okay?" He almost reached for his cell phone to call 911.

Robey put her hand over her heart. "I'm having a heart attack."

Bama laughed and held up his hand. "Take a breath. It will pass."

She took a big breath and let it out slowly. "I'm okay now. I'm okay."

Bama smiled seeing the playful glint in her brown eyes. "You weren't kidding when you said you like to make your own money."

"I love making money. I'm good at it."

Her eyes were a little glazed over like she just had some really great sex. Which got him to wondering if he could put that kind of look in eyes. Hell what he would give to get a shot at that. "Why?"

"I never had any." She took another bite of her hot dog and put it down.

He hoped he didn't sound like he was bragging. "And I've had it."

She was still sizing him up as she swallowed her food. Her head tilted to the side. "An honest to God rich boy. So you take it for granted?"

He was glad she finally said something, because he was feeling like a bug under a microscope. It almost as if she saw everything about him. "No. Money controls you. I saw it with my dad, with my mom's father. My grandfather died at fifty five over his desk and it nearly put my dad in an early grave chasing the buck as well."

She seemed to consider his words carefully before she spoke. "I'll give that, but having money and knowing how to make it work for you puts you in control of your life. That's a good thing."

Bama placed his elbows on the table and leaned closer to her. "Then why did you quit your job, if making money is so important to you?"

Those beautiful lush lips turned down into a tight frown. "If I didn't my boss would have walked all over me for the rest of my life."

He sort of felt bad for her. It must have been a hard choice for her to come to. And he suspected she still wasn't all the way okay with it either. "And you would have been out of control." God would he liked to see that. He'd bet his last dollar that when she let go Robey Wade was one hot ride. And in that moment he decided he wanted to find that out for himself. How he was going to go about it was still a mystery, but he'd figure it out. And the wait would be one of the best parts. He smiled.

****

As Robey dabbed the corners of her mouth with a paper napkin something she couldn't name shifted between them. "That's not a question is it?"

Shaking his head, he smiled. "No it isn't."

There was a seductive tilt to his full lipped smile. If she wasn't so sadly mistaken he was flirting with her. Her insides tingled. "I'll tell you what, how about you and I agree to disagree, on this point." She understood his point of view on money and she was okay with it for him, but it would never work for her.

Running a large hand through his shaggy blond hair he smiled. "I'm cool."

God, he had the most beautiful hands. Large well groomed and tanned, she bet he was really good with those hands and not just at making surf broads. "Good, now that I'm done with my hot dog, what do you want to do next?"

His blue eyes sparkled. "It's a surprise."

She reminded herself that this was his party. He brought her to Pinks so she could give herself over to him springing something on her. Really she could. She made herself smile. "That's okay by me." There that wasn't so bad now was it, girlfriend.

He stood up and waited for her to join him. Then they walked to his car, a Lexus Hybrid. Okay so this guy wasn't ashamed of spending his money and he was environmental aware. Julia told her she would have to get a car to live in Southern California. But first she'd have to learn how to drive. As she got into the passenger seat, she wondered how hard could it be. When he got into the driver's side she asked, "Can you recommend a good driving school?"

"You don't know how to drive?"

Robey fastened her seat belt. "Well driving and surfing were two things I never needed to know living in New York City."

"I'll give you that." He turned on the car. "But why ask me, Julia knows more people in this town than I do."

"Because Julia will end up paying for it and I can buy a car and pay for the lessons." She took a pair of sunglasses out of her purse and slid them on.

Now she looked like a movie star. Normally not his kind of woman, but for her he'd make an exception. "You're sister is good people."

"Yes she is, but sometimes she still tends to mother me."

That he could believe. Julia had tried to convince him he'd be the next big Hollywood "It" boy and when he gently refused her she didn't take it personally and they'd remained good friends. "Not always a bad thing."

Robey held up her hands in agreement. "True, but my mother did teach me the value of self-reliance."

"I'll have a list for you."

She flashed him a million dollar smile that made him want to move the Earth for her. "Thanks.

They got to movie theater and found their seats. As she watched the movie, she began to understand what it was that people saw in surfing. There was a sort of freedom to the whole riding the waves thing. She still wasn't sure if it was for her, but she would give it a shot.

This after all was a new chapter in her new life. She had to let herself be open to new things. This guy was sending out the signals that he was interested in her. Of course she'd play it slow and easy. He was so laid back he'd run for the hills if she just jumped on him. Although that could be an interesting test, she thought. That would testing his I go with the flow attitude.

For a few seconds she let naked pictures of Bama slide around in her head. She wondered if his skin was tanned all over. He wore board shorts that fit loosely they didn't hide all that much of his lean body, or if his skin was as smooth and supple as it looked. Her throat went dry. She was really having herself a doosey of a fantasy right now. The temperature shot up about one hundred degrees. Cool your jets girl or you'll combust, and then you'd never get to find out all about that hot bod sitting next to you.

Robey felt herself smiling. She took a sidelong look at Bama in the movie theater. His fingers threaded through her and she relaxed. His skin was calloused but very warm. His hand felt so strong and capable. She liked that. Few men impressed her with their strength. Oh Robey, she thought, this is going to be an adventure.

She figured she could have done a whole lot worse, but she suspected not a whole lot better.

Chapter Four

Cold water lapped on to the board and moved over Robey's body. She lay on her stomach and practiced paddling as Bama held the board. So in other words she was going nowhere fast. Which was okay with her. There was a lot of water between her and the shore. With who knows what was underneath it.

"With the exception of sheer terror on your face, you really are getting the hang of paddling."

Robey turned her head to glare at him over her shoulder. What's so hard about this? I've mastered paddling, can I go home now. "I thought I was smiling with the joy of my new found freedom."

Bama shook his head. "Nope, that's your cranky face."

She bit off a giggle because it would have ruined her mad. "Stop trying to make me laugh."

"Why?"

"Because I might lose the expression of sheer terror on my face."

His blue eyes widened. "That would be bad, why?"

She was going to slap that sexy smile right off his face. "Haven't you heard in the face of a dangerous situation, fear is a healthy emotion?"

"I didn't get the memo, besides; you're about fifteen feet away from shore. What could happen?"

Robey was still paddling and if he let her go she would be on the shore in about five seconds. "I have no idea, I'm in an alien environment and the music from Jaws is playing in my head. And aren't Great Whites native to these waters?"

He started laughing.

The deep sound of his voice warmed her up and she didn't need the wetsuit anymore. "I don't recall telling a joke."

Bama stopped laughing and cleared this throat. "You know they don't really like how we taste."

That was supposed to make her feel better? She let it settle for a moment. Nope she was still terrified. "Yes, but he has to bite me to find out I don't taste good. That's all I'm saying."

His head nodded and his lips pursed. And these little crinkles around his eyes appeared. "I'm going to give you that one."

A gentle wave lifted her up and she felt her body wobble. "And you know what according to this shark guy on the Discovery Channel, I look like a big fat slow seal to them. I'm thinking those guys don't get a lot of dark meat. So I'm kinda exotic to them."

"I'm not sure, but wasn't that a tad racist?"

Lifting her hands in the air, she snorted. "Don't care. Life in jeopardy here."

"Okay I'm going to let you go and you and the board just cruise on into the shore."

A bolt of panic struck her. She was going solo. She wasn't ready couldn't he just walk her into the shore. Breathe Robey. Breathe. And paddle like hell. "What if I need to steer this thing."

"The tide will take you into the shore all by itself. Just relax and go with it. What's your mantra?"

"I'm not going to die. I'm not going to die." Oops that was supposed to be an internal thought.

He put his hand on the flat of her back to steady her. "You're other mantra."

She could feel his touch through the rubber of her suit. God this man had her number. She didn't want him to let go. "Go with the flow. Go with the flow."

"There you go." He pushed her board and let go of it. "I'll be right behind you."

Her body was as stiff as the board she was riding. Water sloshed over her and she held on for dear life praying the board would move faster. She refused to let go and fall off, just to prove him wrong. She could do this. For some reason the board stared veering to the right and not heading toward the shore. Her instinct was to jerk it in the correct direction. Which she did and instantly she felt herself roll.

Where the hell was Bama?

The board started rocking. And she tried to fight it and the next thing she knew she was underwater. But she was still clinging to the board.

Long seconds passed. Robey was about the let go of the board, when she felt it roll one more time. She knew the second her head was out of the water and she opened her eyes.

"Are you--"

"I didn't let go. I didn't let go."

Bama was bent over her and he was prying her fingers off the board. "Yeah, great."

He pulled her up to her feet. Excitement rushed her. Or maybe she was thrilled to be alive, she didn't know. "I was going with the flow."

Bama gave her a shaky smile. "I'm going to give you that, but you could have let go."

Robey took a deep breath and steadied herself. "I was afraid it would hit me in the head or I'd lose the board."

He pointed to the cord around her ankle. "I was afraid you were going to drown."

"I can hold my breath for a long time."

"Well that was a good first try."

"That rocked." Pumping her fist in the air, she felt as if she conquered the world. "I was scared as hell, but I did it."

"Great!"

The blood coursed through her veins and she was on this high, she'd never experienced before. Robey threw her arms around his neck and pulled his head down and laid the biggest kiss on his mouth.

Bama almost lost his footing as Robey threw herself at him.

The instant her soft mouth touched his he felt as if he were drowning and she was the only thing worth living for.

She was wet and she tasted like salt and her body was shaking and all he could do was cling to her and kiss her back.

He forgot everything except the taste of her mouth and feel of her body.

He didn't want to let go.

Her arms suddenly dropped from his neck and she slid down his body. "Oh my God!"

Was he that bad? Did she have to stop? He was just getting started. "What?"

Her hands went to her cheeks and her eyes were wide with shock. "I shouldn't have done that."

Yes you should and you should do it more. He knew he couldn't say that, but otherwise he didn't know what to say.

"Say something."

"You're a good kisser."

Chapter Five

Was that all he had to say? She wanted him to resist or something like that.

His head bobbed up and down. "When you go with the flow you're committed."

She had to think about that for a moment. Was that bad or good? She didn't know. "Umm, I don't think … I really shouldn't have …"

A big sexy grin split his face. "I'm hella impressed."

That still wasn't the right answer. Did he like it or not. That just made him seem like he was just impressed with her technique, not that he liked what she did or how it made him feel. This man was confusing. "Does that mean you want to kiss me again?"

"Hell yeah." His wet blond hair slapping his cheeks.

Robey reached up and pushed his hair off of his face. "I've wanted to kiss since I met you."

He smiled and this dimple appeared on his left cheek. "Haven't you learned anything?"

Shrugging she hoped she came up the right answer something in the near future, because this man was driving her insane with wanting. "I learned how to paddle."

"Not about surfing, but about me."

Then she got it. With the waves crashing around her ankles and their wet suits sticking together, she stood on her tip toes and kissed him again. She went slower this time savoring his intoxicating taste. His arms went around her and he pulled her even closer.

Robey let her lips mingle with his, then she opened her mouth and his tongue slid inside her working his surfer boy magic. Her head was spinning and her body forgot all about the cold Pacific Ocean swirling around her ankles.

He tasted like sunshine and wind. Her hands slid to his cheeks and she realized he hadn't shaved. Damn that was so hot. Her brain started thinking about those stubbly cheeks between her thighs.

"Way to go dude."

Robey felt his chest start to rumble and she dropped her hands and took a step back. This was her moment; she was going to take the surfer by the board. Lifting her leg, she undid the velco band keeping her board attached to her ankle. Slapping it in his hand, she walked out of the ocean. "I'll see you later on tonight." She said loud enough for him to hear her over the crash of the waves.

"Robey," he called after her.

She turned and smiled. "Pick me up at seven."

"For what?" His eyebrows jiggled.

As if he didn't know. He was going to get lucky tonight. Or maybe it was her who was going to be the lucky one. She unzipped her wetsuit and revealed a bit of cleavage. "I'm going with the flow."

He put his hands on his hips. "That's a big leap."

Yes it was but one she was ready to take with him. "I'm a big girl, Bama. I think I'm ready to take that leap." She turned around and ran back up the beach toward the car she hired to take her home.

This going with the flow thing wasn't so bad at all.

Bama parked the car in front of his house. He didn't let go of the steering wheel because his hands were still shaking. Part of him couldn't believe that he had finally gotten Robey to his house.

She unfastened her seatbelt. "Nice place to hang your hat."

Looking up at the imposing façade of his white stucco beach house, he agreed. He didn't buy the house because of the ritzy address, he was close to the ocean. "Wait until you see the view."

She got out of car. "I could give a damn about the view." She smiled. "Well at least not the ocean."

Who was this siren with the long hair and chocolate skin ready to make all his fantasies come true? "Stop!"

One of the perfectly groomed eyebrow rose. "What?"

Slamming the door he walked around to her and gripped her upper arms. "I know this is breaking the guy code, but are you sure you want to do this?"

Her face just kind of scrunched up.

The expression of disbelief on her face was almost comical. He had to bite his cheek so he wouldn't laugh.

"Don't you?"

"Since about five seconds after I met you."

Her head tilted to the side. "Then why are you questioning things?"

"I'm stupid."

"No comment."

"This is a going with the flow kind of thing."

"Actually I let you know what I wanted. I'm in control."

He loved the smug expression on her face. It was too sexy for words. And come to think about she was and he was good with that. "Well I'm going with the flow."

"Not so stupid after all."

Bama closed the front door and watched her climb the stairs. As she walked up she started unzipping the back of her black dress. She stopped and turned. "Where's the bedroom?"

He pointed up. "Third door on your right."

Robey slipped the black halter dress off her shoulders as she moved up the free standing spiral steps. The black material fluttered to the step and all she was wearing were a pair black heels and a black thong with a bow in the back.

Robey reached the bedroom and kicked off her shoes. Her heart was racing and she was wet already. She turned and Bama was right behind her. Even though the room was dark she could see he'd lost his shirt. Before she could say anything his mouth was on hers. Their tongues warred together as if they couldn't get enough of each other. God she wanted this.

He raised his head. "Condom."

She giggled. "This is your territory."

"That makes you my prey."

"Travis you are so wrong."

He gave her a sultry chuckle. "So its Travis in bed?"

"Yeah it is."

"Good no one calls me that."

That made it special. She liked that. "Travis. Travis."

He got them over to the bed and he pushed her down to dark covered mattress. Then he walked around the bed to a night table and opened a top drawer. He took a couple of condom packets and tossed them on the bed. Then he turned on the table lamp flooding the room in muted light.

She picked up one of the packs and ripped it open and he took off his pants. Putting the condom in her mouth she adjusted it on her tongue. Motioning with her finger to move closer, she grabbed his lean hip with one hand and his throbbing cock in the other. Carefully she rolled the condom over his hardness and began to work her mouth over his flesh.

"Damn Robey," he choked out.

Good, she thought as she cupped his heavy balls and began to squeeze him. His whole body was shaking. She liked that he was excited. It just inspired her even more. Slowly she sank her nails into his sac and his entire body shuddered. Working her mouth over him, she felt herself getting so wet; she was squirming on the bed. The room was still a bit dark to really see his face, but if the moans coming out of his mouth were any indications he was having a really good time.

Bama sank his hands in her hair and pulled her mouth off of his cock. "I have other things to do."

"Like what, Travis?"

He picked her up and moved her to the middle of the bed. He crawled in between her splayed thighs. Then he leaned over and took her mouth in a sweet soft kiss.

Robey lifted her hands and slid them around his neck and then into his silky hair. His body leaned into hers and every muscle from his broad chest to his corded thigh was pressed into her. And his thick cock massaged her belly. She was dripping by the time his mouth started working its way down her neck. "Travis ..." she couldn't finish her sentence when his mouth closed over one of her nipples. Hell, she could barely breathe.

"Yeah baby?"

Robey squeaked.

And he laughed. Then moved his mouth over to her other nipple all the while he was working her drenched thong down her legs.

Squirming she was doing all she could to help him, but she heard fabric rip and she was free. Then one long finger slid slowly inside her filling her. Then he added another finger and he began to pump inside her. His mouth was still teasing her nipples as she put one hand on his and then she was helping him pump inside her. Robey just gave herself over to the pleasure of his touch and before she knew it she came with a scream.

"Oh baby we're just getting started."

She was going to be dead before dawn. Then he moved over her and she felt his cock work itself inside her. He pumped a few times then thrust himself all the way in. Robey's back arched to get him further inside her. He was so big and so hard she thought she was going to die from all the heat and pleasure. "Travis, oh God."

He just kept thrusting inside her until she was completely lost and felt herself slip over the edge and she cried out. After a few more thrust, he joined her.

He lay as she tried to catch her breath.

"Robey, you are the best ride."

"That was better than making money."

"Give me a couple of minutes and I'll make you see Ben Franklin all over again."

Hang ten baby.

Chapter Six

As she moved around the black and white kitchen, Robey's body was still humming after her night with Travis. Okay Bama. She just liked calling him Travis in bed. And he seemed to like it to. She popped four slices of bread in his silver space age toaster. Was it going to make toast or take her to the moon? This thing must have cost like a bazillion dollars, at her Brooklyn apartment; she had a regular old Proctor Silex that she wasn't intimated by. She poured the orange juice and finished adding cheese on top of the scrambled eggs. By the time she had the tray all set, the toast popped up, she buttered it and put it on the plate to take upstairs. After his stellar performance the man deserved breakfast in bed and a second helping of her. The phone interrupted her thoughts and without thinking she picked it. "Hello Anderson residence."

"May I talk to Bama please?"

She clamped the phone between her and her shoulder and headed back up to the bedroom. "May I ask who calling?"

"Sam Winslow from Winslow Sport."

Robey nearly dropped the phone. The number one sporting goods company in the galaxy, Winslow Sport? She didn't want to say that, but it really was the biggest sporting good company in the universe. "Of course. Give me just a minute to buzz him." She stopped balanced the tray on a step and braced it with her leg and hoped to God she could find the hold button. She heard some movement and looked up to see naked Bama strutting down the stairs. She covered the phone's mouthpiece with her hand. "Put some clothes on, its Sam Winslow!" She forced herself to take a breath. "Of Winslow Sport. Oh my God'"

Bama smiled. "Can he tell I'm naked on the phone?"

She rolled her eyes and Bama and his big boner climbed down the rest of the stairs. He took the phone and laid a big kiss on her and she prayed Sam Winslow the sporting goods god hadn't heard her moan.

"Hey Sam."

Robey sat down on the step and nervously began to munch some toast.

"No man I'm still considering the offer."

Winslow Sport made him an offer? For what she didn't know. Hell she didn't care. That was money in the bank. "What?"

"Excuse me a second." He covered the mouth piece. "Honey, take a breath. Okay."

She nodded her head and took a breath then gulped down the entire glass of orange juice. And looked up at him again she was on eye level with his big juicy penis. It was kinda winking at her and she almost lost track of what was going on.

"Yeah, you know I'm not about the business thing, but I'll get back to you in a couple of days." He smiled. "Thanks man, keep it light." He sat next to her on the step. "Close your mouth honey."

Was he nuts? Sam Winslow could sell sand to the Arabs. This guy was a rainmaker and Bama was hemming and hawing. Oh please help me now Jesus. "Do you know who Sam Winslow is?"

"Yes."

She shook her finger at him. "He's like the number one sporting goods company."

Bama shrugged. "And I taught his son to surf."

Calm yourself girl. Calm yourself. "Does he want to buy your company?"

"No he wants to finance me, and move me into a bigger market."

She fanned her face. Actually dollar signs started doing the Cha Cha before her eyes, and this wasn't even her deal. This could be worth gazillions for a whole lot of people if this was handled correctly. This couldn't be happening. "You have to think about it?"

His broad shoulders shrugged as if he were choosing the underwear to put on for the day. "I'm not about the money."

Robey held her arms out. "Look at this house. It's about money."

Bama shook his head. "No I'm close to the beach and I love the view."

Okay she knew that about him, but still. "But--"

"Do you want to talk business or do you want get down to business?" His blond eyebrows jiggled and he pointed to his cock.

Well what the hell kind of question was that. She was already wet again. She didn't even need any foreplay. Hell he could do her on the stairs in the plate of eggs as far as she was concerned. "Just give me a sex here."

Bama laughed. He knew sex would get her off the business trip. "What?"

Covering her face with her hands, she groaned. Oh she had it bad. "A sec. I need a second to think?"

Bama shook his head. Damn he liked her. "That's a Freudian slip if I ever heard one." Slipping his hand over her leg, he felt her tremble under his touch. Damn she was a hot woman.

"I'm seeing dollar signs." Her hands slid off her face and she gave him a sheepish smile.

Putting his hand over his heart, he frowned. "You have to think about having sex with me? After last night? Am I that bad?"

"No I don't have to think about having sex with you, I have to think about all the money you could be making."

He leaned over and nipped her ear. He knew how much she liked that. "I'd rather think about you and me all sweaty and sticky." Which he already was but wanted to be more of.

"We'll have sex in a minute."

Good. Although he didn't think he had a minute left in him. "Promise?"

"Yes, but we need to talk about this." She moved the tray to another step so he could sit next to her.

"Why do we need to talk about having sex? Doing it is much more fun." Okay so he was a guy. Bama had no problem living with that.

"Not that about the deal with Winslow Sport."

He could stall Sam for the next year if he wanted to. All he wanted to do was get Robey back into bed. "I don't want to talk about it. Okay?"

"Do you want get busy with me again?"

He pointed to his cock. "That would be a yes."

"Then we need talk."

He took a big breath. Hold on big guy we'll get you some action soon. "Alright."

"Why aren't you about the money?"

"It takes up too much time."

"Hire me, I'll do it." She covered her mouth the second the words left her lips.

"What?"

"Never mind. I just started seeing dollar signs and got ahead of myself. I can't work for you. I'd rather sleep with you, but I can't believe your giving up this kind of opportunity." She sighed. "But you're not me and I probably wouldn't like it if you were, but that's like pitching for the Yankees and …"

Now a thought was forming in his head. That wasn't such a bad idea. He'd get the girl and the cash and not have to do the work, at least not for the money. "Could you just breathe for a second?"

She held up her hands. "I'm done. Let's eat and then fool around."

Hell why not? He could do a lot of good with the money and Robey

Flow

would be there to help him. "Okay here are the ground rules. You can put this deal together, but no business talk in bed."

Her mouth fell open for a moment. And a look of sheer joy came over her face. "You want me to do this for you. But don't you need to think about it?"

He just made her a very happy woman and happy women were generous. "I'm going with the flow." He picked up a piece of toast and took a bite. It was little buttery for his taste, but his baby made it for him. Screw carbs. He burn them up in about five minutes with her anyway.

She held up her hands and took a deep breath. "But your naked, how can you make a sound business decision butt naked with a boner?"

I think I just did. "I can multitask."

She sneered. "Most man can't."

He wasn't most men. "Okay I'm telling you what you want to hear so we can go back upstairs and have some hot monkey love." That was pretty true.

"You're not letting me handle this because of the sex are you?"

He was letting her handle this because he was kinda in love with her. "Hell no. I'm having sex with so you'll handle the deal for me." He was going to think about that last thought when he was alone and not distracted by her in one of his tee shirts. he promised himself.

"Okay, I can live with that."

He grabbed the tray and stood. "Hurry up I want to eat my eggs off your butt."

"That's just freaky." But she started walking up the stairs to his bedroom.

So what if it is. He was okay with that. "But it sounds fun."

234

Chapter Seven

So it all came down to this. Her first solo ride on the real ocean, not those baby waves she'd been practicing on. She glanced at Bama sitting next to her on his board. A wave gently lifting her and she let it instead of fighting it. Maybe she could unzip her wet suit flash him some breast and they could forget about this whole thing and get back into bed. Boy had her girly parts taken over a big portion of her life lately.

"Are you going to get your wave anytime soon?"

Robey squelched down the panic roiling in her stomach. "I'm waiting for the right one."

"You've let six people go ahead of you." Bama pointed to the guy she just waved on ahead of her.

"Six people who were ready to settle for inferior waves. Not my fault they're not as choosey as me." That sounded good to her. Hope it worked for him.

He coughed.

She'd swear he said bullshit under that fake cough, but she'd let it go. It's not as if she hadn't been dragging him into surfing world domination for the last several weeks. She'd almost got the deal with Winslow Sport finalized and his name on the paperwork. And he'd been pretty cool about it. That and keeping all her girly parts happy. The least she could do was get over her insane fear, ride a wave and then hang up her surfboard forever.

"Are you just doing this for me?"

Her head whipped around to face him. Busted. "Why are you asking?"

"You don't have to."

His voice was so calm like he was talking to a kid and she wasn't sure if she resented that or not. "Yes I do."

"Why?"

"Because you've pretty much have let me drag you into the big business with hardly any fuss and the least I could do is ride one stupid wave." There she said it.

"If you not doing this for you then hang up your board."

Now he sounded like her mom and she felt like a whiney crybaby.

"Your mouth is saying that, but I see the glint of disappointment in your eyes." Okay not really but she didn't want to the bad guy in all of this.

He shrugged his big shoulders. "It's not about me."

Robey motioned another person to go ahead of her. "I want to do something for you."

"Honey, you've done a lot for me the last few weeks."

Now he had to be all understanding which made her feel even worse. Now she had to ride this damn wave. "You let me do the deal."

He jiggled his eyebrows. "I wasn't talking about that."

"Ohhh." Okay now she got one of those little tingles again. God she loved when he talked like this. Damn what this man could do to her.

"Hanging it up Robey this isn't for you."

"But--"

His fist hit the board. "Don't do this for me. Do it for you."

She bit her bottom lip. "Are you upset with me?"

"Not really. Does it matter?"

Another wave lapped at her legs. "Yes it does."

"All I'm saying is that you do this for you, or go back to the beach if you scared." He ran a hand through his shaggy hair.

"I am not scared." She wanted to scream at him that she loved him and wanted to be a part of his world and this was his world and she just needed it to work out the way it was supposed to.

"Yeah you are." His voice was so calm. "You're afraid of letting go."

She was afraid to admit it. Because that put him in control and then he could hurt her so she denied it. "No I'm not."

"Whatever."

"I'll prove it." She started paddling out to the break point. Hell she was going to do this. She was more than some money making cash machine. She could be fun, she could let go. The wave came at her and shegot into to position and got her right knee on the surf board. Her fear was almost overwhelming, but she steadied herself and popped up into a stand. Forcing herself to relax she rode the wave letting the force of the wave take her where it wanted to. Then all of a sudden, she began to relax and enjoy the ride. Pride was welling up in her, this wasn't so bad. The wave began to die and she let herself take in her surroundings and out of the corner of her eye and dorsal fin popped up about three feet away from her.

Shark!

Terror gripped her. Her body was trembling as the fin moved closer to her. She was going to die. Oh God! Oh God! She was losing control of the board and she was going to fall in the water. She felt herself wobble and then she started falling. It was like she was moving in slow motion until her head hit the board and she felt herself slid into the water. She was going die and everything went black.

Bama watched her paddle off, knowing he shouldn't have been so hard on her, but he didn't want her doing things to please him. He liked her control freak ways. Hell she made him want to be a better man. She had fire. The kind he wouldn't mind spending the rest of life next to. He was cool with everything she'd done with Winslow Sport. And it was for the most part pretty painless for him, which he should have told her.

That was a good pop up. She rode the wave like a champ. Maybe after she got a taste of her first solo ride, she'd be down with surfing. Not that it mattered. He wanted her whether she ever got on a board ever again. Her stance was good. Go baby go. He felt himself smile as he watched her ride the wave. Then he saw a dolphin's dorsal fin pop up close to her. She began to fight the ride. He started paddling toward her. Then he saw her fall and hit her head and slide off the board

He undid the Velcro leash and plunged into the cold water and what seemed like forever he reached her board. Going underwater he found her and ripped the Velcro leash off her ankle and brought her up to the surface. In case there was a neck injury he pushed the board under and stated paddling her toward the shore. The lifeguards met him about ten feet from the shore and he steadied her on the board and began to pump the water out of her chest. After what seemed like forever, she sputtered and she coughed out the water. Her eyes opened.

His heart was beating so fast. He couldn't believe he almost lost her. "Baby, are you okay?"

"Shark." Her eyes were terror filled.

Okay he couldn't help himself he started to laugh. "That was a dolphin."

"What?" She tried to sit up, but he held her down.

"Curved dorsal is a dolphin not a shark."

Her head fell back on the sand and she winced. "Freaking Flipper ruined my ride."

Relief washed over him. If she was letting out her inner smart ass she was going to be okay. He still had a chance. "He was trying to ride with you. Didn't you listen to my wildlife lecture?"

"Hell no." She rolled her eyes. "You weren't wearing a shirt. The blood was pounding in my ears. And the sun was in your hair. How am I supposed to think about bullshit stuff like that?"

There was a round of laughter from the people gathered around them. "We're going to have a hell of a story to tell our grandkids."

Her brown eyes went wide. "We're having grandkids? When did that happen?"

Damn he couldn't believe he let that slip. "Oh shit, I did that all wrong."

Robey held up her hand. "Let's back up here."

Bama looked up at the lifeguards hovering over them. "Dudes, can you give me a sec here."

"Sure man." The two guards lefts.

Robey sat up. She was smiling. "So tell me about these grandkids you and I are going to have."

Which as far as he was concerned was a good sign. "I love you Robey."

Propping herself on her elbows she just stared at him. "Well that was unexpected."

Bama put his hand on her cheek glad that her skin was warming up and her color was returning to normal. "But was it bad?"

She shook her head. "No it was perfect."

Curling his finger around a loose strand of her hair he wondered if she was she in love with him too. "So what are you saying?"

Her eyes took on this dreamy quality. "I'm seriously uncontrollably in love with you too."

He smiled. It just didn't get better than this now did it? "Tight."

"And?" Her voice had a sing song quality to it.

Although he was the happiest man on this side of the world, he didn't want to ask her here, when she was wet and cold and almost died. He wanted the moment to be perfect. "I wanna take a shower and get all clean before I go any further. And I think a trip to the hospital might not be a bad idea for you."

"Well just so you know. I'm going to say yes." She sat up and put her arm around his neck.

"Just so you know, I already have the ring." Julia helped him pick the perfect one the other day. It was in the glove compartment of his car.

"Kiss me surfer dude," she whispered near his mouth.

And he did.

The End

Watch for Julia Wade's story in
Caliente
coming 2009
from Parker Publishing